W9-BBV-324

ALSO BY ANNE TYLER

If Morning Ever Comes

The Tin Can Tree

A Slipping-Down Life

The Clock Winder

Celestial Navigation

Searching for Caleb

Earthly Possessions

Morgan's Passing

Dinner at the Homesick Restaurant

The Accidental Tourist

Breathing Lessons

Saint Maybe

Ladder of Years

A Patchwork Planet

Back When We Were Grownups

The Amateur Marriage

Digging to America

Noah's Compass

The Beginner's Goodbye

A Spool of Blue Thread

Vinegar Girl

Clock Dance

Redhead by the Side of the Road

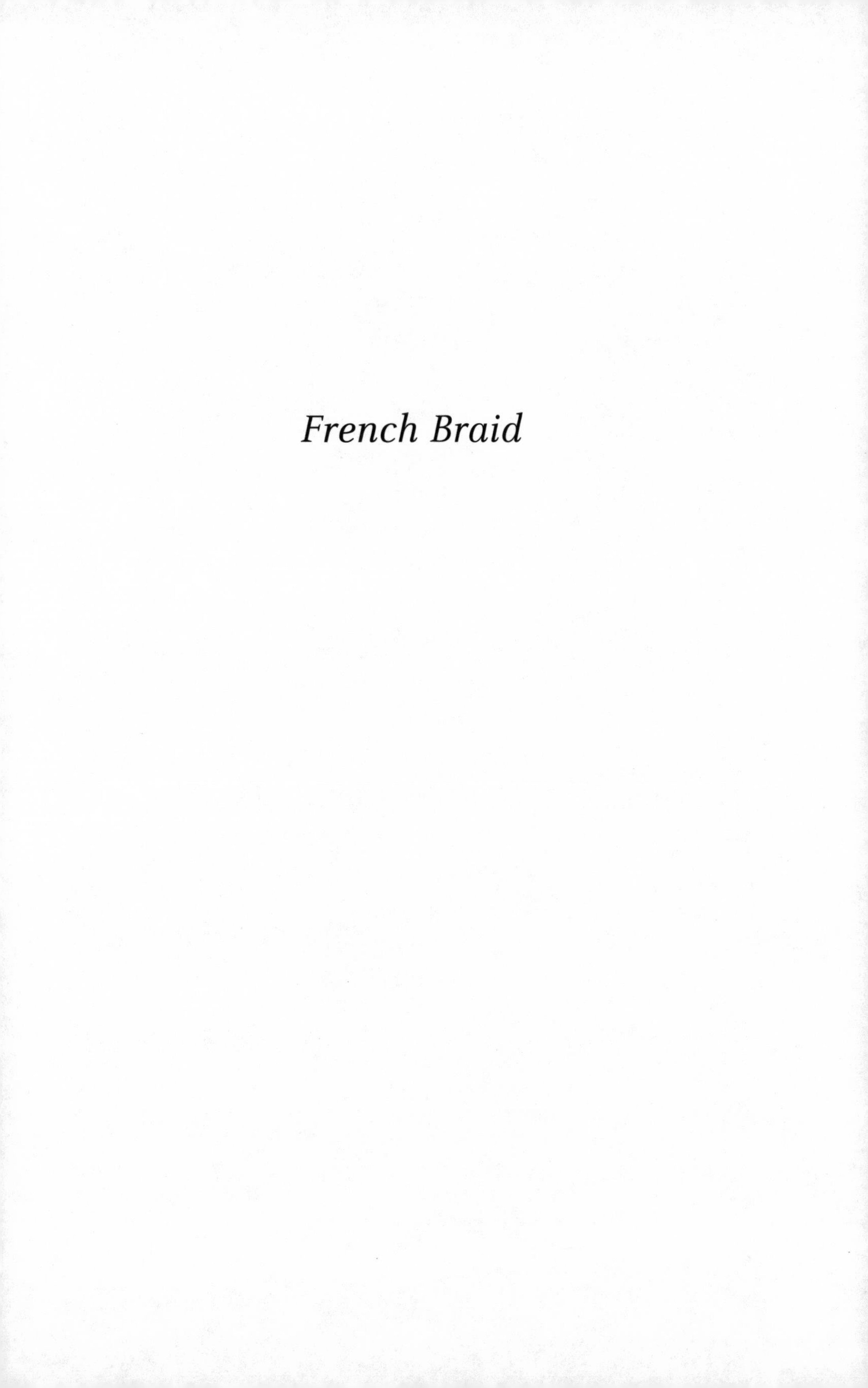

French Braid

French Braid

ANNE TYLER

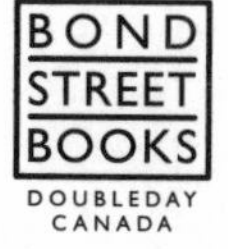

Bond Street Books and colophon are registered trademarks of
Penguin Random House Canada Limited

Library and Archives Canada Cataloguing in Publication

Title: French braid / Anne Tyler.
Names: Tyler, Anne, author.
Identifiers: Canadiana (print) 20210333324 | Canadiana (ebook) 20210333332 |
ISBN 9780385698696 (hardcover) | ISBN 9780385698702 (EPUB)
Classification: LCC PS3570.Y45 F74 2022 | DDC 813/.54—dc23

This book is a work of fiction. Names, characters, places and incidents are products of the author's imagination or are used fictitiously. Any resemblance to actual events or locales or persons, living or dead, is entirely coincidental.

Grateful acknowledgment is made to Peermusic III, Ltd. for permission to reprint an excerpt of "The Song That Never Ends" by Norman Martin. Copyright © 1988 by Norman Martin Music. All rights reserved. Administered and reprinted by permission of by Peermusic III, Ltd.

Cover photograph © Design gallery / Shutterstock
Cover design by Kelly Blair

Printed in the United States of America

Published in Canada by Bond Street Books,
a division of Penguin Random House Canada Limited

www.penguinrandomhouse.ca

10 9 8 7 6 5 4 3 2 1

French Braid

1

THIS HAPPENED back in March of 2010, when the Philadelphia train station still had the kind of information board that clickety-clacked as the various gate assignments rolled up. Serena Drew stood directly in front of it, gazing intently at the listing for the next train to Baltimore. Why did they wait so long to post their gates here? In Baltimore, they told people farther ahead.

Her boyfriend was standing beside her, but he was more relaxed. Having sent a single glance toward the board, he was studying his phone now. He shook his head at some message and then flicked on down to the next one.

The two of them had just had Sunday lunch at James's parents' house. It had been Serena's first meeting with them. For the past two weeks she had fretted about it, planning what to wear (jeans and a turtleneck, finally—the regulation grad-student outfit, so as not to seem to be trying too hard) and scouring her mind for possible topics of conversation. But things had gone fairly well, she thought. His parents had greeted her warmly and asked her right away to call them George and Dora, and his mother was such a chatterbox that conversation had not been an issue. "Next time," she'd told Serena after the meal, "you'll have to meet James's sisters too and their hubbies and their kiddies. We just didn't want to overwhelm you on your very first visit."

Next time. First visit. That had sounded encouraging.

Now, though, Serena couldn't even summon a sense of triumph. She was too limp with sheer relief; she felt like a wrung-out dishrag.

She and James had met at the start of the school year. James was so good-looking that she'd been surprised when he suggested going for coffee after class. He was tall and lean, with a mop of brown hair and a closely trimmed beard. (Serena, on the other hand, came very close to plump, and her ponytail was almost the same shade of beige as her skin.) In seminars he had a way of lounging back in his seat, not taking notes or appearing to listen, but then he would pop up with something unexpectedly astute. She had worried he would find her dull by comparison. One-on-one, though, he turned out to be easy company. They went to a lot of movies together and to inexpensive restaurants; and her parents, who lived in town, had already had the two of them to dinner several times and said they liked him very much.

Philadelphia's train station was more imposing than Baltimore's. It was vast, with an impossibly high, coffered ceiling and chandeliers like upside-down skyscrapers. Even the passengers seemed a cut above Baltimore passengers. One woman, Serena saw, was followed by her own redcap wheeling a cartload of matching luggage. As Serena was admiring the luggage (dark-brown, gleaming leather, with brass fittings), she happened to notice a young man in a suit who had paused to let the cart roll past him. "Oh," she said.

James looked up from his phone. "Hmm?"

"I think that might be my cousin," she said in an undertone.

"Where?"

"That guy in the suit."

"You *think* it's your cousin?"

"I'm not really sure."

They studied the man. He seemed older than they were, but not by much. (It might just have been the suit.) He had Serena's pale hair and her sharply peaked lips, but while her eyes were the usual Garrett-family blue, his were a pale, almost ethereal gray, noticeable even from several yards' distance. He was staying where he was, looking up at the information board now, although the luggage cart had moved on.

"It might be my cousin Nicholas," Serena said.

"Maybe he just resembles Nicholas," James said. "Seems to me if it was really him, you could say for certain."

"Well, it's been a while since we've seen each other," Serena said. "He's my mom's brother David's son; they live up here in Philly."

"So just go ask him, why not."

"But if I'm wrong, I would look like a fool," Serena said.

James squinted at her dubiously.

"Oh, well, too late now anyhow," she said, because whoever it was had evidently found out what he needed to know. He turned to set off toward the other side of the station, hitching the strap of his overnight bag higher on his shoulder, and Serena went back to consulting the board. "What is the gate number usually?" she asked. "Maybe we could just take a chance and head on over there."

"It's not as if the train will leave the minute they announce it," James told her. "First we'll have to line up at the top of the stairs and wait awhile."

"Yes, but I worry we won't get to sit together."

He gave her the crinkly-eyed smile that she loved. "Isn't that just like you" was what it meant.

"Okay, so I'm overthinking this," she told him.

"Anyhow," he said, switching the subject. "Even if it's been a while, seems like you'd know your own cousin."

"Would you know all *your* cousins, out of the blue?" she asked.

"Yes," James said.

"You would?"

"Well, sure!"

But he had lost interest, she could tell. He sent a glance toward the food court along the opposite wall. "I could use a soda," he told her.

"You can buy one on the train," she said.

"You want anything yourself?"

"I'll wait till we're on the train."

But he missed her point. He said, "Grab us a place in line if they post the gate while I'm gone, okay?" And off he went, without a thought.

This was the first time they'd taken a trip together, even this little day trip. Serena was slightly disappointed that he didn't share her travel anxiety.

As soon as she was alone, she drew her compact out of her backpack and checked her teeth in the mirror. Dessert had been a sort of fruit crumble with walnut bits in the topping, and she could still feel them lingering in her mouth. Ordinarily she'd have excused herself after lunch and ducked into the powder room, but time had gotten away from them—"Oh! Oh!" Dora had said. "Your train!"—and they had all left for the station in a flurry, James's father driving and James sitting next to him, while Dora and Serena sat together in back so that, as Dora had put it, "we gals can have a nice cozy chat." That was when she'd said what she'd said about Serena's meeting James's sisters. "Tell me," she had said then, "how many siblings do *you* have, dear?"

"Oh, just a brother," Serena said. "But he was nearly grown before I came along. I've always *wished* I had sisters." Then she had blushed, because it might have sounded as if she were talking about marrying into James's family or something.

Dora had sent her a little tucked smile and reached over to pat her hand.

Serena had meant that literally, though. Ensconced in her parents' small household, she had envied her school friends with their swarms of relatives all mixed up and shrieking with laughter and fighting for space and attention. Some had stepsiblings, even, and stepmothers and stepfathers they could pick and choose at will and ostracize if things didn't work out, like rich people discarding perfectly okay food while the undernourished gazed longingly from the sidelines.

Well, you just wait and see, she used to tell herself. Wait until you see what your *future* family's going to look like!

The train to Baltimore was five minutes delayed now, according to the board. Which probably meant fifteen. And they still hadn't posted the gate number. Serena turned to look for James. There he was, thank goodness, walking toward her holding a drink cup. And next to him, lagging slightly behind, was the man she'd thought might be her cousin. Serena blinked.

"Look who I picked up!" James said as he arrived.

"Serena?" the man asked.

"Nicholas?"

"Well, hey!" he said, and he started to offer his hand but then changed his mind and leaned forward, instead, to give her a clumsy half-hug. He smelled like freshly ironed cotton.

"What are *you* doing here?" she asked him.

"I'm catching a train to New York."

"Oh."

"Got a meeting tomorrow morning."

"Oh, I see," she said. She supposed he meant a business meeting. She had no idea what he did for a living. She said, "How are your folks?"

"They're okay. Well, getting on, of course. Dad might have to have a hip replacement."

"Oh, bummer," she said.

"What I did," James told Serena, rocking slightly from heel to toe, "I noticed him by the newsstand, so I stopped a few feet behind him and said, very low, 'Nicholas?'" He looked pleased with himself.

"First I thought I was imagining things," Nicholas said. "I kind of glanced sideways, not turning my head—"

"When it's a person's own name they're quicker to catch it," James said. "You probably wouldn't have heard me if I'd said 'Richard,' for instance."

"My mom's having hip trouble too," Serena told Nicholas. "Maybe it's genetic."

"Your mom is . . . Alice?"

"No, Lily."

"Oh, right. Sorry. But it was you I sat next to at Grandfather Garrett's funeral, I think."

"No, that was Candle."

"I have a cousin named Candle?"

"You *guys*!" James said, disbelievingly.

"Kendall, her name is really," Serena went on, ignoring him. "She just couldn't say her own name when she was learning to talk."

"You were there, though, right?" Nicholas asked.

"At the funeral? Oh, yes."

She'd been there, but she'd been twelve years old. And he had been, what? Somewhere in his mid-teens; a world of difference back then. She hadn't dared to exchange a word with him. She had studied him from afar as they all milled in front of the funeral home afterwards—his self-contained expression and his pale gray eyes. The eyes came from his mother, Greta, a standoffish woman with a limp and a foreign accent, or at least a not-Baltimore accent. Serena remembered those eyes very well.

"We were supposed to go to lunch with everyone after the service," Nicholas was telling her, "but Dad had to get back for a school play."

"Speaking of getting back . . ." James interrupted. He jabbed a thumb toward the board above them. "We should head to gate 5."

"Oh, right. Okay, we'd better be going," Serena told Nicholas. "I'm so glad we ran into you!"

"Good seeing you too," he said, and he smiled at her and then lifted a palm toward James and turned to walk away.

"Tell your family hello, hear?" she called.

"I'll do that," he called back.

Serena and James gazed after him a moment, although a line was already forming next to the sign for gate 5.

"I have to say," James said finally, "you guys give a whole new meaning to the phrase 'once removed.'"

As it turned out, their train was not all that full. They easily found two seats together—Serena next to the window, James on the aisle. James unlatched his tray and set his drink cup on it. "*Now* do you want a soda?" he asked. "I think the café car's open."

"No, I'm okay."

She watched the other passengers making their way down the aisle—a woman prodding two small children who were dawdling in front of her, another woman struggling to heave her suitcase into the overhead rack until James stood up to lend her a hand.

"He had your coloring, sort of," he said when he'd sat down again, "but I never would have picked him out of a crowd."

"Excuse me? Oh. Nicholas," Serena said.

"Have you got just a huge multitude of cousins, is that it?"

"No, only, um . . . five," she said, mentally counting first. "All of them on the Garrett side. My dad was an only child."

"I've got eleven."

"Well, lucky you," she said teasingly.

"Still, I'd know any one of them if I happened to see them in the train station."

"Yes, but we are just all so spread out," she said. "Uncle David up here in Philly, Aunt Alice out in Baltimore County . . ."

"Ooh, way far away in the county!" James said, and he gave her a dig in the ribs.

"I mean, we tend to see each other only at weddings and funerals and such," she said. She paused, considering. "And not even all of those. But I don't know why, exactly."

"Maybe there's some deep dark secret in your family's past," James said.

"Right."

"Maybe your uncle's a Republican. Or your aunt belongs to a cult."

"Oh, stop," Serena said, and she laughed.

She liked sitting close to him this way—the armrest between them raised so that their bodies were lined up and touching. They had been going out for eight months now, but he still seemed blessedly new to her and not to be taken for granted.

The train gave a preliminary lurch, and the last of the passengers settled hastily. "Good afternoon," a conductor said over the loudspeaker. "This is train number . . ." Serena took her ticket from her backpack. Outside her window, the darkened platform slid by and then they emerged into daylight; they picked up speed; crumbling concrete structures passed, every single inch of them splashed with graffiti that looked like shouting.

11

“So, what did you think of my folks?” James asked her.

“I liked them a lot! I really did.” She let a pause develop. “Do you think they liked *me*?” she asked finally.

“Of course they did! How could they not?”

This wasn’t as satisfying as it might have been. After a moment, she said, “What did they like about me?”

“Hmm?”

“I mean, did they say anything to you?”

“They didn’t have a chance to. I could tell, though.”

She let another pause develop.

“You two board in Philly?” a conductor asked, looming over them.

“Yes, sir,” James said. He reached for Serena’s ticket and handed it to him along with his own.

“My mom went all out on the lunch,” he said, once the conductor had moved on. “That chicken dish was her pride and joy. She serves it only to special company.”

“Well, it was delicious,” Serena said.

“And Dad asked in the car if I thought you’d be sticking around awhile.”

“Sticking . . . oh,” she said.

“I told him, ‘We’ll just have to see, won’t we!’”

Another dig in the ribs, and a sly sideways glance.

Over dessert, his mother had hauled out the family album and shown Serena James’s childhood photos. (He’d been a cute little thing.) James had grimaced apologetically at Serena but then had hung over the album himself, alert to all that was said about him. “He ate nothing but white foods until he was in his teens,” his mother had said.

“You’re exaggerating,” James told her.

“It’s a wonder he didn’t get scurvy.”

“He seems pretty healthy *now*,” Serena had said.

And she and Dora had looked over at him and smiled.

Their train was speeding through a wasteland of scratchy yellow weeds and rust-stained kitchen sinks and tractor tires and blue plastic grocery bags, endless blue plastic grocery bags. "If you were a foreigner," Serena told James, "and you'd just landed in this country and you were taking the train south, you would say, 'This is *America*? This is the Promised Land?'"

"Well, you're a fine one to talk," James said. "It's not as if Baltimore's such a scenic paradise."

"No, I just meant . . . I was talking about the whole Amtrak route," Serena said. "The Northeast Corridor."

"Oh."

"I didn't realize it was a competition," she said in a joking tone.

"Oh, I know how uppity you Baltimoreans are," James said. "I know how you guys sort people out by what high school they attended. And then *marry* someone from *your* high school in the end."

Serena made a big show of looking to her right and left. "You see anyone from my high school sitting here next to me?" she asked.

"Not at the moment," he admitted.

"Well, then!"

She waited, curious to see what he would say next, but he didn't pursue the subject, and they traveled awhile in silence. Behind them, a woman with a soft, coaxing voice was talking on her phone. "So how are you *really*?" Serena heard her say. And then, after a pause, "Now, hon. Now, sweetie. Go ahead and tell me what's wrong. I can hear there's something."

"Just look at poor Nicholas," James said all of a sudden. "His dad moves him away from Baltimore, and so the rest of the family stops speaking to them."

"That's not *us* doing that!" Serena said. "It's them. It's Uncle David, really. My mom says she can't understand it. He used to be so outgoing when he was a little boy, she says. Aunt Alice was kind of a killjoy but Uncle David was one of those sunshine children, all happiness and glee. And now look: he left early from his own father's funeral."

Grandfather's funeral, Nicholas had called it: "Grandfather Garrett's funeral." But Pop-Pop had never been "Grandfather"! How could Nicholas not have known that?

"And then your aunt," James went on. "The farthest *she* moved was Baltimore County, but *oh,* no. *Oh,* no. Never going to speak to *her* again."

"Don't be silly; we speak to her all the time," Serena said, exaggerating only a little.

She didn't know why she felt so defensive. It was the stress, she supposed. The stress of meeting his parents.

When the subject of this trip had first come up, the idea was that they'd go for a weekend. James had talked about where they could get the best Philly cheesesteaks, and whether she'd like to visit the art museum. "You're going to love the Chamber of Horrors," he'd told her.

"Chamber of Horrors?"

"That's what my family calls my bedroom."

"Oh. Ha."

"Wall-to-wall Eagles posters. Sandwich crusts under my bed from 1998."

"But . . . not to *stay* there, though, right?" she asked him.

"Stay?"

"I mean . . . not to sleep in the Chamber of Horrors overnight."

"Hey. I was kidding," he said. "Well, at least about the sandwich crusts. I believe my mom did come through with the vacuum cleaner once I'd moved out."

"But I would be in the guest room," she said, meaning it as a question.

"You *want* to be in the guest room?"

"Well, yes."

"You don't want to stay with me in my room?"

"Not in front of your parents," she said.

"In front of my—" He stopped. "Look," he said. "I guarantee they assume we're sleeping together. You think they'd make a fuss about that?"

"I don't care if they assume it or not. I just don't like to be so public about it when I'm first being introduced to them."

James had studied her a moment.

"They do *have* a guest room, right?" Serena asked.

"Well, yes."

"So what's the problem?"

"It just seems kind of . . . artificial, saying good night in the upstairs hall and going our separate ways," he said.

"Well, I'm sorry," Serena said stiffly.

"Plus, I'll miss you! And Mom and Dad are going to be baffled. 'Good grief,' they'll say, 'do these kids not know about sex?' "

"Ssh!" Serena had said, because they'd been sitting in the library where anyone might be listening. She glanced around the room and then leaned across the table toward him. "We'll just go on a Sunday, then," she said in a lower voice.

"What's that got to do with it?"

"We'll say we're tied up on Saturdays and so we're coming in on a Sunday, and since I have a class Monday mornings we'll have to make it a day trip."

"Geez, Serena. You're saying we'd travel all that distance just for a few hours? Just to pretend we're not really so much of a couple after all?"

But that was what they'd ended up doing. Serena had gotten her way.

She knew she had disappointed him. He probably thought she was a hypocrite. But still, she felt she'd made the right decision.

They were nearing Wilmington now. Scattered, abandoned-looking houses were gradually giving way to clean white office buildings. The conductor passed down the aisle collecting ticket stubs from the slots above certain seats.

"Take that thing your mother said about my brother-in-law," James said suddenly.

"What? What thing are you talking about?"

"Back when I first came to dinner, remember? I told your mother that one of my brothers-in-law came from Baltimore, and she said, 'Oh, what's his name?' and I said, 'Jacob Rosenbaum, but everyone calls him Jay.' 'Oh,' she said, 'Rosenbaum: he's probably from Pikesville. That's where most of the Jewish people live.' "

"Well, Mom's a little behind the times," Serena said.

James gave her a look.

"What?" she asked him. "Are you calling her anti-Semitic?"

"I'm just saying Baltimore can be kind of us-and-them, is all."

"You're still going on about *Baltimore*?"

"Just tossing it out there," he told her.

"Your brother-in-law's folks might certainly live in Pikesville," Serena said. "But they might also live in Cedarcroft, right next door to my parents. It's not as if our neighborhoods are *restricted* or anything."

"Oh, sure, I know that," James said hastily. "All I meant was, seems to me that Baltimoreans like to . . . categorize."

"Human beings like to categorize," Serena told him.

"Well, okay . . ."

She said, "How about what *your* mom said, when we were leaving?"

"Huh?"

" 'Next time you should come for a weekend,' she said. 'Come for Easter weekend! All of us get together then, and you can see what a big family feels like.' "

Without intending to, Serena adopted a perky, chatty-housewife tone, although in fact that wasn't at all what Dora had sounded like. And James caught it; he sent her a quick, sharp glance. "What's wrong with that?" he asked her.

"It was just a little bit judgy, is all," Serena said. "Like, 'Poor, poor Serena. We're the ones with the *real* family. You're the poor little *pretend* family.'"

"She didn't say 'real family.' You just now told me she said '*big* family.'"

Serena didn't argue, but she let the corners of her mouth turn down.

"We're the ones with the wide-open family; you're the poor little narrow family"—that was what Dora had actually been saying, although Serena wasn't going to argue with James about it.

The trouble with wide-open families was, there was something very narrow about their attitude to *not*-open families.

The train was slowing now. "Wilmington!" the loudspeaker said. "Watch your step, ladies and gentlemen, and be sure to check around for . . ." Outside Serena's window, the sunlit platform glided into view, dotted with passengers looking so pleased and anticipatory that it seemed they believed that boarding this train would be all they had ever hoped for.

Serena was remembering the Christmas present her parents had given James. He had come to their house for dinner the day before he went home for the holidays, and when they sat down at the table a slender, flat, gift-wrapped box had been waiting on his empty plate. Serena had cringed, already embarrassed. Please let this not be something too personal, too . . . presuming! Even James had looked uncomfortable. "For me?" he'd asked. But when he opened it, Serena had been relieved. Inside was a pair of very bright orange socks. A black band ran around the top of each reading BALTIMORE ORIOLES, with a cartoon Orioles mascot at the center.

"Now that you live in Baltimore," Serena's father explained, "we thought you should dress the part. But we didn't want to get you in trouble with folks in Philly, so we chose a pair that hides the evidence as long as you keep your pants cuffs down."

"Very considerate," James had said, and he insisted on putting them on then and there and strutting shoeless around the dining room before they started eating.

He'd had no idea that in fact, neither one of Serena's parents was a sports fan. They probably couldn't tell you the name of a single Oriole—or Raven, either, for that matter. The sheer effort they must have expended in thinking up this gift for him just about broke Serena's heart.

Next to her, James said, "Hey."

She didn't answer.

"Hey, Reenie."

"What."

"Are we going to start fighting about our relatives now?"

"*I'm* not fighting."

The train gave a lurch and began rolling forward again. A man with a briefcase walked down the aisle looking lost. In the seat behind them, the woman with the coaxing voice said, "Sweetheart. Honey Pie. We're going to bring this up with management on Tuesday. Hear what I'm saying?"

"I can't believe she's still on the phone," Serena murmured to James.

It took him a moment, but then he answered. "*I* can't believe it's a business call," he murmured back. "Would you have guessed it?"

"Never."

"You can't tell *me* women in business behave the same as men."

"Now, now, let's not be sexist," she said with a laugh.

He reached over for her hand and laced his fingers through hers. "Face it," he told her, "we've both been under a strain. Right? Parents can be such a drag!"

"Tell me about it," she said.

They rode along in a comfortable silence awhile.

"Did you catch that thing my mom said about my beard?" he asked suddenly. "Talk about judgy."

"What thing?"

"When she was showing you the photo album. She gets to my high-school days and 'Here's James at his graduation,' she says. 'Doesn't he look nice? It was before he grew his beard.' She cannot let it go about my beard. She hates it."

"Well, she's a mother," Serena told him. "Mothers always hate beards."

"The first time I came home with it, freshman year in college, my dad offered me twenty bucks to shave it off. 'You too?' I asked him. 'What *is* this?' He said, 'I personally have nothing against a beard, but your mother says she misses seeing your handsome face.' 'Fine,' I told him, 'let her pore over my old photos, if she wants to see my face.'"

"Well, you did look very attractive in your graduation picture," Serena told him.

"But *you* don't think I should shave my beard, do you?"

"No, no. I like your beard." She gave his hand a squeeze. "I was glad to see the Before version, though."

"How come?"

"Well, now I know what your face looks like."

"You were worried what my face looks like?"

"Not *worried,* but . . . well, I've always thought that if, let's say, I grew up and met the man I was going to marry and he happened to have a beard, I would ask him if he'd mind shaving it off one time before the wedding."

"Shaving it off!"

"Just one time. Just for two little minutes so I could see his face, and then he could let it grow back again."

James released her hand and drew away to give her a look.

"What," she said.

"And how about if he said no?" he asked. "How about if he said, 'This is who I am: a guy with a beard. You can take me or you can leave me.'"

"But then if he . . ." She trailed off.

"Then if he what?" James asked.

"If he . . . turned out to have a weak chin or something . . ."

He went on looking at her.

"Well, *I* don't know!" she said. "I'd just want to find out what I was getting into, is all I'm saying."

"And if he had a weak chin you'd tell him, 'Oh, *I'm* sorry, it seems I can't marry you after all.'"

"I'm not saying I wouldn't still marry him; I'm saying I would go into the marriage *informed,* is all. I would know what I was dealing with."

James stared glumly at the back of the seat ahead of him. He made no move to take her hand again.

"Oh, *Jaaames,*" Serena caroled softly.

No answer.

"James?"

He turned toward her abruptly, as if he'd come to some decision. "Ever since we started planning this trip," he said, "you've been putting up little . . . walls. Setting limits. No staying in the same room together; has to be on a Sunday . . . Four measly hours we were there! We spent more time traveling than visiting, pretty near! And I don't get to see my folks so very often, you know. I'm not like you, living in the same city with them and practically in the same neighborhood, dropping in on them whenever you need to run a load of laundry."

"Well, that's not *my* fault!"

As if she hadn't spoken, he said, "You know what I was thinking when we were riding up to Philly? I was thinking that once you'd met my parents, you'd decide we might as well stay over. We could take an early-morning train back in time for your class, you'd say, now that you'd seen they were okay."

"I already knew they'd be *okay*, James. I just felt—and besides, I didn't bring my toothbrush! Or my pajamas!"

He didn't so much as change expression.

"Well, next time," she promised him, after a pause.

"Fine," he said, and he drew his phone from his pocket to check the screen.

They were passing a stretch of the Chesapeake Bay now—a wide sheet of water, matte gray even in sunlight, with lone birds hunched motionless on posts sticking up here and there. The sight made Serena feel melancholy. Homesick, almost.

This was all because of her cousin, really. Running into him had sent a kind of jagged feeling down the center of her chest, a split between the two parts of her world. On the one side James's mother, so intimate and confiding; on the other side Nicholas, standing alone in the train station. It was like taking a glass bowl from a hot oven and plunging it into ice water: the snapping sound as it shattered.

"Could we ever maybe have a family reunion?" Serena had once asked as a child.

And her mother had said, "Hmm? A reunion? I suppose we could. Though it wouldn't be a very *big* reunion."

"Would Uncle David and them come?"

"Uncle David. Well. Possibly."

Nothing about that reply had sounded promising.

Oh, what makes a family not work?

Maybe Uncle David was adopted and he was mad that no one had told him. Or he'd been written out of a will that had included both his sisters. (Even in her childhood, Serena read a lot of novels.) Or some sort of family argument had spun wildly out of control, the sort where outrageous remarks were made that a person couldn't forgive. That seemed the most plausible explanation. You can't think later what the argument was about, even, but you know that things will be changed forever after.

"Well," Serena had told her mother, "at least Aunt Alice might come."

"Maybe," Lily had said. "Although you know your aunt Alice. How she's always tut-tutting me whenever we get together."

Serena had given up.

The fact was, she reflected, that even when the Garretts did get together, it never seemed to take, so to speak.

Without moving, she slid her eyes in James's direction. He was reading a screenful of text. (He had the most extraordinary ability to read entire books on his phone.) Absentmindedly, he was chewing his lower lip.

Serena's best friend in high school had been a boy named Marcellus Avery. This wasn't a romance; it was more a kind of mutual aid society. Marcellus had weirdly white skin and very black hair, and everybody made fun of his name. And Serena weighed about ten pounds too much and could not for the life of her cope with any sort of ball—baseball, tennis ball, soccer ball, any sort at all—in a school where sports were paramount. At lunch they would sit together and talk about how shallow all their classmates were, and on weekends he would come to her house and they would watch foreign movies in her parents' TV room. Once, though, he had let his hand settle oh-so-casually next to her hand on the couch between them, and when she didn't move hers away he had leaned imperceptibly closer and planted a soft, shy kiss on her cheek. She still remembered the velvety feel of the fuzz above his upper lip. But nothing more had happened. In a moment they had drawn apart and stared fixedly at the TV again, and that was the end of that.

The funny thing was, though, that now Serena realized he had been absolutely beautiful to look at. His head had had the most perfect shape, like a marble statue's head, and for some reason it had always made her think of how much his mother must love him. She wondered where he was today. Probably snatched up in marriage by someone, she thought—some woman smart enough to recognize his worth. And here Serena sat, next to a boy who was no different from her classmates back in high school.

All she could think about was how long it would be before this train ride came to an end and she could be on her own again.

2

THE GARRETT FAMILY did not take a family vacation until 1959. Robin Garrett, Alice's father, said they couldn't afford one. Also, in the early days he refused to leave the store in anyone else's hands. It was Grandfather Wellington's store, was why—Wellington's Plumbing Supply, turned over to Robin's care only grudgingly and mistrustfully after Grandfather Wellington had his first heart attack. So of course Robin had to prove himself, working six days a week and bringing the books home every Saturday for Alice's mother to examine in case he'd slipped up somewhere. Face it: he was not a born businessman. By training he was a plumber; he used to buy his parts at Wellington's just so he could catch a glimpse of young Mercy Wellington behind the counter. Mercy Wellington was the prettiest little thing he'd ever laid eyes on, he told his children, and all the plumbers in Baltimore were crazy about her. Robin hadn't stood a chance. But miracles do happen, sometimes. Mercy told the children she'd liked his gentlemanly behavior.

Then after Grandfather Wellington died and the store became

Robin's—or really Mercy's, legally speaking; same thing—he had acted even more tied to it, more obligated to oversee every last nut and bolt of it, and so they still took no vacations. Not till he hired an assistant manager whom he referred to as "young Pickford," a good-natured sort without a lot of brains but steady as a rock. That was when Mercy said, "All right, Robin, now I'm putting my foot down. We are going on a family vacation."

Summer of 1959. A week at Deep Creek Lake. Rustic little cabin in a row of other cabins just a walk from the lake itself. Not actually on the waterfront, because Robin said that was too pricey, but close enough; close enough.

In 1959 Alice was seventeen years old—way past the stage where traveling with her family could be any kind of thrill. And her sister, Lily, was fifteen and madly in love with Jump Watkins, a rising senior at their high school and a champion basketball player. She could not possibly leave Jump for a whole week, she said. She asked if Jump could come to the lake with them, but Robin said no. He didn't even bother giving a reason; he just said, "What? No," and that was that.

So for the girls, the trip was nothing much to look forward to. It had arrived too late in their lives. For their brother, though . . . well, David was only seven, the absolutely perfect age for a week at a lake. He was a joyful child anyhow, delighted to take part in anything new and different. From the moment he heard they were going, he started counting the days on the calendar and planning what to bring with him. He must have envisioned the lake as a sort of oversized bathtub, because he proposed to pack his plastic tugboats, his wooden sailboat, and his little wind-up plastic diver. Mercy had to explain that they might float away from him in all that water. "I'll get you a beach bucket at the dime store instead," she promised, "and a shovel." So after that, he went overboard in the other direction and started singing sea songs. "My Bonnie lies over the ocean . . ." he sang in his clear little voice, and he renamed his cowboy doll Bobby Shafto. (He was always renaming his cowboy doll, which he still took to bed with him nights, although he hid him in the closet whenever he had playmates over.) "Bobby Shafto's gone to sea," he sang, wafting the doll over his head in a horizontal, swimming position. "Silver buckles at his knee . . ."

They set out on a Saturday morning, after stopping at the kennel first to drop their dog, Cap, off for boarding. Alice was the one who drove. She'd had her license only a while and she was always begging to drive, although generally her father said no because she was too "headlong," as he put it. Today, though, he allowed it. He sat beside her in the front seat, pointing out stop signs and curves and oncoming cars that she could see perfectly well for herself, thank you very much. In back were Mercy, David, and Lily—David in the middle, because he was still small enough not to mind the hump in the floorboard.

They were a family of blonds, but Mercy and David were golden-haired blonds, pink-and-white-skinned and vivid (such a waste, in David's case), while Robin and the girls were slightly darker. All of them had blue eyes, and all of them were shortish, even Robin. Alice knew this bothered him, because sometimes when he was dealing with taller men at the store she saw him draw his shoulders up and hold his head higher than usual. He would practically stand on tiptoe. This always made her sad, although she supposed he didn't realize he was doing it.

It was a half day's trip through mostly rural areas, once they'd left the city. David could still be entertained by glimpses of horses and cows and their young ones, and he and his mother made a game of spotting tractors, but Lily was in a sulk and slouched silently in her seat, glaring straight ahead of her. As they drew nearer to the lake, they began to see signs reading TOURISTS in front of some of the private homes, and tarpaper shacks selling bait, and gravel lots full of motorboats with their prices chalked on their windshields. Scattered cafés no bigger than sheds offered fried chicken and meatloaf and dollar lunches. The Garretts had packed a lunch to eat once they arrived, but they did stop at a roadside stand for produce, and then again at a cinderblock cube beneath a two-story-tall electric sign reading FAT HARRY'S GROCERIES. Lily didn't go into Fat Harry's with them; she stayed in the car, with her arms folded stubbornly across her chest. "The more fool *you*," Alice told her when they all returned. "Mom let us get ice cream and we chose butter brickle." Lily hated butter brickle; she always said the chips felt like something that shouldn't be in there. But she didn't even bother reacting, just went on staring straight ahead.

What with all the produce they'd bought and now the groceries, it was a fairly uncomfortable ride for the final five miles of the trip. Their trunk was stuffed with suitcases and linens and Mercy's painting supplies, so their purchases had to be crowded around them inside the car—Fat Harry's grocery bags all but hiding Mercy and Lily from view, and a giant watermelon resting on David's lap. Paper sacks from the farm stand covered the floor in front of Robin, leaving barely enough room for him to set his feet.

They had to locate their cabin from a mimeographed sheet of instructions that had been mailed to them by the owner. "Take a right on Buck Smith Road," Robin read aloud. "Continue two and one quarter miles. Take a left at the sign for Sleepy Woods." Sleepy Woods turned out to be six log cabins lining the highway, a couple with boats jacked up on trailers in their side yards. The Garretts' cabin was number 4. It was small but efficiently organized, all on one floor, with a bedroom for the girls and another for their parents, this one with a foldout cot set up for David.

The combination kitchen and living area smelled of wood smoke from the fireplace, but the bedrooms smelled like mildew and so Mercy opened the windows. Outside, the smell was all pine and sunshine. Pine trees towered overhead and the ground was slippery-smooth with brown needles. Alice could see why the place was named Sleepy Woods. She thought she could sleep very well here.

First they ate their lunch at the wooden table in the kitchen, because all of them were starving. They had tuna-salad sandwiches and carrot sticks, with peaches from the farm stand for dessert. Then Robin started unloading the things in the trunk, and Mercy sent the girls to make up the beds while she put away the groceries. David was the only one without a task, so he went out back to let Bobby Shafto climb trees. He shimmied him up various trunks and set him astride low branches, in the meantime singing, "He'll come back and marry me-ee . . ."

Once the trunk was emptied, Robin and David changed clothes and walked down to the lake to try it out—Robin in baggy red trunks and a T-shirt and regular black work shoes with black socks, David in a short white terry-cloth robe bought especially for this trip and his little brown fisherman sandals. The path to the lake was a kind of logging trail through the woods, two sandy ruts with a grassy strip in the middle. For several minutes after they left they could be seen flickering in and out of patches of sunlight, Robin with their towels draped around his neck and David swinging his beach bucket so that the shovel inside made a clanking sound they could hear even from the cabin.

Alice tried to chitchat with Lily while they were making up the beds—"I call dibs on the one by the window" and "I sure hope this cot is more comfortable than it looks"—but Lily didn't answer and kept her same grumpy expression. When they'd finished, Alice unpacked her things and put them in the bureau ("I call the top two drawers"), and Lily took a pad of paper and a ballpoint pen from her suitcase and settled against the propped pillow on her bed and started writing. To Jump, presumably, not that she bothered explaining that.

Alice gave up on her. She put on her swimsuit and a big shirt and collected her camera—a Brownie Starflash she'd been given for her last birthday—and went back out to the kitchen, where she found Mercy hunting a pitcher for the tea she'd just brewed. "I'll look for one while you go change," Alice told her, and Mercy said, "Oh, thanks, honey," and disappeared into her bedroom. She emerged a few minutes later in a shirred latex swimsuit such as Esther Williams might wear, and a peach kimono fluttering open at the front and cork-soled sandals with giant pompoms on the toes. "Where's Lily?" she asked, and Alice made a face and said, "Writing a letter." Mercy just gave an airy little laugh. She seemed to view Lily as some belle from *Gone with the Wind*, with boys galore lining up to "dance attendance," as she called it.

They left the cabin and set off down the path that Robin and David had taken earlier. It was hot but not unbearably so—a good ten degrees cooler than Baltimore, Alice would guess. Tiny insects buzzed around their heads whenever they passed through shade, and squirrels scrabbled up the trees.

The lake was bigger than Alice had expected. You could see the opposite shore, but it looked very far away, and the near shore curved to the left and disappeared behind a clump of bushes, so she knew there must be more lake in the distance. A heavyset woman lay tanning on a towel, and an old man, fully dressed, sat facing outward on a canvas chair at the end of a rickety dock. The only one in the water was Robin, swimming a determined breaststroke parallel to the shore with his expression grim and set. David stood watching from the water's edge. He had taken off his robe but he was bone-dry; clearly he had not so much as dipped a toe in. "What do you think of the lake?" Mercy asked, coming up behind him, and he turned and asked, "Is Daddy going to drown?"

"No, no, no," she assured him, "Daddy's a *good* swimmer." David turned away again and resumed watching his father.

"You planning to get wet?" Alice asked him.

He said, "Pretty soon I am."

"Want me to take you?"

"No, that's okay."

Alice removed her shirt and tossed it onto the sand next to her camera. "Well, here goes," she said, and she began wading in. The water was lukewarm but turned cooler the farther she waded, and when she finally ducked under it was cold enough to make her gasp.

Viewed from here, the shoreline had the quaint, static look of a scene in her mother's book of French paintings—the old man on the dock shaded by a giant straw hat, the woman just a flattened strip of color against the sand. David was squatting now to fill his bucket. Mercy was taking dainty steps deeper and deeper until finally she launched herself forward in a breaststroke considerably more graceful than Robin's. She had spent her girlhood vacationing in Ocean City, was why. She was no stranger to water. But after a few yards or so, she stopped swimming and stood up. "Come on out!" Robin called to her, but she said, "I don't want to get my hair wet." She had the kind of hair that took forever to dry, thick and wavy, with ringlets spilling from a chignon piled high on top of her head. She said, "I was thinking I might fetch my sketch pad and take a little walk in the woods. Can you keep an eye on David?"

"Sure thing," Robin said. "I'll teach him how to swim; how's that?"

"Oh, good," Mercy said. She turned and started wading back, her arms held straight out at her sides and her hands lifted like little birds, while far beyond her, up at the edge of the woods, a small version of Lily could be seen shading her eyes to observe them. She didn't come any closer, though. She didn't even have her swimsuit on, and after a moment she turned away and disappeared again.

The difference between this scene and the ones in the French paintings, Alice thought, was that the paintings all showed people interacting—picnickers and boating parties. But here everybody was separate. Even her father, a few yards away from her, was swimming now toward shore. A passerby would never guess the Garretts even knew each other. They looked so scattered, and so lonesome.

All three of the children, even David, knew that their mother hated to cook. She claimed she *loved* to cook, but what she meant was, she loved to make desserts. And her desserts were the fancy kind: not cookies or chocolate pudding but delicate pastry cornucopias filled with sweetened whipped cream, and towering structures of meringue studded with candied violets. Things she'd served in her youth to her gentleman callers, Alice surmised. Beautiful to look at, but not what her children wanted to eat.

Or Robin, either, although he never admitted it. He would say, of some lacy concoction, "Why, honey! How did you *do* that?" But he wouldn't have more than a sample spoonful of it.

This meant that Alice took on more of a role in the kitchen than most girls her age. She opened a can of Dinty Moore or boiled some frankfurters, to begin with, but gradually she moved on to simple casseroles and then to recipes from *Woman's Day* or the food page of the newspaper—dishes with "Espagnol" in their names or "à la Française." "Oh, why, sweetheart!" her father would say, poor man. "Did *you* fix this?" He was a meat-and-potatoes guy himself. But she knew he was grateful to her for pitching in.

For their first supper at the lake—Mercy not back from sketching yet, David cranky with hunger—Alice heated some tinned corned beef hash and topped it with grated cheddar and a sprinkle of chives from a bottle she'd found in the cupboard. (Previous renters had left all manner of odds and ends behind—jams and dried beans and barbecue sauces and various mysterious cans that she looked forward to exploring.) She sliced up several farmstand cucumbers and doused them in a mixture of Mazola and cider vinegar. David, meanwhile, begged for something to hold him over. Crackers, cookies—"Anything!" he said dramatically, but then turned down the slice of cucumber she offered.

"Where's your mother?" her father asked her. It was a constant refrain of his: "Where could she *be*?"

Alice said, "Still out sketching. Let's start without her." Then she slapped plates on the table, and counted out silverware, and raced around hunting napkins till she realized they'd forgotten to bring any and started tearing off sections of paper toweling instead.

Alice often liked to imagine that a book was being written about her life. A narrator with an authoritative male voice was describing her every act. "Alice sighed" was a frequent observation. "Go call Lily for supper," she told David, and David said, "She's not here," and Alice said, "Where is she?" and David said, "She went off with a boy."

"Alice sighed heavily," the narrator said.

It was true that Lily was off with a boy. Trent, his name was; apparently they'd met when she happened to stroll past his family's lake house. She showed up with him toward the end of the meal. By that time Mercy was back from sketching, pine needles clinging to the folds of her skirt, and the four of them were starting in on their butter brickle ice cream. "Where have you *been*?" Alice asked Lily, while their mother sat up straighter and sent Trent an extra-bright smile. He was a handsome, heavy-browed boy in a U of Maryland T-shirt, and Alice figured him to be several years older than Lily. Lily said, "This here is Trent, and him and me are going to this burger place in town so I won't be needing supper."

"Isn't that nice!" Mercy said, at the same time that Robin asked, "How're you getting there?"

"Oh, Trent has a car," Lily told him.

"You a safe driver, son?"

Lily said, "Daddy!" but Alice thought he was right to ask, and also she didn't like the prompt, easy way Trent answered him. "Yes, *sir*, an excellent driver," he said. Something smarmy about him, Alice thought. Robin, though, said, "Okay, then, I guess. Don't keep her out too late," and Lily gave a twiddly wave with just her fingertips and the two of them left.

It always puzzled Alice, how the boys would flock to Lily. Oh, she was pretty enough, in a round-faced, dimply sort of way, but that didn't explain why they grew so alert when she walked into a room. It seemed she gave off some kind of high-pitched signal that only male ears could detect. (Grown men as well as boys. Alice had noticed more than one friend's father sending Lily that same sharp arrow of awareness.) Alice herself was asked out only on occasion, only for official events like school dances. She knew she lacked Lily's powers of attraction. She wasn't even sure she wanted them. (She *really* disliked the look of that Trent guy.)

"Well," Robin said, once the two of them had left, "so much for Jump Watkins, heh-heh," and Mercy told him, "Oh, now, she just likes to socialize." Then they went back to eating their ice cream.

The next morning, though, all through breakfast, it was Trent this and Trent that with Lily. Trent came from DC; he played varsity tennis; next year he was joining his father's sporting-goods business. "How *old* is he?" Alice asked, and Lily said, breezily, "Twenty-one. Why?" and then rushed on to talk about his family's lake house, just down the shore. It was huge, she said, and they owned it outright, and there was a stag's head above the fireplace. "You've been inside?" Mercy asked, and Lily said, "Yes, and I met both his sisters and their boyfriends." Then she excused herself and went to get dressed, because she and Trent were taking a spin in his family's motorboat.

Mercy's plan for the day, she said, was to paint what she had sketched yesterday. While Alice was still clearing the breakfast dishes, Mercy set her new travel-size kit of acrylics and her pad of canvas paper on the kitchen table—the only workspace available. "Will you be finished by lunchtime?" Alice asked her, and Mercy said, "Oh, my, yes," but Alice had her doubts. Her mother tended to get all caught up in her painting once she began. Most likely they'd be eating lunch on their laps in the living room, if things proceeded as they usually did.

Alice herself went for a swim, taking David with her, and Robin said he'd be joining them because it was a "shame to waste the lake," as he put it, but first he wanted to see what he could do about the loose window screen in his and Mercy's bedroom. Clearly, he was feeling edgy with so much free time on his hands.

Today David brought a collection of toys to the lake—a half-dozen or so little plastic GIs rattling around in his bucket. Except he kept calling them "veterinarians." Alice thought at first he meant veterans, but no, when they reached the lake he dumped all the GIs out on the sand and told her, "This one here is Herman; he does the *big* animals, cows and horses. This here is Don and he does the cats and dogs."

"Where are their patients?" Alice asked him.

"It's not time yet to see the patients. First the veterinarians have to have a meeting. 'Well, Don,'" he said in a growly deep voice, "'I'm off to the Pimlico racetrack to see to that horse with the broken leg. What are *you* up to today?'" And then, in a slightly higher voice, "'That mother cat they brought in is just about to have her kittens and I'm about to deliver them.'"

Alice failed to see the point of this game. There was no action involved, unless you counted the way he made each soldier jump up from the sand a few inches when it was that one's turn to speak. But at least he was entertaining himself, and gradually his cases grew more detailed and developed into actual stories. (One dog, for instance, needed to be put down because he'd bitten a little boy, except that then the veterinarian proved the little boy was lying and so the dog's life was saved and the veterinarian decided to adopt it.) Alice smoothed on her special homemade mix of baby oil and iodine, rumored to speed the tanning process, because the sun here was much weaker than it would have been in Ocean City. Then she stretched out prone on her towel and leafed through a copy of *Mademoiselle*—the college issue, all about what young women would be wearing to college this fall.

Eventually, her father's work shoes and black socks appeared in front of her, and she raised her eyes to find him peering down at her. "Why aren't you in the water?" he asked.

"I'm waiting till I get hot enough."

"David? Want to come in with me?"

"I can't; I've got an emergency here," David said.

Their father was silent a moment, perhaps trying to figure this out. Then he tugged off his T-shirt and dropped it on Alice's towel. "Well, *I'm* going in," he said.

Alice sat up and gazed after him as he walked away. Several people were in the water this morning—a young couple, a man supervising a toddler, and someone unidentifiable swimming far from the shore. Not till Robin reached the very edge did he bend to take his shoes and socks off, and he set them side by side on the sand but spent some time watching the other swimmers before he began wading in.

He was not a born vacationer, Alice thought. There was something effortful about him. He kept his elbows raised above the water, and his shoulder blades stuck out from his back like fryer wings.

The beach itself was more populated today. The heavyset woman was back, lying on her striped towel as if she had never left, and a couple with a baby under a giant umbrella, and another couple with a whole crowd of boisterous children. The only boy among them looked to be about twelve or so—considerably older than David, but Alice gave it a try, even so. "Think you'd like to go talk to that boy over there?" she asked David. But he flicked the merest glance toward the boy, who was striding down to the water now. "No," he said. "He's too old."

"He looks really nice, though."

But David had already turned back to his veterinarians. He held one of them up over his head to watch a distant motorboat pass. "I saw three ships a-sailing by," he sang, "a-sailing by, a-sailing by . . ."

Alice reached for her Brownie Starflash and raised it to one eye and squinted. She wondered if it was Trent and Lily in the boat, but she couldn't tell from here.

You would think, judging from Mercy's fondness for her book of blurry French paintings, that her own paintings would be equally blurred—less scenery than a shorthand for scenery. The fact was, though, that they were not that way; or not entirely, at least. Take the one she was working on when the three of them got back to the cabin. Her pine trees were vague green pyramids, her forest floor an expanse of brownish wash, but then in the foreground, at the lower left corner, her cast-off pompom sandals were as sharply defined as if they were sitting under a magnifying glass. The running stitches outlining each strap, the pores in the cork of the soles, even the tiny sweat bee that had alighted on a frond of one pompom: nothing had been left to the imagination. Alice found the contrast disturbing; the abrupt transition from hazy to specific made her eyeballs feel tight. Were the sandals meant to be a message? A clue to something? A symbol? Oh, she just didn't get it!

But then, she never did. So she said what she usually said: "That's nice, Mama," and went off to change out of her swimsuit. Behind her, she heard David ask, "Could your paintings be in a museum, ever?" And Mercy said, "Oh, *no* no no," and gave one of her tinkling laughs. "I just paint for me," she said, and she sent him off to get dressed.

It was obvious that Trent didn't have a steady girlfriend, Lily said, because the Ivy League buckle on the back of his khakis was unbuckled. "Maybe it's unbuckled by accident," Alice told her. "Maybe he's just sloppy."

"Are you kidding? It's a *statement*," Lily said. "Everybody knows that much."

"Couldn't you just ask him straight out if he's going steady?"

Lily gave her a look.

By now it was the fourth day of their stay, and Lily had spent every one of those days exclusively with Trent. From the sound of it, they mostly hung out at his family's lake house. "What do you do there?" Alice asked, and Lily said, "Oh, just swim and stuff." The only time Trent appeared at the Garretts' was when he stopped by to pick Lily up, sometime in the mid-morning. (He drove, although it was only a walk.) "Hey there, gorgeous," he would greet her. And then, "Hey, Mr. Garrett. Mrs. Garrett, aren't *you* looking fine!"

Robin, nursing his third cup of coffee, would merely grunt, but Mercy would say, "Why, thank you, Trent. How are you today?"

"I'm doing great, thanks."

Alice he all but ignored. He would lift a hand a few inches in her direction and let it flop again. And to David he just said, "Hey, kid."

"Hey," David said, but he didn't look up from what he was doing.

This particular morning David announced, after Trent and Lily had left, "Trent says things that aren't real."

Alice said, "Mm-hmm."

But Mercy said, "What, honey? What are you talking about? What did he say that wasn't real?"

"I don't know, but it wasn't," David said.

"Oh, now. I think he's cute," Mercy said.

It was strange, Alice reflected, that a grown woman couldn't see as clearly as a seven-year-old. But then, David often seemed weirdly smart about people.

As for Robin, all he offered was, "At least he's mannerful; I'll say that."

There was a brief silence.

"Alice loved her father very much," her narrator said, "but sometimes she despaired of him."

Then Robin drove to the Esso station to put some air in the tires, and Mercy traveled about the cabin collecting her sketching supplies. David, seated on the rug with a coloring book, told Alice, "I like Jump Watkins better than Trent. Don't you?"

"Ah, well, Trent is a college man, don't you know," Alice said.

"He's not a *man*," David said.

Before Alice could explain that she had been speaking sarcastically, their mother added her own two bits from the kitchen. "Maybe not to *you,* hon," she called, "but I can see Alice's point: he's way more sophisticated than Jump Watkins is."

David and Alice exchanged a glance, but they didn't say anything.

That was the night when Lily came back so late that everyone except Alice had already gone to bed. Alice was listening to the radio in the living room. (The cabin didn't have a television set. She was losing her mind with boredom.) The program she had hit upon was some kind of request show; a DJ read out people's letters and then played the songs they asked for. "Here's one for Jerry from Kate, she misses him very much," he said, and "The Man in the Raincoat" started up. Alice found this interesting. (What kind of person must Jerry be, if "taken my money and skipped out of town" brought him to Kate's mind?) Then a pair of headlights swung across the dimly lit room, and a moment later she heard footsteps crossing the porch and Lily walked in the door. "You still up?" she asked Alice. "What time is it?"

"You're asking *me* that?" Alice said. But when she heard her own tone, more a mother's tone than a sister's, she covered it quickly with "Have a good evening?"

"I had a wonderful evening," Lily said. She flung herself on the couch next to Alice. She smelled of cigarettes—probably Trent's, since her one attempt at smoking had made her throw up. "I did kind of ask about the going-steady thing," she said. "He'd paid me this really sweet compliment; I'm not going to repeat it; and I said, 'I bet you tell your girl back home that, too,' and he said, 'What girl back home?' and I said, 'Oh, now, I know you must have a steady girlfriend,' and he said, 'Why would I be sitting here with you, then?' So!"

"So," Alice said.

Lily's mouth looked swollen, and her cheeks were flushed. She seemed extra perky and excited; sort of artificial. "Alice," she said, "can I ask you a favor?"

"What's that?" Alice asked warily.

"Suppose if Trent takes it into his head to, I don't know, propose or something."

"Propose!"

"Or, I don't know. It could happen. I mean, this is not some little puppy-love thing. This is serious! So I'm just saying, suppose you happen to get wind of it. He asks you my ring size or something."

"Lily—"

"Just let me say this! If he should mention it to you, could you let him know I've always wanted to be proposed to in a gazebo?"

"*What?*"

Lily leaned toward her, clasping her hands tightly in her lap. "Ever since I was a little girl," she said, "I've pictured a guy in a gazebo asking me to marry him. I know it sounds silly, but . . . and guess what! Where Trent's folkses' lake house is, there's this house next door even bigger and it's got the prettiest little gazebo in the backyard. I couldn't believe it! I happened to glance over when we were on his patio and I could not believe it."

"Lily," Alice said, "Trent is not going to propose to you."

"You don't know that!"

"You're fifteen years old. Not even old enough to drive yet. And you met him just four days ago. Besides which, another thing is . . . Trent is not somebody you should trust."

"You don't even know him!"

"I know him well enough to see he's a guy on the make. He's stuck here with just his family, none of his friends nearby, and he spies this little underage girl hanging around all starry-eyed and 'Ho-ho-*ho*!' he says to himself. 'What have we *here*?' he says."

"Now, that is just mean," Lily told her. "You're just jealous *you* don't have anyone. Talk about *stuck* someplace! Just because you've got no one yourself, you want to ruin things for me."

And she jumped up and stomped off to their bedroom, slamming the door behind her.

She'd been loud enough so that Alice half expected their parents to hear. She *needed* them to hear. She glanced hopefully toward their room, but their door stayed shut and silent.

"See if you can get your boy into the water," Robin told Mercy over breakfast the next morning. "It appears he wants to stay on dry land and admire the lake from a distance."

Mercy turned to look at David. He was dusting his Cheerios with spoonfuls of cocoa powder; he called such experiments "cooking." "Is that true?" she asked him. "You don't like going in the water?"

"It's got a squelchy bottom," he told her.

"How would you even *know* that?" Robin demanded. It came out like a sort of explosion. "You haven't even put your feet in yet!"

"I've put my feet in," David said. He stirred his Cheerios industriously.

"Half the time he doesn't so much as take his sandals off," Robin told Mercy. "He goes out to the end of the dock with his fishing rod, he calls it—piece of grocery twine tied to a stick. Not even a hook on the end. Sits there swinging his feet a good six inches above the water and sings those songs of his. While *Charlie*, now, Bentley's boy . . ."

Bentley was Robin's new friend—the father of the boisterous children Alice and David had spotted on their second day at the lake. The two men had struck up a conversation and found they had a lot in common; Bentley owned a contracting business and had recently installed his own plumbing in his family's new addition. In fact Alice was surprised to hear that her father had even noticed whether David went into the water or not, because he and Bentley liked to stand waist-deep with their arms folded across their chests and talk about sewage or something. Every now and then Charlie would plow past them with a showy Australian crawl, sending up a violent backwash, but Robin and Bentley just absently blotted their faces on their bare shoulders and went on talking.

"Maybe Charlie could teach David how to swim," Mercy said.

David stopped stirring his Cheerios. "Charlie's too old," he told her.

"Oh."

"What are you talking about?" Robin said. "He's not but ten or eleven, at most."

David said, "I think he must be twelve."

"Eleven, twelve . . . At least he's not scared to get wet!"

"Oh, Robin, let it be," Mercy said. "David will learn to swim when he's ready, just the way the girls did."

"The girls learned *way* before this. Alice learned when she was four."

Actually, she'd been eight. But her father hadn't worried about it.

There were advantages to being a girl and having nothing much expected of you.

Another advantage was that her mother announced after breakfast that she planned to take her girls shopping in the little town nearby. (Alice enjoyed shopping.) The fact that Lily was in bed still, and that when they woke her she said she couldn't go because Trent was coming to get her, didn't faze Mercy in the least. "So? He'll just have to wait," she said. "It'll make him appreciate you."

Then she added that, who knew, they might find Lily a new swimsuit. Lily had been complaining that her current suit was childish. "A bikini?" Lily asked.

"Well . . . a two-piece, at least."

"I don't want just a two-piece. No one but mothers wear two-pieces."

"We'll see," Mercy told her.

"Oh, goody!"

"We'll *see*, is all I said."

"Daddy, will you tell Trent to wait for me if he comes before I get back?" Lily asked.

"No can do, hon. I'll be down at the lake, teaching your brother to swim."

"Leave Trent a note," Mercy suggested. "Stick it in the screen door."

Lily didn't look happy, but she said nothing further. Apparently she figured a bikini was worth inconveniencing him.

Alice drove. Her mother sat next to her and Lily sat in back, sunk so low in her seat that her face didn't even show up in the rearview mirror. They took the little highway they'd come in on, continuing in the same direction. They passed small houses set close to the road with rustic wooden signs out front carved with names like FISHIN' FIEND and RETIREMENT ACRES. The whole way, Mercy chattered merrily. She was in a very happy mood. "When I was a girl," she told them, "I used to imagine how I'd take shopping trips with my daughter after I was married. Little did I dream I'd have *two* daughters! I pictured how we'd try on clothes together, and experiment with different shades of lipstick, and conspire to hide all our packages from her father when we got home."

"Will Dunnville have that kind of store, though?" Lily asked. "Won't it just have country kind of stores?"

"Oh, surely they'll have *some* nice places. This is a tourist area! Rich people come here!"

Lily had been right to wonder, though. Main Street turned out to be the road they were already traveling on, except with sidewalks. There was a hardware store and a drugstore, a dingy-looking café, and then a shop called Hi-Fashion with a single mannequin in the window wearing a marcelled plaster hairdo from the 1940s and a green gingham housewife dress. They went in anyhow. A bell clanked over the door. "Do you-all carry swimsuits?" Mercy asked the woman behind the counter, and the woman—kind-faced and pigeon-bosomed—perked up and cried, "Oh! Yes! We do have swimsuits! Over there on that rack!" But all the suits were one-piece, many with skirts. "This one's kind of cute," Mercy told Lily hopefully, fingering a pink-striped seersucker with boy-cut legs.

"Oh, *please*," was all Lily said. Mercy didn't push it.

They thanked the woman and walked out. They went to the drugstore, where the lipsticks were kept in a locked glass case and it felt like too much work to ask the young man at the register to open it. "But aren't these headbands pretty?" Mercy asked. They were crescent-shaped, covered with fabric in different colors. Nothing special, but for a moment Alice's eye was caught by a wide black grosgrain one. It would be good for when she dressed up, she thought. She stopped to lift it from the rack. "Alice flung her long hair carelessly over her shoulder," her narrator said. But she already owned a headband in black velvet, and really, that was dressier. She replaced it and continued toward the door, with Mercy and Lily following.

Out on the sidewalk, they paused to look across the street. A lawyer's office, a chiropractor, a shoe store displaying men's work boots. A small, dark grocery store called Robinson's with nothing but a brass scale centered in the window. "Oh, my," Mercy said wearily. Then she said, "Sometimes I think, is this *it*?"

Her daughters turned to stare at her. She thought it *sometimes*? Not just on this one occasion?

But then she gave her shoulders a shake and "Well," she said, "maybe we can find us a treat in that fancy grocery store."

So they crossed and went into the grocery, which was indeed fancy, with imported jellies and spices and corked bottles of flavored vinegars. Mercy said, "How about we choose some chocolates for dessert tonight?" and while she and Lily were deliberating, Alice strolled around the rest of the store. The fruits in the produce section were cradled in individual nests of green tissue and they were very expensive, and anyhow the family had all the fruit they needed from the farm stand; but she did select an avocado pear because you didn't often see those in Baltimore. When she set it on the counter where Mercy and Lily had set their chocolates, Lily said, "Seriously?" which gave Alice second thoughts, but then the customer ahead of them—an older woman buying a tiny can wrapped in gold paper—reached over and picked it up to examine it more closely, and Alice felt a stab of possessiveness. So she said, "*Yes,* seriously. All the more for us if you don't want to try it." And Lily said no more.

When Mercy had paid the cashier—a severe-looking woman who exchanged not a single word with them—they stepped out into the sunshine. Mercy was carrying their purchases in a tiny forest-green Robinson's bag. "So," she said. "Shall we get on home?" The girls didn't bother answering, just followed her down the sidewalk.

In the car, Mercy twisted around to tell Lily, "*Here's* an idea. Once we're back in Baltimore, we'll buy you a swimsuit at Hutzler's, how's that."

"A bikini?" Lily asked.

"Well . . . yes, okay, why not?"

Mercy turned and faced forward again. Alice checked the rearview mirror and found Lily looking smug and secretive.

When they reached the cabin, Trent's red Chevy was parked in their usual space. "Darn," Lily said, and she started tugging on her door handle even before their car had stopped behind his. "He's been *waiting* for me."

"All the better!" Mercy said. "Let him see you're worth it!" But she might as well not have spoken; Lily was already out of the car and halfway up the porch steps.

Alice and Mercy, following, had nearly reached the steps themselves when Robin appeared in the doorway. There was something strange about him. He didn't have his shoes and socks on, Alice realized. He was in his swim trunks and T-shirt—both noticeably wet, and plastered to his skin—but his archless, knobby white feet were naked, and he wore an odd sheepish expression as if he were embarrassed. "Hey there, hon!" he told Mercy brightly.

She stopped short at the top of the steps. "Robin?" she said suspiciously.

"How was your shopping trip?"

"What's wrong?" she asked.

"Wrong? Nothing's wrong!"

"Why are you dressed that way?"

"Oh, I was just, we were just down at the lake, don't you know, and David had a little incident."

"Incident?"

"He panicked and thought he was drowning."

"*What?*"

She pushed past him and hurried into the house. Alice and Lily followed; their father stood aside for them and then followed too, letting the screen door shut very gently behind him.

In the living room, Trent was lounging on the couch with one leg slung carelessly along the length of it, Alice's *Mademoiselle* open on his lap. He raised an index finger to Lily and said, "Hey, babe."

"Hi, Trent!"

"Where is he?" Mercy asked Robin.

He gestured silently toward their bedroom.

The door of the bedroom was shut, although in the daytime

it always stood open. Mercy flung open the door and rushed in, still carrying her Robinson's bag. "Honey?" she said. "Are you all right?"

David said something muffled that Alice couldn't make out. Meanwhile Lily was asking Trent, "Have you been waiting long?" and Trent said, "Well, longer than I cared to, let's put it that way."

Alice peered into the room. She saw David curled on his cot, wearing his trunks but nothing else, clutching his cowboy doll to his chest. Mercy sat on the edge of the cot, stroking his back. "Did you have a little scare?" she asked him.

He nodded, and then gave a sniff.

"Come on out to the living room with me," she suggested.

He just clutched his doll closer.

"You don't want to come out and sit in my lap?" she asked. "Maybe try one of the chocolates the girls and I brought you from town?"

A shake of his head.

She sat straighter and studied him for a moment. Then she rose and returned to the living room. She asked Robin, "What on earth happened?"

"Oh, well, me and Bentley were just, you know, standing there keeping a watch on him—"

"Did you throw him in?"

"What?"

"Did you throw him into the water?"

"*No,* I didn't throw him into the water! Why would I do that?"

"Like some sink-or-swim thing? You and Bentley doing some he-man thing?"

"What are you *talking* about?"

She walked over to the rocker and sank down into it. Trent had abandoned the couch by now; he was waiting by the front door while Lily rolled her towel into a cylinder around her swimsuit. "I'm going to Trent's house," she told Mercy, but Mercy just looked at her blankly.

"He wasn't in any danger, Mercy, I swear it," Robin said. "Me and Bentley were standing right there on the end of the dock. All I had to do was jump into the water and lift him up by one arm and he was *fine*. Soaked my shoes pretty good, though."

"Bye, Mama," Lily said. She and Trent left. Alice asked her mother, "Shall I put some things out for lunch?" But Mercy just dropped her shopping bag to the floor and rocked her chair back.

David did emerge from the bedroom, after a bit. He appeared while Alice and her parents were eating lunch; he crept quietly into the kitchen and hoisted himself onto his chair and plucked a slice of bologna from the platter. He still had his trunks on, but he'd added a sweatshirt, and he'd brought along his cowboy doll, which he laid facedown across his lap. Even Mercy knew enough not to make a fuss. She just moved the sack of bread a little closer to his plate and went on telling Robin about their trip into Dunnville. "Dullville, they *ought* to call it," she said. "I was expecting they might cater some to the tourist trade, but they don't."

"Missing out on a good thing there," Robin said. "Some guy with a little business sense could come along and make a killing."

"Well, sooner or later, I suppose—careful, honey," she broke off to tell David. "You're getting mustard on Bobby Shafto."

"Bascomb," David corrected her. Bascomb was who the doll had been before he became Bobby Shafto. (The Garretts' mailman was named Bascomb.)

"Oh, *excuse* me," Mercy told the doll. David moved Bascomb from his lap to the seat of his chair and went back to spreading mustard.

"In town I bought us an avocado pear," Alice told him. "I thought we could have it on Friday with our special last-night supper, how's that."

"Okay," David said.

But he didn't sound very interested.

"Now, an avocado pear is one thing I just never have understood," Robin said. "In what way is it a pear, I ask you. Is it even a fruit? Doesn't it seem more a type of vegetable?" He looked over at David. "What do *you* think, son?"

David shrugged almost imperceptibly and screwed the lid back on the mustard jar.

They let him be, after that. He would come around in his own good time. Robin walked over to Bentley's cabin after lunch to help out with a little electrical problem, and Mercy set up her paints on the kitchen table, and Alice changed into her swimsuit and went down to the lake. She did invite David along, but when he didn't bother answering she dropped the subject. She left him curled up on the couch with Bascomb, and when she returned an hour or so later he was sound asleep. Mercy told her he'd slept the whole time Alice had been gone. "It's a kind of healing process, I think," she said. "Clearing a troubling memory out of his brain. He'll be his normal self when he wakes up again." And she smiled at Alice and stirred her paintbrush around her white porcelain palette.

Lately, she'd been painting different sections of the cabin. A suggestion of pink-splotched wallpaper in the girls' room, with the facets of one cut-glass bureau knob minutely outlined by a brush with a tip like a pinpoint. A baseboard in the living room dissolving into the floorboards, distinct specks of something Alice took to be sand scattered all around it, except Robin said it was not sand but evidence of carpenter ants.

"I believe I'm more an interior kind of painter than an exterior kind," Mercy told Alice. "I was thinking this vacation might, oh, expand my vision, but when I was out there in the woods I felt so overwhelmed, you know? Like I was drifting in space."

"I do like the cabin paintings the best," Alice said.

She had the sudden peculiar feeling that she had somehow become older than her mother—her dainty little mother drifting in space. Because the awful truth was that Alice did not much like *any* of her mother's paintings, although she would never be unkind enough to tell her so.

The next morning, it was raining. Robin was the one who minded most. He said, "An arm and a leg this week cost us, and now a whole day of it is going to go to waste."

"Oh, not really to *waste*," Mercy told him. "We're still having ourselves a holiday, aren't we? Still spending time together as a family."

"Hmph."

"Besides, it'll do you good to get out of the sun for a while."

It was true that Robin's face had turned a bit ruddy. (All that standing about in the lake with Bentley.) At this rate, he would be the only one of them coming home from vacation with something to show for it, because Alice's baby-oil-and-iodine mixture had not had much effect, and Mercy and David hadn't been outdoors enough. As for Lily, well, Alice had to wonder how much of Lily's time at Trent's had really been spent swimming. She was still very pale. This morning when she arrived at the breakfast table—the last one up, as usual—Mercy asked her, "What are you going to do today now that you have to be inside?"

"Why would I have to be inside?" Lily asked.

"Because it's raining."

"It is?" Lily looked toward the kitchen window. "Well, darn."

"Maybe you could stay home for once and we could all play board games. They've got every kind of game here. Monopoly, Parcheesi . . . You should see what's in my closet!"

"Oh, Trent and me will think of something," Lily said offhandedly. She reached for the strawberry jam.

Mercy studied her. Then she said, "Have you heard from Jump since you got here?"

"How would I have heard from Jump?" Lily asked. "He doesn't have my address."

"Yes, but you were going to write him as soon as you'd figured out the mail situation."

"Well, I didn't," Lily said. "And even if I had, I doubt he'd have time to answer before I got home again."

She smoothed jam across her toast. Mercy raised her eyebrows at Alice and took a sip of coffee.

After breakfast, Robin went into town to cruise the hardware store, and David got busy with his veterinarians, and Mercy tidied her bedroom while the girls did the breakfast dishes. "All I can say is, it better not be raining tomorrow," Lily told Alice as she dried a plate.

"What's happening tomorrow?"

"It's our last day, silly. I'm spending the whole time with Trent. We're going to sit out on his patio; I've already got it planned. Next door to guess-what. The gazebo."

Alice dunked a skillet in the dishpan. "Well," she said, "I haven't mentioned gazebos to Trent, so don't hold your breath."

"That's okay, I'm thinking it will just naturally occur to him. We'll be sitting there; he'll wonder what I'm looking at; he'll turn and see the gazebo . . ."

Alice had a sudden image of Lily glancing meaningfully from Trent to the gazebo, Trent to the gazebo, the way Cap liked to gaze from the humans sitting around the table to the roast beef on the sideboard. She snorted.

"What?" Lily demanded. "What's so funny? You don't believe me? The two of us think alike, I tell you. He's every bit as romantically minded as I am."

"I seriously doubt *that*," Alice told her.

"Alice, I mean this. If Trent doesn't propose before I leave here I'll just die. I really will die, I swear."

"It's not going to happen, Lily."

"Yes, it will," Lily said, "because it has to. And that's all I'm going to say about it."

Then she tossed her dish towel onto the drainboard and stalked out, even though the dishes weren't anywhere near finished.

The only game David wanted to play was Go Fish, it turned out, which was fine with Mercy but not so much with Alice, because Go Fish could drag on so long. It certainly did today. They must have flipped the deck half a dozen times, and they were still at it when Trent showed up. "Come play cards with us, Trent!" Mercy told him. She seemed to think they were back in the olden days, when suitors would agree to such things. Trent tactfully pretended not to hear. "Ready, babe?" he asked Lily, and she nodded and followed him out the door. She was carrying her towel-and-swimsuit roll, as if she imagined the weather might change.

Alice waited till David was absorbed in drawing cards, and then she asked her mother, "Do you think they're chaperoned, in that house?"

"Chaperoned!" her mother said. She sounded amused, as if Alice were the one who was back in the olden days. "Goodness, they've got his whole family around. I hardly think they lack for company."

So Alice gave up. Anyhow, it was her turn to play a card.

On Friday, the sun returned. Everybody took heart. Lily went off with Trent, and Alice and Robin had a swim, and Mercy sat on her towel with David. Alice suggested to Robin that they try swimming to the opposite shore, but he told her it was too far. Secretly, she was relieved.

After a while Bentley arrived, so she left the lake to the two men and headed toward dry land. She found David and Mercy beginning a sand castle, and she spread her towel next to them and sat down to apply her tanning mix.

The sand here was normally too loose for sand castles, but yesterday's rain had made it easy to pack it into David's bucket and turn out cylindrical towers. As soon as Mercy discovered that, she went back to the cabin and returned with more equipment—teacups and Jell-O molds and square Pyrex storage containers—so that they could build a whole city. Mercy could get very caught up when it came to making things. She collected branching twigs for David to use as trees; she began constructing a city wall with pebbles. Her face shone with sweat and Skolex cream, and her hair slipped loose from her topknot without her noticing.

The rest of Bentley's crew came down, his wife and their gang of children. Tania, the wife, spread their towels nearby while the children went to play in the water. The little ones were content to stay in the shallows but, wouldn't you know, Charlie had to plunge straight in and swim out toward the men and then beyond them, kicking up a storm.

This apparently reminded Robin that he hadn't taught David to swim yet. "Son?" he called from the water. He cupped his hands around his mouth and called, "Davy? Come on out, son!" But David kept his back to the lake and went on planting twigs. "Tell your boy he should come out!" Robin called to Mercy.

"Your father's asking for you," Mercy told David.

"I want to go back to the cabin," he said. He stood up and brushed off his hands.

"Now?" Mercy asked. She looked surprised. She sent a glance toward the lake, but Robin and Bentley were having a conversation.

"He does seem a little flushed," Tania commented from her towel. "Did you bring a sun hat for him?"

"Why, no, I—"

"I bet *I* have one. Somewhere, here . . ."

Tania started rooting through her tote. David turned and looked beseechingly at Alice. "I'll take you," she told him.

She got up from her towel and reached for his hand. Mercy sat back on her haunches, still holding a pebble, and asked him, "Don't you want to finish our city?"

"No, thank you," David said.

"Well . . . okay. I'll finish it for you," she decided.

She leaned forward to set her pebble in place on the city wall, and David and Alice left.

For lunch, Alice set out odds and ends—everything they needed to use up before they went home. Half a pack of bologna, half a container of coleslaw, a hamburger from last night's supper, briefly reheated in a skillet . . . Robin was the one who ate the burger. "These came out pretty good," he told Mercy. "Right?" Because he'd grilled them himself in the backyard, shielding them with a sheet of cardboard so they wouldn't get rained on.

He was eating lunch in his swimsuit, and so were Mercy and Alice. David, though, had changed into shorts and a T-shirt the minute he'd reached the cabin. Clearly he wasn't planning to go back down to the lake. Their mother must have realized this, but she pretended not to. "Wait till you see what I've done with our city," she told him. "I'll show you after lunch. It's a masterpiece!"

"That's nice, Mama," David said quietly.

Mercy cocked her head at him, but she didn't say anything more.

"Next time, though," Robin announced, "I'll let the coals sit a bit longer before I put the meat on. Tonight when I grill our . . . What am I grilling?"

"Pork chops," Alice told him.

"Tonight when I grill our pork chops I'm going to wait till the coals are purely gray, solidly gray with no glow to them."

"I've already got them marinating," Alice told him.

"Marinating?"

"They've been sitting in this marinade I mixed from things I found in the cupboard. Really I just made it up, but I think it'll be delicious."

Robin frowned.

"You are such a creative cook, honey," her mother told her.

"I even found wine in the cupboard. Red. Well, just a little bit in the bottom of a bottle, but it was enough with everything else I added."

"How *old* was this wine?" Robin asked suspiciously.

"Wine doesn't get *old*, Daddy. Well, it does, but that's fine for marinades. All the magazines say so."

He went on frowning. He said, "I haven't forgotten the eggplant."

Alice had once served the family Eggplant Parmigiana. Her father had taken a mouthful and then stopped chewing and asked, "What *is* this? What is this slippery part?"

"It's eggplant," Alice had told him.

"Oh, dear God," he'd said, and he had set his fork down.

Perhaps remembering this too, Mercy told him, "The nice thing about marinades is, they enhance the meat's normal flavor. They don't add their *own* taste; they just enhance the taste of the meat."

Actually, Alice wasn't so sure about this. There were a lot of unusual ingredients in her marinade, including black sesame oil and some cute little bottled peppers with a long Italian name. But she told her father, "You're going to love it."

"Okay . . ." he said in a faint voice.

Mercy patted his hand.

After lunch Mercy and Robin went back down to the lake—Mercy had agreed to take a dip with him, seeing as this was their last day—and Alice said she would be along with David once she'd cleaned up the kitchen. She didn't look at David as she said this, and David didn't contradict her.

Once their parents were gone, Alice threw out any leftovers they hadn't managed to finish and washed the dishes. Then she and David played several games of Crazy Eights. David said that they ought to keep score; play till the first person reached a hundred points. Ordinarily they didn't count points, but just stopped when one of them ran out of cards. So she knew he was trying to put off going to the lake. "Tell you what," she said, laying the deck aside. "Why don't you and me figure out what to do with that avocado pear."

"Yes!" he said, as if it had been weighing on his mind all along.

"I'm thinking a salad. What's your opinion?"

"A salad. Goody."

"What else should be in our salad?"

"Um, lettuce, bananas . . ."

"Bananas!"

"Or . . . I don't know . . ."

"Tomatoes, maybe?"

"Yes, tomatoes."

Alice rose and went to the icebox to check the crisper drawer. "Well," she said, "we do have lettuce, but no more tomatoes. I guess we need to buy some."

This wasn't a made-up errand; she really should have planned her side dishes better. But now that she thought about it, she was just as glad to be done with swimming. "Let me get out of my suit," she told David, "and we'll drive to town."

"Okay!"

So she went to change clothes in her room, and then she took her purse from her bureau drawer and her father's car keys from the mantel, and they left.

The greenery along the road had a freshly washed look after yesterday's rain. A lot of vacationers were out riding bicycles, and she drove extra carefully to avoid them.

"I miss my bicycle," David told her.

"Well, you'll be home tomorrow."

"And I miss Cap and I miss Jimmy next door and I miss my lamp with the covered wagon on it."

"You'll see them soon enough."

She glanced sideways at him. He was sitting in the front seat next to her, his face turned toward his window so the nape of his neck was exposed. It looked spindly and sad, somehow.

In town, the sidewalks were almost empty. It was the last day for lots of people, no doubt. Alice was able to park directly in front of Robinson's. And inside the store, they found they were the only customers. Alice led the way to the produce section, where she let David choose two tomatoes. No more than that, she instructed him; they were killingly expensive. "Highway robbery!" she whispered. (A pet phrase of their father's.)

David asked, "Do we have enough money?"

"Yes, I believe we can swing it."

This felt like a whole different place, now that she had David with her. When the severe-looking cashier saw him, she brightened and picked up a jar of lollipops. "Take two," she urged him. David had never liked hard candies—he said they made his teeth feel furry—but he selected a red lollipop and a green one. "Thank you, ma'am," he said. Alice had no idea how he'd known to add the "ma'am." It wasn't something that children were taught in their part of Baltimore.

In the car heading back to the cabin, he asked, "Do I like avocado pears?"

"You love them," she said.

"When did I have one?"

"Well . . . I don't know," she said. "But I'm pretty sure you *will* love them, because you're an adventurous kind of person."

He let his head tip back against the back of his seat, and he looked over at her and smiled.

When they reached the cabin, they found Trent's Chevy parked out front, all its windows open. "Hmm," Alice said. "So much for the gazebo."

"What?"

"Nothing."

They got out of the car and went inside, but there was no sign of Trent and Lily. They must have gone down to the lake. Alice set her Robinson's bag on the kitchen counter. "Here," David told her, and he handed her his lollipops, which she stowed in the cupboard among the cans and jars for whoever stayed here next. Then she took her purse to her bedroom.

Except her bedroom door was shut, and when she turned the knob, it wouldn't open. She shoved her shoulder against it. She turned the knob again. Nothing happened.

From inside she heard movement—a scurrying sound, a murmur. She tried the knob once more and this time it was grabbed from inside and twisted violently, and the door fell open and Trent walked out, tucking his shirt into his khakis.

Alice drew back a few steps. Trent crossed the living room. "Hi, kid," he told David.

"Hi," David said.

Trent walked out the front door, letting the screen door slap shut behind him.

Alice tossed a glance into the bedroom—Lily sitting on the very edge of her bed, buttoning her blouse, not looking in her direction. Then she spun around and strode after Trent. She arrived on the porch just as he was getting into his car, and she reached him before he could close the driver's-side door. "Stop," she told him.

He stopped.

"You will leave this place and not come back," she said. "You will never see Lily again. My uncle is a policeman, and my family will have him arrest you if we ever catch you anywhere near her."

Too late, she realized she should have said "judge." Her uncle was a judge. Judges had more power. But Trent looked ruffled anyhow. He said, "Fine! I'm leaving!" Then he slammed his door shut and started the engine quicker than she would have thought possible, and the car lurched backward and then forward and swerved out onto the road.

Alice went back into the cabin. She was shaking. Her bedroom door was closed again, but she didn't try to open it. Instead she returned to the kitchen. She set her purse on the table.

"We forgot to buy salad dressing," David told her.

"We can make our own," Alice said.

Her voice was thin and quavery, but she didn't think David noticed.

The marinated pork chops turned out beautifully. Even Robin agreed. He'd drawn the corners of his mouth down when he first saw them—damp and inky-looking, strewn with stray bits of spices—but they emerged from the grill a nice crusty brown, and when he took his first bite he said, "Well . . ."

"Good, huh?" Alice asked him.

"I've got to admit," he said, and Mercy said, "They're delicious!" David, who was often distrustful of meat, cut himself the smallest bite and chewed it gingerly, with just his front teeth, but a moment later Alice saw him take another bite, so she knew he thought it was okay, at least. And he ate a lot of his salad.

Lily was not at the table. She was in her room with the door shut. They'd called her name twice and she still hadn't come out, so Mercy rose to go knock. No answer. She opened the door and stuck her head in. "Honey?" she asked. They heard Lily say something. Mercy was silent a moment, and then she said, "Well, suit yourself," and closed the door and returned to the table. She seemed more amused than distressed. "Young love," she said lightly to Robin, and she picked up her fork.

"What: you're going to let her skip supper?" Robin asked.

"She'll be all right," Mercy said. She speared a tomato wedge.

"Why are you humoring her, Mercy? It's the last night of our vacation! We're eating a special dinner! She needs to come out and join the family like a civilized human being!"

"Oh, Robin. She's brokenhearted. You remember how it feels."

"No, I do *not* remember. She's fifteen years old. She's going to fall for some new boy before the week is out; you watch."

"She says nobody understands her and she wants to die," Mercy told him. Then she asked, "Can I have the rest of your salad?"

She meant the three chunks of avocado pear sitting alone on his plate. He'd picked his way around them as fastidiously as Cap would pick around any vegetables in his food bowl. "Go ahead," he told her, and he drew back to give her room to stab a chunk with her fork.

So Lily was forgotten, and it was probably just as well. She'd only have sat there sulky and tear-stained, dampening the atmosphere. Which was very festive, really. Mercy was teasing Robin now with a forkful of avocado pear, and Robin was pretending to shrink away in horror, and David was grinning at both of them.

"Alice took another bite of pork," her narrator said, "and savored its subtle seasoning."

3

On the morning of September 6, 1970—a Sunday, clear and cool but nowhere near fall-like yet—Robin and Mercy Garrett drove their son, David, to Islington, Pennsylvania, to start his freshman year at Islington College. They settled him in his room, they introduced themselves to his roommate (a nice enough boy, by the looks of him, though not half as nice as *her* boy, Mercy felt), and they said their goodbyes and left.

For most of the drive home, they were quiet. Occasionally they would say things like "Those walls could have used a coat of paint, in my opinion" (this from Robin) and "I wonder if David will remember a single word of my laundry instructions" (from Mercy). But generally, they stayed sunk in that sort of silence that radiates unspoken thoughts—complicated, conflicting thoughts cluttering the air inside the car.

Then, on the Baltimore Beltway, fifteen minutes from home, Robin said, "I suppose we should kick up our heels tonight, now that we're back to just the two of us. Go out for a fancy meal or, I don't know, have wild sex on the living-room floor or something"—a dry little laugh here—"but you know? I'm feeling kind of let down, to be honest."

"Well, of course you are, honey," Mercy told him. "We've lost the last remaining chick in our nest! It's natural we would feel low."

And she did feel low; no question about it. In many ways David was the child closest to her heart, although she'd expected to feel closer to her girls. After Alice and Lily left home it was just David and his parents, and the chaos died down and sometimes Mercy was able to hold actual brief conversations with him. Besides which, Alice had always been so bossy and confident, and Lily was such a, well, mess, really; but David had a sort of stillness about him and a listening, attentive quality that Mercy had come to appreciate, these past few years.

But. Even so. Mercy had a plan in mind, and of the many emotions that she was feeling as they drove home, the predominate one was anticipation.

On Monday morning, as soon as Robin left for work, Mercy went to her closet and retrieved a flattened Sunkist carton she'd picked up at the supermarket. She opened it out, reinforced the bottom with packing tape, and started filling it with clothes.

Not *all* her clothes. Oh, no. To look in her bureau drawers, once she'd rifled them, you would never suppose anything was missing. Knit tops remained, but just the ones she didn't wear very often—the faded ones, the unbecoming ones. Underpants remained, but just the ones with the waistbands going. The carton was not over-large—she had to be able to carry it for several blocks—and she didn't pack it too tightly. Plenty of clothes still hung in her closet that she hadn't even looked at yet.

But she had all the time in the world for that.

She folded the flaps of the carton shut, hefted it to one hip, carried it down to the kitchen, and let herself out the back door.

It was Labor Day, and although Robin had gone in to work as usual, a lot of the neighbors were still asleep. She walked down her street without encountering a single other person, and once she'd turned onto Belvedere the few pedestrians she saw were strangers. They didn't give her so much as a glance.

On Perth Road, she took a right at the third house from the corner—a white clapboard house with a patchy little front lawn—and followed a worn path around back to the garage. A fragile-looking wooden staircase ran up one side. She climbed it and unlocked the door to her studio.

It wasn't the sort of studio originally meant to be lived in. At some point someone must have fixed it up for a teenage son itching to leave home, or a husband longing for a den. Not counting the tiny bathroom carved out of a rear corner, the space was a single open square with one window overlooking the patio. The kitchen area was merely a linoleum-topped sink counter with a hot plate sitting on top of it and a miniature fridge alongside. There was a small Formica table and a single chair that Mercy never sat in, because she liked to stand when she was painting. Tubes of acrylics and jars of brushes and various-sized pads of canvas paper were strewn across the table's surface—the only clutter she allowed herself. The couch was a daybed with a faded brown corduroy slipcover, and the bureau beside it bore a tasseled lamp that couldn't take a bulb over forty watts. More linoleum on the floor, but in a different pattern from the linoleum on the counter. No curtains; just a yellowed paper shade. No rug. No closet.

Mercy loved it.

Robin had balked, at first, when she'd proposed renting it. That was three years ago, when both girls were already long gone. He'd said, "Why not paint in the girls' room? The girls' room is standing empty!"

"The girls' room is our guest room," she told him.

The Garretts never had overnight guests. Mercy's few relatives lived nearby and Robin's were mostly dead, and they knew nobody out of town. But Robin couldn't argue further, because even though he was the family's sole earner, the store belonged to Mercy and so she had some say in their household finances. She wondered how the conversation would have ended if that hadn't been the case. He was proud to have a wife who painted, she knew, but she suspected he thought of it as a hobby, like embroidery or crochet.

This was about to change, if Mercy had anything to say about it.

She removed the few items in the chest of drawers—extra art supplies, an out-of-date *Life* magazine—and replaced them with the clothes she'd brought. She had also brought a toothbrush and a tube of toothpaste, a shower cap, a comb, and a bottle of shampoo. She put these in the bathroom, which till now had been outfitted only with a bar of soap and a hand towel. Then she sat down on the daybed and stared out the window. This was what she planned to do here: sit and think, all by herself. Or *not* think. Be a blank. In addition to painting, of course.

From where she sat, all she could see was the top of the oak tree that towered in the Motts' backyard. Beyond that was sky, but she couldn't see the sky right now, because the oak was still fully leafed out. The leaves hadn't even started to turn; they were a deep, lustrous green, and they gave her a feeling of peace.

Finally she stood up and retrieved her empty carton and went home.

On Tuesday she brought a bath towel, a washcloth, a set of linens, and a flannel blanket. She stripped the daybed of its cover and made it up and fitted the cover on again, leaving the pillowcase on the bureau for when she had a pillow. She'd forgotten there was no pillow here—just a row of corduroy cushions propped against the wall. She would have to buy one on Saturday when she had the car.

And if Robin happened to be down in his basement workshop on Saturday, she might even load some of the heavier items—a few dishes, a saucepan or two, the clock radio from the girls' room—and drop them off at the studio while she was out and about.

She experienced a kind of inner leap at this thought, a sense of enthusiasm she hadn't felt in years.

Wednesday was the first day they could hope for a letter from David. That is, assuming it took only a day for mail to travel from Pennsylvania. But since it was western Pennsylvania, it might take longer. Also, there was no guarantee that he would write so soon. She had asked him to; she had begged him to. "Drop us a line the minute you're settled," she had told him, "just to say if you're okay." And Robin had added, "You know how your mother worries, son." But you never could predict with David.

Anyhow, even so, she lingered at home that morning and waited for the mailman. All for nothing, it turned out. Robin called from the store to check, even, which proved that she was not the only one who worried. She said, "I wish we could phone him. I did make a note of the number for his dorm."

But Robin said, "What, and listen to the money ticking away while they try to track him down?"

"No, I know. You're right," she said.

So instead, she phoned the girls. Alice was a stay-at-home mom now—she and Kevin had a nine-month-old baby—so she was easy enough to reach, but hard to keep on the line. "What do you expect? David's a *guy*," she told Mercy. "You'll be lucky if you hear—no! Robby! Take that out of your mouth!" (They'd named the baby Robin, even though she was a girl.) "Give it to Mommy, sweetheart. Mom, I have to go. She's eating kibble out of the dog's dish."

Lily was more difficult to reach. This was surprising, since she was between jobs at the moment. (She was between jobs an awful lot, it seemed to Mercy.) But maybe she'd landed something new. At any rate, her telephone just rang and rang, so eventually Mercy hung up and went to her studio after all.

Today she took with her a choice selection of skirts. She had never been a pants person. She wore skirts or dresses. But dresses required hangers and the studio had no closet, whereas skirts could lie flat if necessary. She had given this some thought. She had deliberately left room for them in the long bottom drawer of the bureau.

The studio had developed a different smell since yesterday. It had a slightly floral scent that she identified as *her* smell. Or her brand of laundry detergent, at least.

While she was there, she tried calling Lily again on the phone in the kitchen. This time, Lily answered. "Hello?" she said. There was something wary in her voice, as if she feared bad news.

"Hi, honey!" Mercy said brightly. "How you doing?"

There was a silence. Then, "I'm just going to say this straight out, Mom," Lily said. "I'm expecting."

"Oh!" Mercy paused. "Expecting . . . a baby?"

She heard a snort of something like laughter.

"Well, that's wonderful, honey!" she said. Lily had always claimed that she and B.J. had no interest in children, but of course people could change their minds.

"I was planning to bring it up at David's goodbye supper," Lily said, "except then I chickened out."

"I bet B.J. is excited," Mercy said, testing.

"It isn't his," Lily said.

Mercy took this in.

Lily said, "I knew you would react this way."

"What! I'm not reacting! I'm just adjusting, is all. What are you going to do?"

"What *can* I do?"

"Does he know?" Mercy asked.

"No."

"He doesn't know you're expecting, or he doesn't know it's not his?"

"Neither one," Lily said.

"Well," Mercy said drily, "that would certainly explain why you didn't want to tell us in front of him."

"That was why I *did* want to tell you. So you-all could be, you know. A buffer zone."

"Are you saying he might get violent?" Mercy asked.

"B.J.? Not a chance."

Mercy wondered how she could be so sure. B.J. was a motorcycle mechanic, and he favored black leather jackets and leather boots with chains around the ankles. But she said, "Well, that's *some* comfort."

"Why on earth is it," Lily said, "that you always, always manage to miss the point."

"Miss the point! What point? You tell me you're having a baby, and I would naturally wonder about the father's reaction." She paused. She said, "Father *figure*'s, I mean."

"Well, B.J. is not the father or the father figure, either one."

"Okay," Mercy said. "Who is?"

She felt pleased with herself for sounding so unshockable. However, Lily didn't seem impressed. "Oh, just a guy from Dodd," she said offhandedly.

"From . . . the real-estate place?" Mercy asked. That was the latest job Lily had quit, or maybe been fired from—a receptionist position at Dodd, Goldman.

Lily said, "Right. He's an agent there."

"Ah," Mercy said, but she was taken aback. A real-estate agent didn't sound like Lily's type at all. She said, "What's his name?"

"*Mom!*"

"What? He's the father of my grandchild! I need to know his name!"

"Oh, God," Lily said, and then she started crying.

Mercy said, "Lily, honey. Lily. Stop. We need to think this through. We need to think calmly and collectedly. Have you told *him* about the baby?"

"He's married," Lily said.

"Buried" was how it came out through her tears.

It was Mercy's turn to say, "Oh, God."

"Of *course* you'd have to act all scandalized," Lily said.

Mercy let this pass. She waited while Lily blew her nose. Then, "So," she said finally. "Just to consider this from every angle . . . Does B.J. really need to know that he is not the father?"

"What! You mean I should lie to him?"

Mercy felt herself flush. She said, "Not lie, exactly. Just fail to tell the truth. It might be a . . . kindness to him."

"But that's just wrong!" Lily said.

"Oh. Yes, sorry, I—"

"Besides which," Lily said, "it would have to be immaculate conception, if B.J. was the father."

"Oh."

"We've kind of gone off each other."

Mercy wondered why she hadn't noticed that. The family saw very little of them—they'd eloped during Lily's sophomore year at community college, where B.J. was not even a student, and they lived in a little apartment downtown—but she had always thought they seemed happy.

However: "If I could just get away from here," Lily was saying now. "Get away somewhere and think for a while. Go on a cruise or something."

"A cruise!" Mercy said. It was such a bizarre notion that she wondered if she had misheard, for a second.

"Or at least get away from *them*, from B.J. and Morris both, until my head is clear."

Morris. Mercy filed the name in her memory. So many unexpected people seemed to edge into a person's life, once that person had children.

"I was thinking last night that I might ask if I could camp out in your studio awhile," Lily said. "Sleep on the couch, heat a can of soup on the hot plate . . ."

Mercy stirred uneasily. "Oh, well," she said. "Actually, your and Alice's old room would make more sense. Since it has real beds and all."

"*My* room! Do you know how defeated I'd feel, moving back into my childhood bedroom?"

"Well, no need to make any rash decisions," Mercy told her. "But, listen! Maybe you should see a doctor, find out if you're really pregnant. It could be that you're just late."

"Three *months* late?"

"Oh."

Recent sightings of Lily raced through Mercy's mind—Lily stopping by the house to borrow the blender, Lily at David's goodbye supper. Had she been wearing extra-loose clothing? But she'd always been the sloppy type. "Well," Mercy said, "you should see a doctor anyhow. How do you feel, by the way?"

"I feel fine," Lily said. "What do you hear from David?"

Mercy dragged her mind back to the reason she'd called. "Not a word," she said. "I was thinking we might get a letter today, but the mailman's already been and he didn't bring a thing."

"I wouldn't hold my breath," Lily told her.

"No, well . . ."

"Now, promise not to tell Dad about you-know-what, okay? Wait till I decide what I'm doing."

"All right, honey," Mercy said. "I know you'll figure this out."

And they said their goodbyes and hung up.

It was a lot to take in, Mercy reflected—not just Lily's pregnancy, but the disastrous state of her marriage and the unexpected appearance of what's-his-name.

Morris, that was it.

She was ashamed to admit that her main concern was how to dissuade Lily from moving into the studio.

When they didn't hear from David on Thursday, Mercy sent him a postcard from her stash of museum cards—a Seurat. "We miss you!" she said. "We need to hear you're okay! Please write." She didn't give him any news from home, because she wanted him to wonder. Besides, at the moment she didn't have any news that she could share. Lily's condition was still a secret, and her own move to her studio should first be announced to his father.

She sort of dreaded that.

She dropped the postcard into the corner mailbox on her way to the studio. Today she was bringing footwear. She had exchanged her Sunkist carton for a canvas tote by now, and she filled it with a pair of dress shoes, a pair of sandals, and her slippers. What she hadn't planned ahead, though, was where to stow them once she'd arrived. She cast her eyes around the room, which still had a satisfyingly stripped-down look. It was crucial not to add any extras. Eventually, she stashed everything in the deepest of the drawers beneath the kitchen counter. It wasn't as if she meant to do any serious cooking here, after all. She could afford to give up one drawer.

Today, for the first time all week, she walked over to the table and studied the single painting that stood propped against a jarful of brushes. This wasn't a work in progress. It was completely finished. The subject was her own house—the dining room, specifically. A vague gleam of dining-room table and a blur of rug and a forest of sticklike chair legs, except one chair was the high chair that her children had once used, and those legs were microscopically detailed, every knob and indentation, as was the stuffed rabbit in overalls, little Robby's rabbit, lying facedown across one rung where Robby had thrown it.

Next to this painting was a stack of postcards featuring the same painting in miniature. The white edging at the bottom bore her name and her studio phone number, followed by "Let a Professional Artist Paint Your House's Portrait."

She was *sort* of a professional. Wasn't she? Or should she have said a "trained" artist? She had deliberated some time over that, and still she wasn't sure that she had made the right choice.

She'd been trained at the LaSalle School, down on 26th Street. She'd spent a year and a half there, and she had dreamed of studying in Paris someday. Now she couldn't imagine how that would have come about. Her father was not a rich man by any standard. Had she thought she would get a grant of some kind? Or apprentice herself to some famous French painter? All she could recall now was a mental image of the attic room she had fancied she would live in—the steeply slanted ceiling and the narrow window with its view of Parisian rooftops.

Still, the LaSalle School was a very respected institution.

She was planning to display these postcards in neighborhood grocery stores and on laundromat bulletin boards and next to the register at Wellington's Plumbing Supply. But not till she had told Robin.

On Friday they heard from David. Finally! He wrote on ruled notebook paper and he sent it in one of the envelopes Mercy had stamped and addressed for him and tucked in his suitcase pocket. "Dear Mom and Dad," he wrote. "I like it here a lot but I have to take remedial math which I am not happy about. Love, David."

She phoned Robin at the store and read it to him. "Huh," he said. "I guess now he wishes he'd paid more attention in math class."

"He paid attention!" she said. "It's not his fault he's not mathematical!"

"Huh."

Robin was still unhappy that David planned to major in English. (He wanted to be a playwright.) To hear Robin tell it, English was the most useless subject possible. (And let's not even talk about playwriting.)

She called Lily next. One of the benefits of hearing from David was that it gave Mercy an excuse to get in touch with her. "So," she said, after she had read the letter aloud. "How are you feeling, sweetie?"

"I'm feeling fine."

"I mean—"

"Yes, I know what you mean."

"So did you . . . have you thought about—"

"Don't *push* me, Mom! Okay? I can handle this!"

"Yes, of course you can, but—"

"I'm sorry now I told you."

Well, at least she wasn't crying anymore. That was an improvement. Mercy cleared her throat. "I'm wondering," she said delicately, "whether you might consider having a nice long talk with B.J. and telling him the truth straight out and asking if the two of you could start over."

"Mom, you do not have the slightest inkling what I'm dealing with here."

"No," Mercy said, "I don't. I certainly don't. But you're going to need someone to support you, sweetie. And I do know this much: marriages have stages. They have incarnations, almost. You can be in a good marriage and you can be in a bad marriage, and they can both be the same one but just at different times."

"Well, mine is bad and then it's more bad," Lily said.

"Oh, that can't be true!"

"We have absolutely nothing in common."

"Lots of couples have nothing in common," Mercy told her.

"That may be fine for *you,* Mom, but I'm not going to settle."

"Settle!" Mercy burst out. She felt stung. "Well, aren't *you* special!"

Click. Lily hung up.

Good riddance, Mercy thought. And then she spent some time stalking around the house making exasperated *tch!* sounds and coming up with other, more pointed things that she could have said to Lily.

Ever since Robin had been able to afford an assistant, he had made a practice of taking Saturdays off. This was Mercy's idea. She'd told him he should spend more time with his children. As it turned out, though, his children were fairly busy with activities of their own, and so he ended up retreating to the basement, where he happily puttered away at various projects while Mercy took the car and ran errands. Then in the evening they would have a nice dinner together, occasionally at a restaurant but more often at home. Robin said the way restaurants marked up their prices was highway robbery.

This Saturday, they stayed home. Mercy fixed Polish sausage links with hash browns, a favorite of his, and she opened a Natty Boh for him without his asking. She herself had a glass of Chianti, and she put some Frank Sinatra on the record player, and she wore the V-necked dress he liked and a little makeup, although not so much that he could say he preferred her to look like her natural self. He did notice the effort she'd gone to. "Well, isn't this nice," he said when he sat down. "A vase of flowers, even!"

"It's our first Saturday night as an *old* couple," she said jokingly. "I thought we should make an occasion of it."

"Aw, honey, you could never look old."

She unfolded her napkin and laid it across her lap. "Speaking of old," she said, "I'm thinking I'll just be twiddling my thumbs now that I don't have anyone to do for anymore."

"You've got me to do for!"

"Yes, but . . . and so it occurred to me I might step up my painting some."

"*Excellent* idea," he said. He helped himself to the mustard.

"Even try making some money, if I can."

He set the mustard jar down. He said, "Now, Mercy, we're doing fine for money. There is no need whatsoever for you to go out to work."

"Oh, I'm not going out to work! I'm just thinking I could sell my paintings to customers."

He knotted his eyebrows. He said, "Well, fine, honey, but I'm not sure if—"

"Here's the thing," she said. "You know how house-proud some people are. Even you and me! Why, I am just always so pleased when our wisteria starts blooming up the left-hand side of the porch and passersby stop and tell me how pretty it's looking."

"Yes, well . . ."

"So, house portraits! Get it? Portraits of people's houses! I would advertise; I'd say, 'Artist willing to come to your house and figure out its aura.'"

"Its what?"

"Its special, unique character. You know? Like, well, if I was to paint our own house I'd zero in on that wisteria. Or, remember the picture I did a while back, the one of little Robby's high chair in the dining room?"

He cocked his head.

"I mean, the general dining room is just suggested, more or less, but then special attention is paid to the high chair with its legs that go in and out and are kind of, say, carved."

"Lathed," Robin said.

"Yes, lathed, and Robby's stuffed rabbit is lying underneath it."

"I know the picture you're talking about," Robin said, but he still had his eyebrows knotted.

"I'd show them that and I'd say, 'What would be special in *your* house? Wouldn't you like me to paint it?' And I'm thinking it would mean more to them if I was the one to pick it. If I was to *read* their house, like reading their horoscopes or their palms, and I was to say, 'Here is your house's soul. Its defining feature. Its essence.'"

"Okay," Robin said. His forehead cleared. He nodded. "Yeah, sure, honey. You should go ahead and do that."

Then he picked up his fork and started mixing the mustard in with his sausage links.

"It would mean more time at the studio, I'm sorry to say," Mercy said.

"Well, you've got plenty of that."

"I might even have to spend the night, now and then."

"Have to what?" he said. He set his fork down.

This was the hard part.

"Well, *you* know," she said. "I'd get going on a project, get all involved and caught up in it . . ."

"Huh," he said.

"So I figured if I kept a blanket handy in my studio, I could curl up on the daybed and grab myself forty winks instead of walking home alone in the dark."

There was a silence, if you didn't count Frank Sinatra singing "Strangers in the Night."

"Mercy," Robin said. "Are you leaving me?"

"Oh, no!" she said, and she reached across the table to set a hand on his wrist. She said, "No, dear one, I would never leave you! How could you think that?"

"But you're telling me you don't want to sleep with me anymore."

"I just meant, like, now and then. Like if, let's say I had a deadline of some sort."

He didn't speak. His lips were slightly parted and he was searching her face; he looked stricken. It filled her with pity. She tightened her hold on his wrist and said, "Dearest one. You're my husband! How could I possibly leave you?"

"But no one's going to set you a deadline for just a *painting*," he said.

All at once she didn't pity him so much. She let go of his wrist. She said, "Paintings can have deadlines."

"This is just your way of walking out on me."

"No, it's my way of getting a little . . . independence," she said.

"You want to be *independent*?" he asked. He pronounced the word at a distance, somehow, as if he found it distasteful.

"Robin. Listen. Remember Alice's wedding, when she was making out the guest list? And she said to me, she said, 'Kevin's dad's new wife doesn't seem to have a whole lot on the ball, so could you take charge of her at the reception and talk housewife to her, please?' "

"Okay . . ."

"Like *I* didn't have a whole lot on the ball, either! You know?"

"She didn't mean—"

"She'd invited all the other teachers and her headmistress, even, so thank goodness *I'd* be around, she was saying, because I was just a housewife."

"It's only a word," Robin told her. "It's not an insult. I am just a plumber; so what? We all get put in other people's pigeonholes. It's shorthand, is all it is."

"It's shorthand for 'a nobody.' You know?"

But she should stop saying "you know," because the point was that he *didn't* know; he didn't have any idea.

He said, "I couldn't bear it if you left me, Mercy."

"I'm not going to leave you. I promise."

"It sure sounds to me like you are," he said.

"Doo-be-doo-be-doo," Frank Sinatra sang.

Silly man.

For the next little bit, then, Mercy continued sleeping at home. She got up in the mornings and made Robin's breakfast; she tidied and bustled around until he went to work. (Oh, leave! Just leave! she told him in her mind. How long can it take to just *go*?) Then, the instant he was out of the house, she was off to her studio. She didn't have much to carry anymore. All the essentials were there now, and even those seemed excessive, because she'd envisioned her future life as taking place in an empty room. It was almost disturbing to find that a certain amount of clutter was creeping in by necessity: the teakettle on the hot plate, the dishcloth draped over the sink rim.

By now she had distributed a number of her postcards. She'd even had one response, not by phone but in person, when a customer chanced to see her tacking a card up at the dry cleaner's. "You paint portraits of houses?" the woman asked, and Mercy said, "Yes! Are you interested?"

"Well, I ask because my husband and I just bought a house in Guilford."

"I could paint that!" Mercy said. "I could come over, walk through it, get a feel for its personality . . ."

"It's only a thought," the woman said.

"Take a card," Mercy told her, and she pressed one of her postcards into the woman's hands. "That number is my studio; you can reach me there most weekdays. Just keep trying if I don't answer."

Then she left, because she didn't want to seem pushy. But two days later the woman did call. She said that once they had the place fixed up exactly the way they wanted, they might ask Mercy to visit, and Mercy agreed that it was best to give the house time to become its true self. "Its true self," the woman repeated, and there was something approving in her tone that gave Mercy hope.

Meanwhile, David was not writing them. Mercy sent a couple of letters asking specific questions—"How is your math class?" "Are you liking your roommate?"—but she didn't get any answers. Typical, Robin said. "The boy has just washed his hands of us," he said. "I could have told you he would do that."

"Oh, Robin! How can you say that? He's always been so close to us!"

"He hasn't been close since grade school," Robin said, and Mercy dropped the subject, because they were never going to see eye to eye about David.

Alice and Lily hadn't heard from him, either. But they were less concerned, because they had issues of their own. Alice's Robby got roseola and kept Alice up all night for three nights in a row. Lily was almost unreachable, and when she did answer her phone, it was only to say no, she'd heard nothing from David, and no, she'd made no decisions. Goodbye.

Then, one Friday evening toward the end of the month, while Mercy and Robin were watching the local news, Lily rang the front doorbell. (Lily never rang the doorbell; she would just walk in.) Robin was the one who answered, and Mercy heard him say "Lily!" And then, puzzlingly, "Hello?"

Mercy rose from the couch and went to join him. She found Lily introducing a fortyish man in a business suit. "Dad, this is—hi, Mom! Mom and Dad, this is Morris Drew."

"Hello, Morris," Robin said, but in a questioning tone. It was up to Mercy to step past him and hold out her hand. "How do you do, Morris?" she said. "Won't you come in?"

Morris's handshake was firm and professional. He was an ordinary sort of man—medium height, plumpish build, thick glasses with round lenses—and Mercy knew she was going to have trouble fixing his face in her memory. "It's a pleasure, Mrs. Garrett," he said. His accent was that nonaccent that radio announcers favor.

They came inside, Morris giving the doormat a token shuffle even though it was a dry evening. Mercy went over to turn off the TV. (A man had been glimpsed walking what looked like a wolf in Druid Hill Park.) Robin said, "Well!" and rubbed his hands together. Lily and Morris sat down on the couch. Robin chose his recliner chair, but he didn't tip it back; he stayed upright, alert, as if braced for trouble. Mercy sat in the rocker.

"Morris and I have some news," Lily said immediately. "We're getting married."

Robin said, "What—?"

What about the marriage she already had? he would be wondering. Mercy was the only one who knew enough to wonder about the marriage *Morris* already had. It seemed there was quite a lot to explain here, and to adjust to and settle in with. But Lily must have decided that the simplest approach was to glide right past it all. "It won't be happening right away," she told them, "but I thought you might like a heads-up. Morris is keeping an eye out for the right house to come on the market."

Robin wore a stunned look.

Mercy jumped into the breach. "When you've found a place to your liking," she told them, "I'll come and paint its portrait for your wedding present."

"What? Okay," Lily said, and inquired no further. "Thanks, Mom," she said.

And Morris said, "Thank you, Mrs. Garrett."

So Lily's approach worked, apparently. Just that quickly, all those inconvenient obstacles simply disappeared.

Or at least on the surface they did. Robin stayed almost completely silent for the remainder of their visit, letting Mercy carry the conversation, and when Lily kissed his cheek as they left he just stood mute and allowed it. But in fact he was baffled and indignant, and the instant the door closed behind them he wheeled on Mercy as if it were all her fault. "What is *happening* here?" he fumed at her. "How is it that a married woman can show up on her parents' doorstep and introduce her new fiancé and we don't blink an eye?"

"Now, honey," Mercy said. "Nobody outside a marriage has any real notion what goes on *inside*; you know that yourself."

"I don't know any such thing," Robin said.

Well, of course he didn't. Their own marriage was as clear as glass, an open book, exactly what it seemed. If you didn't count the fact that Mercy had now spent several nights away from him.

The first night, she'd told him she might be late because she was working on a tricky painting. The second night—a week or so later—she said the same thing. This was calculated. She wanted him to start adjusting by degrees. And it worked, because when she stayed away for a third night without announcing it ahead, he didn't phone to ask where she was or charge over there to confront her. Which was not to say he was happy about it. He was churlish and huffy and difficult; the mornings after these nights he kept sending her sideways glances and opening his mouth to speak and then stopping himself.

But she was always present for those mornings. She made sure to be home before he woke up, and she had his breakfast on the table by the time he came downstairs.

She planned to stop doing that at some point. But not quite yet.

The day after they met Morris, Alice phoned Mercy and said, "So!" and then she waited. "So, I guess you had a visit from Lily," she said finally.

Alice and Lily had never been close. They were just too different from each other, Mercy supposed. But apparently they did confer about their parents now and then, in that furtive, head-shaking way that siblings tend to do, because it was obvious that Lily had asked Alice to put out some feelers. Mercy was cagey, though. She said, "Mm-hmm."

"So what'd you think of Morris?"

"He seemed nice," Mercy said neutrally. "Have you met him?"

"I have."

How many times? On what kind of occasion? Did she find him likable? Trustworthy? What, exactly, did she think was going on here?

Mercy didn't ask a one of these questions. She said, "Maybe I'll have him over for dinner with the whole family."

"Okay . . ." Alice said, plainly waiting for more.

"Are you and Kevin free this Sunday?"

"We're supposed to go to his mom's."

"Next Sunday, then?"

"We can do next Sunday."

"Fine," Mercy said. "I'll talk to Lily." And then she said goodbye, still without delivering any verdict on Morris.

She sort of enjoyed that conversation.

Except that Robin refused to allow a family dinner. He said, "Hold on: what? You want to open up our house to our daughter's paramour?"

"Paramour!" Mercy said. She was surprised he knew the word. "He's her fiancé, honey. We want to welcome him into the family."

"But how can she have a fiancé when she's already got a husband, huh? Where is B.J. in all this?"

Robin had always disliked B.J. Behind his back he called him Elvis. When B.J. and Lily eloped, Robin swore they must have "had to," and he had seemed almost disappointed when no baby appeared.

Speaking of which . . .

If only Mercy could explain about Lily's being pregnant, maybe he would be more understanding.

On the other hand, maybe it would send him clear around the bend.

It was this possibility, rather than her promise to Lily, that kept her from sharing the news.

She called Alice back and told her they would have to put off their dinner. "Oh?" Alice said, and waited to hear the reason.

"I'm really not sure *when* we can do it," Mercy said. Then she hurried to ask how little Robby's pull-ups were going. Robby had reached that stage where she could pull herself up to a standing position but didn't know how to sit down again. She would stand wailing in her playpen, exhausted, till Alice forcibly bent her knees and lowered her to the ground. Whereupon she'd immediately stand again. Alice had a lot to say about that. She forgot to pursue the subject of dinner.

. . .

The name of the woman Mercy had met at the dry cleaner's was Evelyn Shepard, and she phoned in mid-October and invited Mercy to tour her house. "I think we've settled in by now," she said, "and I wanted to see how you might choose to paint it."

"I'd be happy to come take a look," Mercy said.

"If you can stop by when my husband's here too . . ."

"I can do that."

"And maybe bring some samples of your work? I showed him the picture on your card, but—"

"Of course. I'll bring my portfolio," Mercy said.

And she made a mental note to hunt through her desk drawers at the house for the leather-grained cardboard portfolio she'd saved from her days at the LaSalle School.

They chose a Saturday morning, which meant Mercy had the car. She parked down the block from the Shepards' house in order to get an overall impression of it as she approached; she wanted to arrive armed, so to speak. It was a standard three-story colonial, red brick with forest-green shutters. Well, never mind; she usually preferred interiors to exteriors anyhow. She pressed the doorbell and then studied it intently. Her vision seemed to have sharpened and she was alert to every detail. But it was an unexceptional doorbell, a white rubber button set in a fussy brass plaque.

Evelyn Shepard opened the door and said, "Good morning, Mrs. Garrett!"

"Oh, please, call me Mercy," Mercy said.

"And I'm Evelyn. Won't you come in?"

Evelyn wore heels, on a Saturday in her own house. Just low heels, but still. She was slightly younger than Mercy but already matronly-looking, with carefully curled brown hair and a dressy flowered dress belted tightly at the waist. "Clarence?" she called. "The artist is here." She led Mercy across the foyer—Persian carpet, crystal chandelier—and into the living room, which was very large and formal, with a grand piano at the far end. Mercy's eyes were going *click, click, click,* registering all they could. "You have a lovely home," she said politely, and she sat where Evelyn directed, on a slippery satin sofa, but then instantly stood up again when Clarence entered the room. "Oh! Clarence!" his wife said, as if he had surprised her. "This is Mercy Garrett, the artist."

Clarence was older than his wife—gray-haired and mustached, with an ascot blossoming from the open collar of his shirt. Outside of English movies, Mercy had never seen an ascot. The sight gave her confidence. In a flash, she was able to place these people: newly settled in a house designed to be imposing, wearing clothes they'd bought expressly to live up to what they thought it required of them. "Your house is beautiful," she told him, and this time her voice was firmer and she was smiling warmly.

After that it was easy. The Shepards settled on either side of her and she pulled paintings from her portfolio—a sunporch, a breakfast nook, and what she called a "music room." (It wasn't a music room; it was Alice and Kevin's living room, but she instinctively altered her vocabulary to suit the circumstances.) With each one, as the picture's focal point sorted itself out from the surrounding blur, Evelyn said "Ah!" but Clarence remained silent. "So this one," Evelyn said of the so-called music room, "with the photograph on the end table; I'm guessing that's a picture of the house's original owner, am I right?"

She was referring to a photograph propped next to a conch shell: Kevin's father or uncle or something in a visored Army cap, glaring belligerently out of a silver frame with infinitesimal silver beads around the edges. Mercy said, "Yes, an ancestor on the husband's side," and flipped to the next painting: her and Robin's bedroom. A rectangle of bed, a slash of floorboards, and then part of a rocking chair with a nightgown draped over one arm, every wrinkle and stitch painstakingly defined.

"The essence of that house is a *nightgown*?" Clarence asked.

"Hush, Clarence," Evelyn told him.

"And here we have my granddaughter's nursery," Mercy said. ("Nursery!" She liked that.) The sketchiest of vertical lines suggested the slats of Robby's crib, but the braided rug it stood on was so detailed that the rosebud print of Mercy's old sundress showed clearly in one of the strands.

"I just think that's so unusual," Evelyn said on a long sigh of a breath.

Clarence said, "Have you ever tried painting the whole scene in detail, instead of just one part?"

"Well, of course!" Mercy told him. "Anyone can do that. But I am aiming for something a little more meaningful. I want to zero in on the single feature that reveals a house's soul."

He looked worried. He said, "What if you decide that the house's soul is a bathroom or something?"

She laughed. "I can assure you that's unlikely," she told him. Although actually, one of the paintings she hadn't yet shown him depicted the green tongue-and-groove partition enclosing the little "maid's toilet" in Robin's basement workshop. She shut her portfolio with a snapping sound and gave Clarence another smile. "In any case," she said, "you can always say you don't want it after you see what I've done. You'll have absolute veto power."

Evelyn sat up straighter and clasped her hands and gazed expectantly at Clarence.

"Ah," he said. "And . . . may I ask how much you charge?"

She had contemplated raising her price from one hundred to two as soon as she saw that grand piano, but she could tell now that he didn't think much of her work. Meekly, she said, "A hundred dollars."

He sent a look toward Evelyn. "Well," he said. "All right."

"Yes!" his wife said on another outward breath.

"Pending approval of how it turns out, of course," he told Mercy.

"Of course," she said.

On the first of November, a Sunday, Mercy phoned David. She chose late afternoon, figuring that was when he was most likely to be in his dorm; but even so, the boy who answered the phone took a long time tracking him down. "Garrett?" she heard him shouting, and then, farther off, "Hey, Garrett! Where you gone to, man?"

She was using the phone in the kitchen, and now she sat down at the table while she waited. It was a good sign, she thought, that the boy had called David "man." It implied that they were friends. She looked across the room at Robin, intending to tell him this, but he was standing with his back to her in front of the open fridge, as if his only reason for being there was to get himself a snack. Perversely, she changed her mind and said nothing.

The connection was one of those where other conversations on other lines somehow threaded themselves into this one. She heard a tiny laugh, a faint "*What?*" So many happy, carefree lives going on elsewhere.

David said, "Hello?"

"Hi, hon!"

"Hi, Mom."

"How're you doing?"

"Doing fine," he said. "Is everything okay?"

"Well, except we never hear from you."

"Aw, I'm sorry. I'm just really busy," he said.

"Are they giving you much work?"

"Yeah, they're giving me a lot, but so far I'm keeping up."

"That's good to hear."

"How's everybody there?"

"We're fine! You want to speak to Dad?"

"Sure."

"Robin?" she said. She held out the receiver, and Robin turned away from the fridge with a show of surprise. "Your son," she told him.

He shut the fridge door and moved toward her slowly, with feigned reluctance, which made her cluck in exasperation. He took the receiver and said, "Hello?" and then, "Oh, hi, son."

David said something on a rising note, and Robin said, "We're okay. How about you?"

Something-something from David.

"Ask about Thanksgiving," Mercy said in a piercing whisper.

"Huh? What? Your mom wants to know about Thanksgiving."

Another murmur from David.

"Well, *I* don't know. Just whether you're coming home for it, I guess," Robin said, and Mercy gave another cluck and grabbed the receiver from him. "David?" she said. "You know they run a shuttle over the holidays, right? From school to the Greyhound bus station, the Wednesday before Thanksgiving."

"Yeah, but seems to me that's a long way to come for just a couple of days," David said.

"It's not a *couple* of days; it's Wednesday, Thursday, Friday—"

"I was thinking it would be a good time to get my history paper out of the way," David said.

Mercy said, "Couldn't you do that in Baltimore?"

Robin was studying her face.

"Well, but here I've got the library and all."

"Oh," she said.

"How's Robby doing? She learn to walk yet?"

"Walk? I don't know. Just about," she said. It seemed like very hard work, this conversation. "So, I'll give you back to Dad," she said. She held the receiver toward Robin, but he drew away and waved his arms in a crisscross pattern in front of him. She put the phone to her ear again and said, "I guess he must've said all he has to say."

"Okay, so, bye, Mom," David said.

"Bye, hon."

She hung up.

"He's not coming?" Robin asked her.

She shook her head.

"Well. It's only natural," he said. "Got his friends around, his studies . . ."

"I know that," she said.

"This is a good sign, in fact."

"I know," she said.

Who they *did* have for Thanksgiving was Morris Drew.

Lily showed up at the studio one weekday morning, having first looked for Mercy at the house, she said; and she'd barely settled on the daybed before she announced her purpose. "Mom," she said, "I'm not coming to Thanksgiving this year unless I can bring Morris."

This wasn't completely unexpected. She and Mercy had, of course, been in touch by phone over the past few weeks—maybe not as often as Mercy would have liked, but enough for her to know that Lily and Morris were still very much a couple; that B.J. had agreed to a divorce as if he didn't even care; and that Morris's divorce was already underway. Now Lily said they'd bought a three-bedroom house in Cedarcroft and the two of them were moving in as soon as they'd had the roof replaced. "That's why it was such a bargain," she said. "Morris talked the price *way* down. Of course he knows all about such things."

And Morris's poor wife? And where had B.J. gone, exactly? And what was the news of the baby?

But the baby was the only one Mercy felt she could ask about.

The baby was fine, Lily said nonchalantly. (She still didn't seem noticeably pregnant, although she wore an overblouse that made it hard to tell.) She pulled a Polaroid from her purse: a photo of a standard white cottage with an awning above the front stoop. "This time next year, you can come to *our* place for Thanksgiving," she said. "Isn't it darling?"

"Yes, it's—"

"But this year it's not ready yet for guests," she said. She slipped the photo back into her purse. She said, "I know what you're going to say. I know Dad is in a huff. Last night on the phone he told me I could only bring B.J. to Thanksgiving. Like that was even an option! B.J.'s moved down to Fells Point."

"You talked to Dad on the phone?" Mercy said.

"Yes, and he said you were working late. Did he not tell you I called?"

"I guess he didn't have a chance to," Mercy said. (She had spent last night in the studio, and this morning for the very first time she had not gone home for breakfast.)

"But you can persuade him, Mom; I know you can. You can change his mind. All this while he's been claiming B.J.'s so irresponsible, remember? And Morris is *very* responsible. He's going to be such a good provider, and a good father, besides; he's always wanted kids. Won't you make Dad let us come for Thanksgiving?"

"Well, of course I will, honey," Mercy said, and she said it with confidence. There was no way Robin would willingly lose touch with his own daughter. Why, family was more important to him than anything! He had spent too much of his youth without one, was why.

"All he needs," she told Lily, "is for Morris to, maybe, explain a little bit more. You did kind of take your dad by surprise, you know. So here's what: you two come by the house this evening, and we'll leave the men in the living room while we go fix refreshments. Then Morris can tell your dad how he knows this was a shock, never meant for things to work out this way, just fell head over heels in love the instant he laid eyes on you. And then he'll announce about the baby: how he realizes the timing's unfortunate but he's thrilled about it anyhow, totally respects you, totally wants to stand by you . . . Well, *you* know."

Lily was nodding vigorously. "He can do that," she said. "Morris is good at things like that."

Mercy could believe he was. She only wished she could remember what the man looked like.

Well, it all worked out. Robin was stony-faced at first—actually tried to follow Mercy and Lily out to the kitchen, till Mercy ordered him to stay in the living room with Morris. But when they returned with the coffee, Morris was telling Robin why it made sense to spring for slate shingles instead of asphalt, and Robin was nodding and saying, "Durn right it does. Durn right, I say."

So. Morris came for Thanksgiving.

He wore a brown suit and a tie, and Lily wore a brand-new maternity smock. Alice gave Lily a lecture on natural childbirth. Kevin told Morris and Robin about the advantages of enclosed shopping malls. Little Robby refused to sit in her high chair and staggered around the dining room with both fists high in the air, practicing her walking. And Mercy sat at the end of the table smiling, smiling at all of them.

For her portrait of the Shepards' house Mercy chose their upstairs hall, focusing specifically on the grandfather clock standing between two bedroom doors. This was not her first choice, to be honest. Her first choice was an obscure corner of Evelyn Shepard's sewing room: a weathered footlocker dating from Clarence's military service, spilling over with various remnants of fabric in all different colors and weights and patterns. But she knew better than to settle on that.

This clock was massive and ornately carved, its brass pendulum swinging ponderously behind a rectangle of thick glass, its face a disc of creamy porcelain topped by an arc of glittering brass moons in varying phases. Clarence told Mercy he had always cherished it, implying that it had been handed down through his family. Evelyn told Mercy they had found it in an antique store in New Market, Maryland, a year and a half ago. What neither one of them seemed to know (or maybe they just didn't want to know) was that down near the base on the left-hand side, just above the egg-and-dart molding, the initials CTM had been clumsily scratched with some sharp object. Needless to say, Mercy included the initials in her portrait.

She had a long debate with herself before she showed the Shepards the finished painting. If they asked her to remove the initials, would she refuse? Silly, of course: this wasn't worth some lofty moral stance about freedom of expression. But still . . . She wavered. All for nothing, it turned out. Evelyn Shepard loved the picture, and Clarence said it was very nice. They appeared to pay no more notice to the painted initials than they had to the real ones.

Originally, Mercy had fantasized that the Shepards might spread the word—that their commission might lead to others after their friends saw the picture. But that didn't happen. (Could the Shepards have hung it someplace out of the public view? Mercy had no idea.) Who *did* spread the word, to her surprise, was Morris Drew. He telephoned her at her studio a week or two after Thanksgiving and asked if he might take a supply of her postcards to his office. "People buying a new place," he said, "they tend to be very house-proud. I could slip a card in with their papers at the settlement and they might decide to have a portrait painted."

Mercy was touched. And it did have some effect: a young couple with a new condo called to ask her prices and said they would think it over, and then an older woman called to commission a picture for her son and daughter-in-law, who had just bought a lovely Victorian on the wrong side of Roland Park.

You couldn't say Mercy was making an actual living at this. But she hoped she might, someday.

At Christmastime, David finally came home. He seemed more self-assured and more comfortable in his own skin; his hair was so long that it fell across his forehead like a sheaf of wheat, and he had developed a new habit of saying "Right? Am I right?" after almost every sentence. But oh, it was so good to see him! Mercy kept finding excuses to give him a hug, or just to trail a hand across his back as she walked past him. Often he was out who-knows-where with his friends, but still she thought the house had a different feel to it now.

That whole three weeks while he was home, she didn't spend a single night in the studio and she stopped by there only a few times during the day, even. She was forced to rely on the clothes and toiletries she had left behind at the house, which made her realize how thoroughly she had relocated. Well, she'd moved out, really. It had reached the point where Robin would ask, "Will you be here tonight?"—not taking it for granted anymore; and if she said yes, he would get all happy and relieved. And when Alice and Lily phoned, they tried her studio number first now, not even seeming to think about it. Neither girl asked outright what was going on. Neither one said, "Have you *left*? Are you and Dad splitting up?" Maybe they didn't want to know. Maybe, like the

Shepards, they preferred not to see the initials scratched on the clock. While David, of course, had no reason to ask, since as far as he could see nothing had changed.

She was reminded of the first time Lily brought Morris to visit—how she'd announced forthrightly that she was going to marry him, blithely gliding right past the facts that she was already married and that Morris was too, and making no mention whatsoever of her pregnancy. Was it really so easy to convince the world that life was proceeding as usual? Mercy had wondered.

Yes, it was, evidently.

A cold wave struck in January and Mercy bought an electric blanket. First she considered a quilt, but a quilt would have been too bulky under the corduroy slipcover. (She was scrupulous about concealing the fact that the couch was also a bed.) She hid the controls behind one of the cushions so that nobody would suspect.

The linoleum floor was so icy that she could feel it through the soles of her shoes, so she bought heavy suede clogs and fitted them with fake-fleece insoles from the drugstore. The studio's only heat came from an ancient electric radiator affixed to one wall, and she moved the table closer to it so she wouldn't freeze while she was working.

She didn't have much contact with the elderly couple she rented the studio from—just a brief exchange of greetings if they happened to be outside as she was passing through their yard—and now that it was winter they were all but invisible. One evening, though, she heard somebody trudging up her staircase, and she opened her door to find Mr. Mott puffing heavily on the landing. "Evening, Mrs. Garrett," he said.

"Why, hello," she said. "What brings you here?"

"Got a little favor to ask you."

"Oh?"

She stood back to let him step inside, and he removed his knit wool cap while she shut the door behind him. He was a large, beefy man with a bushy white mustache, and he didn't seem in very good condition. "It's about our daughter, Elise," he said. "She's having exploratory surgery."

He pronounced the last two words with extra care, as if they were foreign.

"Oh, no, I'm sorry to hear it," Mercy said.

Apparently taking this for permission, he crossed the room and settled on the daybed. He *fell* on it, almost. She crossed too and sat next to him.

"She's down in Richmond," he said, "her and her boy, and they don't have anyone else. Her husband died a couple of years ago. So me and Mrs. Mott are going to go stay with Dickie while Elise is in the hospital."

"Well, of course," Mercy said.

"We're wondering if you could take care of our cat."

"You have a cat?" she asked, playing for time. She'd never had any dealings with cats.

"Desmond," he said, in an urgent tone of voice.

The name would have amused her if she hadn't been so intent on figuring out what was being asked of her. "So . . ." she said. "So you want me to just . . . bring him his food every day?"

"We were thinking maybe keep him here," he said, and he glanced around the room.

"Here!"

"I notice you're here a good bit nowadays. And we'd feel kind of bad leaving Desmond on his own too long. I mean, for a weekend or so, sure, but—"

"How long did you have in mind?" Mercy asked.

"We don't know yet, is the thing. It might be no time at all! We just don't know. And Desmond is real undemanding, but still . . . In the house all by himself, day and night; and he's not allowed out ever because we don't want him killing the birds . . ."

"Well, but this place is kind of small, really," Mercy said.

"Not *that* small. You could fit his litter box in the bathroom, easy."

"Litter box!"

"And I'd bring you all his supplies."

Couldn't they board him someplace? Weren't there such things as cat hotels? But Mercy decided against asking that. Mr. Mott was fixing her with a steady, imploring gaze. His eyes were a faded brown, the lower lids sagging and reddened.

"I'd be happy to keep him," Mercy said.

Because if you're going to do someone a favor, her father used to tell her, you might as well do it graciously.

Desmond was a gray plaid sort of cat with a squarish face and short, chunky legs. He arrived in a small suitcase with a mesh window at either end, but he jumped out as soon as Mr. Mott set the case on the floor and unlatched the lid. He stalked off toward the kitchen area, his tail straight up in the air and twitching slightly. Mercy got the impression that a twitching tail on a cat did not mean at all the same thing as a wagging tail on a dog.

While Mr. Mott went back to the house for Desmond's supplies, Mercy sat on the daybed and watched the cat sniff his way around the baseboards. Then he leapt nimbly onto the kitchen chair and surveyed the paints and brushes on the table. His back was turned toward Mercy, but something quivery and alert in his posture made her think he was very much aware of her. Eventually he dropped to the floor again with a thud that seemed to shake the whole garage. And here she'd always thought cats were so delicate!

Mr. Mott returned, puffing harder than ever, burdened with a plastic dishpan-looking thing filled with various sacks and bowls. "He should only have this one brand of cat chow," he said, "on account of his kidneys. You can find it easy in most grocery stores. He's not allowed to eat canned food. He'll *tell* you he is, but he's not."

Mercy wondered how he would tell her. Also, it sounded to her as if Mr. Mott was thinking they might be away long enough so she would need to buy more cat chow. This was a little bit worrisome. But she said, "We'll get along fine, Mr. Mott. Don't give him another thought. I hope things go well with your daughter."

And she saw him off with a smile, and waved as she closed the door.

The litter box did fit in the bathroom, but just barely, and it came with a plastic spatula gadget that she laid alongside it. Desmond's water bowl and his food bowl—both unnecessarily large, in her opinion—had to be placed on the kitchen floor beside the counter, where they were clearly visible from anywhere in the studio. This violated her no-clutter policy. It made her unhappy. She told herself that in time she would stop seeing them, but this thought made her even unhappier.

Overall, though, Desmond turned out to be less intrusive than she'd feared. He wasn't a nagger or a whiner; nor was he a lap cat. When she sat on the daybed he sat next to her, rather than on her. He lay curled up like a nautilus, purring. At night he slept between her ankles but on top of the covers, so that the only time she was aware of him was when she stirred her feet or turned over. Then she felt the warm weight of him holding down her blankets.

She developed the habit of talking to him while she was painting. Just brief remarks; no baby voice or anything like that. "Oh, shoot," she would say. "Look what I've gone and done." Or "What's your opinion, Desmond? I'm worried this looks *fussed* over." And Desmond would give her a measured stare before he went back to bathing his left shin.

Often as she was painting she found herself drifting back through her past like someone wandering through an old house. She thought of her father, who used to take her for neighborhood walks on Sundays when she was a child so that her mother, already an invalid, could get her rest. "Notice the rust stains below those eaves," he would say. "Below Mrs. Webb's eaves. I don't know how often I've told her she needs to have her gutters cleaned." And once, when it began to rain, "Have you ever wondered where rain comes from?" "No, not really," she had said bluntly, but he had told her anyhow—all about evaporation, condensation . . . Now she saw that he had adored her, and she felt a deep wave of regret for her failure to realize that before.

She thought of Robin as he was when he was courting her, when he came by the store too often and made little trumped-up purchases just so he could catch a glimpse of her behind the counter. So bashful, he'd been; so tongue-tied and respectful. It was a fad back then for boys to address girls as "kiddo" and treat them with the cool amusement that Humphrey Bogart, say, displayed toward his leading ladies. But Robin had called Mercy "Miss Wellington" until she laughingly told him not to. Some of his pronunciations were backwoodsy—"strenth" instead of "strength," for instance, and "ditten" instead of "didn't"—but he took great care with his grammar, and he made a point of using longer words than he needed to. "I'm wondering if you might ever want to go on a social engagement," he'd said. He meant a movie, it turned out; she couldn't remember now which one. It was such a hot evening that once they were settled in their seats, she had drawn a small jar from her purse and plucked out a cotton disc soaked in toner and blotted her upper lip. Then, on second thought, she had tapped him on the arm and offered him the jar as well, and he had glanced at it in surprise and then taken a disc himself and popped it into his mouth. Mercy had looked quickly away, pretending not to see. She had worried he would try to swallow it so as to save face, but a moment later she sensed a surreptitious movement in the dark as he removed the disc from his mouth and, who knows, perhaps slipped it into his pocket or dropped it beneath his seat.

He had extremely blue eyes that seemed clearer than other people's eyes. They made him look trustful and hopeful. His lips were distinctly etched, double-peaked at the center in a way that she found intriguing. He knew everything there was to know—instinctively, it seemed—about everything mechanical. In that respect, he was very like her father.

He took her down to Canton to meet his one close relative, a great-aunt whom he boarded with in a row house twelve feet wide. She was a sharp-faced, unsmiling woman who might have been daunting if she had not treated Mercy so deferentially. She insisted that Mercy should sit in the only comfortable chair, and she apologized several times over for the supper she served them—a pot of beet soup and then some kind of rolled-up cabbage leaves with ground meat inside. "I know it's not what you'd call upper-class," she said, and Mercy said, "Oh, goodness, my dad's a storekeeper," and Aunt Alice said, "I know." Mercy had a sense of futility then, and in fact for as long as Aunt Alice lived—eight more years—she never seemed fully relaxed around Mercy. She attended their wedding, an understated, street-clothes affair, in a hat with a bird on it and a church dress more formal than the bride's dress.

After Mercy and Robin were married they rented the upper

floor of a little house in Hampden, and Mercy slipped into domestic life as if she had been born to it. Which she had, really. No one she knew back then imagined any occupation for wives besides keeping house and rearing children. When the war began and other women started going off to jobs, Mercy was already pregnant with Alice. Then, two years later, along came Lily, and Mercy no longer wondered what to do with herself. She was busy night and day; she felt panicky, sometimes, and Robin would not have thought of offering to help even if he had been around, which he seldom was. Sometimes it seemed they barely exchanged two words before they fell into bed at night, exhausted.

He was a good husband. He worked hard, and he loved her. And Mercy did love him back. But occasionally, for no particular reason, she used to entertain fantasies of leaving home. Oh, not seriously, of course. They were no more than the idle, he'll-be-sorry fantasies that she assumed must flit through all women's minds on those days when they felt taken for granted. She enjoyed picturing what disguise she might choose—dyeing her hair a vivid black, for instance, and switching to tailored black slacks with creases ironed down the front, and perhaps even taking up cigarettes, because who would ever dream that Mercy Garrett would be smoking? She could sashay right out of the neighborhood, blowing smoke rings all the way to Penn Station, and no one would give her a glance.

At least she had not acted on that fantasy, she thought now. At least she had dutifully stuck around, fixed untold thousands of meals, cleaned house each day and then risen the next day and cleaned the same house all over again. And now she looked back on that time quite fondly, in fact, even though she had no earthly desire to relive it. She could still feel her children's soft cheeks pressing against hers. She could still feel their little hands tucking themselves into her hands. She heard Lily's comically sultry voice singing "Itsy Bitsy Spider"; she heard David's infectious chuckle. Oh, and the birthday card that Alice had made her in third grade! "Dear Mama promise me you will never ever ever die." And that lovely carefree week they had spent at Deep Creek Lake, their very first vacation and, in fact, their last, with the girls almost grown up by then and halfway out the door. It all happened so fast, she thought, even though it had seemed endless at the time. And generally, she had managed well. She had nothing to reproach herself for.

Still, she dreamed now that she lived in some sort of police state and she was walking down a gray street in a gigantic black fur coat. A man in uniform stopped her and said her coat looked to him like the coat belonging to X, a well-known revolutionary, and what should he make of that?

She said, "Well, let's just say it would be very, very difficult to get in touch with X these days."

And she blew out a long whoosh of smoke, and both of them laughed evilly.

Mr. Mott telephoned twice—first a week or so into Desmond's stay, just asking how things were going with him and saying their daughter had had her surgery but would be longer in the hospital than they'd originally expected; and then in early February, apologizing for how much time this was taking but giving no further information. Nor did Mercy ask; she sensed she shouldn't. "Don't you worry about *us*," she said. "We're doing just fine here." And she meant it.

One Sunday morning, she woke to a foot and a half of snow. The round metal table on the Motts' patio wore a dome of snow like an igloo, and their roof so exactly matched the opaque white sky above it that she couldn't see the line dividing them. The two dormer windows seemed to be hanging in empty space.

She felt cozy and secure; she made herself a big breakfast and she ate it in her bathrobe. The cat, meanwhile, perched precariously on the windowsill and stared out at the snow, transfixed. "Quite a surprise, isn't it?" Mercy said, and Desmond turned briefly and raised his eyebrows at her.

The phone rang: Robin, of course. "You okay there?" he asked.

"I'm fine," she said. "How are things at the house?"

"Pretty good. They haven't plowed the roads yet, though. I'm going to come over on foot and bring your boots so you can walk back with me."

"Oh, don't do that! I can manage!"

"It's no trouble; the walk will do me good," he said.

"Robin. Really. I'm smack-dab in the middle of a painting right now. I was planning to work all day anyhow, and I have plenty to eat and drink. I could stay holed up for days!"

"Well, but I was thinking I could light us a fire in the fireplace," he said.

"Yes, do that! Light yourself a fire and get all comfy and be glad you don't have to go anywhere. *I'm* certainly glad!"

"Oh."

"I'm going to get so much done!"

"Oh."

"I'll come by later. Bye!"

But "later" was three days later. By that time, they'd cleared the roads, if not the sidewalks, so she could walk back to the house if she kept to the street. Robin was off at work when she got there; it was early afternoon. She found the kitchen a bit scattered-looking—cocoa tin left out on the counter, dishes stacked in the sink—and from the afghan and pillow lying on the couch she guessed he might have spent at least one night in front of the TV instead of going upstairs to bed.

First she started a load of laundry, adding the clothes she found in the bathroom hamper to those she'd brought from the studio;

and then she tidied the kitchen and mixed a meatloaf, using the ground beef from the fridge. It was her plan to put it in the oven at about four thirty or five, so that they could have it for supper. But it wasn't even two yet, and once she had gone through the mail, and vacuumed the living-room rug, and switched the laundry from the washer to the dryer, she changed her mind. She wrote Robin a note, "Bake at 350º one hr.," and she taped it to the loaf pan, which she set in the fridge at eye level where he couldn't miss it. Then she put on her snow boots and walked back to her studio.

Spring came early that year, at the very beginning of March. Lavender crocuses started speckling the lawn, in among the grass blades where they weren't supposed to be growing. One morning the Motts' huge oak filled up with tiny birds, so many of them that all at once the bare tree seemed abundantly leafed, and they made a busy chittering sound like hundreds of scissors snipping. Desmond stared round-eyed from the windowsill with his chin quivering.

Lily's baby arrived, a boy, and she and Morris moved into their new house. They were planning to have a quiet wedding as soon as their divorces came through. Alice's Robby began talking, and once she started she wouldn't stop; Alice kept a notebook of all her funny sayings. David wrote to say that a skit of his would be staged in the college auditorium.

In April Mercy invited her three closest friends to the studio for tea: Darlene from high school and Carolyn and Bridey, whose children had grown up with her children. None of them knew she didn't live at the house anymore. The few times they'd gotten together lately it was only for a movie or for lunch at a local café; no need for her to explain where she was coming from or going back to.

Her excuse for having them come to the studio was that she

wanted to show them her portraits, but she served real tea from a teapot and cookies she'd bought at the Giant just the same as if she were entertaining at home. The three of them perched in a row on the daybed and sipped from cups that she had carried over in her tote. They all said they liked the portraits very much. Well, what else could they say, of course, but Bridey did ask, "So if you came over to paint *my* house, what part of it would you focus on?"

"I wouldn't know what part, at the outset," Mercy said. "I would just make some quick overall sketches and then come back here to figure that out."

"Why is that? Why wouldn't you need to paint the detailed part while you were there at the house?"

"Because the whole reason I'm painting the detailed part is, that is what's ended up being the only thing I remember," Mercy said patiently. "It's the one part I really saw, it turns out. So I know it must be what's important."

"I see," Bridey said, but she didn't sound very sure.

When the women left, Desmond slipped out of the bathroom, where he'd been hiding, and stalked all around the room's perimeter, reclaiming it as his own.

On a balmy evening in early May, Mercy heard someone climbing her stairs. She figured it had to be Robin; the girls would be fixing supper at this hour. She stood up hastily from the daybed and turned the radio off. (The idea was that she was staying here nights to work, not to sit idle.) But when she went to open the door she found Mr. Mott outside, Mr. Mott puffing and sweating in a short-sleeved seersucker shirt that made his arms look embarrassingly naked. "Why, Mr. Mott!" she said. "You're back!"

"Not *back* back," he said. "Just here to pick up a few things from the house."

"How's your daughter?"

"Not so good," he said.

"Oh, I'm sorry to hear that."

"She's having to have these treatments, series of treatments," he said. "Seems like things have spread everywhere."

"Oh, no."

"Right," he said. Then he looked past her and said, "*There* you are!"—talking to Desmond, who was gazing at him blankly from his spot on the daybed. "How you doing, fella?"

"Oh, Desmond's fine. We're getting along just fine," Mercy said. "Won't you come in and—"

"So we're going to have to move down there," Mr. Mott said. "Move to my daughter's place in Richmond. Got to help out with our grandson. Well, *Elise* can't tend him. Right now she can't even have him to visit her in the hospital, because the slightest little germ could be the end of her. And Dickie is not but eight, you know. So me and Mrs. Mott are going to have to move there."

"But . . . maybe once everything is back to normal . . ." Mercy said.

He just looked at her.

"My nephew will be staying in our place," he said finally. "He's going through a divorce. So you can put the rent through our mail slot same as always and he will pass it on to us."

"Certainly," Mercy said.

"And would you might want to keep Desmond?"

"Keep him? You mean forever?"

"Right."

"Oh! No, I'm sorry, I could never do that."

"We can't take him to Richmond because Dickie is allergic. And my nephew despises cats; I already asked him."

"See, I really don't lead the kind of life to own a cat," Mercy said.

"But you've managed up till now, haven't you? He hasn't been any trouble, has he?"

"No, none at all. Still, I just don't *want* a cat," Mercy told him.

"But what am I going to do, then? How am I going to deal with this? I just have too much *on* me! Everything's crashing in on me and I don't know where to turn, and now I find out the water heater has been leaking all over our basement for I-don't-know-how-long when my nephew swore in God's name that he would keep an eye on things for us. I'm just . . . surrounded!"

He was. She could see that. He was going under. Oh, that helpless, sinking, beleaguered feeling, that weighted feeling of everything crowding in on you and strangling you and demanding from you, all at the same time!

She placed a hand on his arm, the sad puffy skin of his forearm. "It's okay. I'll take Desmond," she told him. "Don't you give him another thought. I'm glad to do it."

"Thank you," he said.

Then he turned to go. She wasn't offended; she knew he had nothing left for the usual chitchat. She just dropped her hand from his arm, and he opened the door and walked out.

The following Saturday morning she walked over to the house to pick up the car, as she did every Saturday. She was the only woman she knew these days who had no car of her own, but she didn't want the encumbrance, and anyhow, Robin would have found it extravagant. She went directly out back to the garage, and she fished her keys from her purse and got in and started the engine.

In her studio, she took Desmond's travel case from the corner behind the door. Unaccustomed to cats though she was, she knew better than to let him spot it ahead of time. She set it on the kitchen counter and unlatched the lid before she went to scoop him up from the daybed. He struggled only briefly—surprised, it seemed, more than upset. She plopped him into the case and slammed the lid shut, lickety-split, and then she carried it outside and down the stairs. It was like carrying a bowling ball, the way the weight inside slid about and tilted and bucked, but she hung on. Meanwhile, Desmond was silent. She had expected him to meow. But it was an expressive silence, she felt, a sort of bristling of the airwaves. Not till she parked at the animal shelter and walked around to the passenger side to reach in for his case did he say anything, and then it was just a single, questioning "Mew?"

She shut the passenger door behind her and hurried toward the building with him.

When she got back to the studio, she gathered his supplies—his two bowls and his sacks of kitty litter and cat chow, his litter box and the slotted spatula next to it—and she carried them out to the garbage bin in the alley and dropped them in. Then she returned to the studio. The silence there was noticeable. She couldn't figure out why, though. It wasn't as if Desmond had been a noisy cat.

She ought to make her weekly grocery trip now so she could return the car to Robin, but first she thought she'd just sit awhile. She sat on the daybed with her hands folded; she didn't even try to look busy. She didn't even turn the radio on. She just sat listening to the silence.

Summer arrived, but David came home for only a few days, because he'd found a job with a theater group. Children swarmed the neighborhood, chanting and laughing and quarreling. The oak tree in the Motts' backyard had filled out with so many leaves that any small birds on its branches chirped invisibly, but larger birds (hawks? some kind of falcons?) could often be seen circling high above it and then wheeling off again. For the first time Mercy wondered if certain birds were famous among other birds for their distinctive flying style—if they took pride in executing a particularly graceful arc or a breathtaking swoop as the others watched admiringly.

She would give her shoulders a shake, finally, and turn away from the window and go back to whatever painting she'd been working on. The carved pineapple on a newel post. The ball-fringe trim on a curtain. The doorstop shaped like a black iron dog with a tail like an upright feather.

Am I missing something? she thought every now and then. Am I overlooking something?

But she would dismiss the notion, and reach once more for a paintbrush no thicker than an eyelash.

4

NOBODY IN THE GARRETT FAMILY made much fuss over Easter. Oh, they did buy inexpensive prefilled baskets for their children if they happened to notice some in the supermarket, and they might drop in on a neighborhood egg hunt just to look sociable, but that was about the sum of it.

So when David phoned on an April afternoon in 1982 and proposed driving down that Sunday for Easter dinner, they were all taken aback. Lily was the one he spoke to. She was at work; she managed the store for her father now that young Pickford had become a survivalist and moved to the wilds of Montana. "Wellington's Plumbing Supply," she said, and David said, "Lily, is that you?"

"David?" she asked. "Is everything okay?" Because David was not a telephone person, to put it mildly.

"Yes, fine," he said, "but I've had a hell of a time tracking anyone down. First I called Mom: no answer. And then Alice, but she didn't answer, either."

"Well, of course not. Alice is harder to find than any of us," Lily told him.

She said this because it hurt her feelings, a little, that he'd tried Alice before he tried her. In fact, Alice was normally very easy to find. But "Carpool, moms' group, PTA . . ." she said.

"So then I figured I'd try Dad," David told her, hurting her feelings even further. "I'm glad I got *you*, at least."

"Huh," she said.

"I wanted to check about Easter."

"Easter! What about it?"

"Well, I thought I might drive down for Easter dinner. Bring a friend."

"A friend?" she asked. (Antenna going up.)

"My friend Greta."

"Ah."

She glanced around the store, looking everywhere for Robin. Where *was* he? This was momentous.

"So will everyone be available, do you think?"

"Of course they will!" she said.

Or they would drop their plans so they *could* be available; she could guarantee it.

"I was thinking we'd arrive about noon or so," he said. "We can't stay over, because we don't get Easter Monday off."

"Oh? Greta works at your school?" she asked.

"Right," he said. "Will you tell the others?"

"Yes, certainly! You know they'll be—"

"Okay," he said. "Bye."

"I look forward to meeting Greta!"

But he had already hung up.

He was thirty years old at the time, an English and drama teacher in a high school just outside Philadelphia. He had taught there for several years. He lived in a house that he rented with an option to buy. In other words, he was settled. Established. And yet he had never, ever, on a single occasion, brought a girl home to meet the family. All they knew of his private life was what he happened to let slip in passing, and when they pressed him for further details—"Spring vacation with your friend Lois? Is this Lois somebody special?"—he grew cagey and changed the subject.

It was no wonder, therefore, that his Easter plans caused a stir. Lily first told her father, whom she found in the stockroom. "Is that so!" was all he said. (But fixing her with a stare, meanwhile, giving the news his full attention.) Then she called her mother at the studio. Still no answer there. So she called Alice, who was home by now and reacted quite satisfyingly. "What on earth!" she said. "Did he say *why*? Did he say something like 'meet the family'? Like 'want you all to get to know this person'?"

"He just said he was bringing a friend."

"Maybe she *is* just a friend."

"Well, but . . . and then he asked if everyone would be available. Also, he said 'we.' There was something about the way he said 'we.'"

Alice was silent a moment. Then, "Greta," she said musingly. "Hmm."

"I wonder if she's foreign," Lily said.

"It's fine with *me* if she's foreign."

"Yes, of course; I'm just trying to get a—"

"We'll have the lunch here, obviously," Alice said.

"What! At your house?"

"Where else?"

"But if he's bringing this Greta home, so to speak," Lily said, "shouldn't it be at his actual family home? Isn't that the point?"

"Get serious, Lily. How long has it been since Mom's cooked a meal?"

"Well, but," Lily said, "I mean . . . Okay, then you should all come to *my* house. I'm right here in town, after all."

Alice herself was not in town; she and Kevin had moved out to Baltimore County. The rest of the family found that incomprehensible: how she could choose to live so far away, how isolated she was, how her children were bound to grow up with no sense of real life. But Alice said, "If it's warm enough we could eat on the terrace, even."

They had a flagstone terrace as big as their house. An entire outdoor kitchen-dining area was attached, complete with cabinets. Lily thought that was show-offy. She didn't say so, of course. She said, "It's bad enough they'll have to deal with the holiday traffic; why make them drive to *your* place?"

"Because we have room for them?" Alice answered. "Because we'll be two, four . . . because we'll be eleven around the table, counting the kids? And you have just that teeny little dining room."

Alice and Lily didn't talk very often—only when there was an issue involving their parents or some such. And they almost never got together. Now Lily was remembering why. (Mostly they just saw each other when David came to town. In fact it seemed ironic that he, of all people, should serve as the family's connector. David, who was the very opposite of connected!)

"I could do it buffet-style," she said.

Alice made a laughing sound that wasn't actually a laugh. "*No*-ho-ho," she said. "Lily. Never serve buffet-style when children are involved."

"But I would—"

"And we have the rec room, besides," Alice said. "So if it happens to be cold, the kids can hang out down there. You know how they all get when they're cooped up."

"Well, anyhow, this is probably beside the point," Lily said, "because I'm pretty sure Mom will say that for something this important—"

"She'll say that for something this important, she just can't think what to serve," Alice said. Alice loved to finish Lily's sentences for her.

"Well, I'm going to ask her," Lily said. "Just as soon as I get hold of her."

"Lots of luck with that," Alice said.

Mercy said that for something this important, she just couldn't think what to serve.

"But I could help you," Lily said. "I could bring the main dish, say, and the salad. All you would have to do is fix one of your special desserts."

"It's not only that," Mercy said. "The food is the very least of it. There's all the cleaning and the fixing up, arranging the flowers, ironing the tablecloth . . . I have to admit I'm not keeping up with the housework nowadays."

It was bizarre, Lily's husband always said, how something so obvious was never, ever talked about: her mother had left home. Sometimes Lily would say something extremely pointed, like "Mom, I think you should know that Dad has this racking cough and I can't talk him into seeing a doctor or even taking off work a few days. I think it might be pneumonia." Then her mother would say, "Isn't he exasperating?" as if she had known about his cough all along, although it could easily have been a couple of weeks since anyone in the family had laid eyes on her. "Well," she'd say, "I'm going to give him a talking-to; how's that." And sure enough, Robin would phone Lily that evening and say, "Your mom is making me go see Dr. Fish tomorrow, so you'll have to open for me. Hate to ask, but you know how she fusses." His shyly boastful tone filled Lily with pity. He was so proud to have a wife who cared about his well-being.

"Has anyone asked her?" Morris said once. "Have they asked, 'Are you and Dad separated? Divorced? Or what, exactly?'"

"I don't see *you* asking," Lily pointed out.

"Me! I don't have the right."

"And I do?"

"Well, you're her daughter."

Yes, but.

In fact, she didn't feel like Mercy's daughter. Or more accurately, she didn't feel that Mercy was any kind of mother. She felt Mercy was like those cats who fail to recognize their own kittens after they've grown up.

Now she said, "Okay, Mom, how about everyone comes to *our* place instead. All you have to do is show up for it, okay?"

"Or maybe Alice's place," Mercy suggested.

"Alice's! Why not mine?"

"Well, you're a working woman, sweetie. Alice has more free time. Let's ask Alice to do it."

"You're only saying that because you don't trust me," Lily said.

"Not trust you!"

"You're never going to change your view of me, are you? I'm the problem child. I'm the college dropout; I'm the faithless wife and the home-wrecker and the unwed mother. You just can't admit that a person is capable of change. But I'm thirty-eight years old now! I manage a whole store! I have a very happy marriage and a son who's on the honor roll!"

"Well, of course you do, honey," Mercy said in a soothing voice. "*I* know that."

There was no denying, right then, that the two of them did sound like mother and daughter.

Morris referred to it as "going to approve the intended." "Get your shoes on, buddy," he told their son on Easter morning. "We're going to approve the intended."

"What?"

"Going to meet your uncle David's new girlfriend."

"Now, we don't know she's his girlfriend," Lily said. "He didn't say straight out that she is."

"Of course she is, or why would he care if we met her?" Morris asked.

He was tying his tie in front of the foyer mirror. Lily was putting on her parka. (The day had turned out cold, sad to say.) She was not half as dressed up as Morris; she wore pants and a turtleneck. And Robby, who'd been watching cartoons in his pajamas until just a few minutes ago, had put on his usual outfit of jeans and a sweatshirt and was only now trying to step into his sneakers without losing hold of the marshmallow egg he was unwrapping. Lily tut-tutted and knelt to fit one of his feet into a sneaker. "You remember your uncle David, right?" she said.

"Sure."

"And he's bringing his friend Greta."

"Is she pretty?"

"We don't know yet."

She tied his sneaker and reached for the other one before she thought to add, "Not that it matters."

"It matters to *me*," he said.

He had just turned eleven, but he seemed much younger—a round-faced, chubby, bespectacled child who took after his father. Lily was surprised he gave even a thought to whether girls were pretty or not.

In the car, she told Morris, "Watch Alice say I put something redundant in my salad."

"Redundant!"

"Watch her say I shouldn't have put tomatoes in when she's serving tomato aspic or something. But I did ask. I said, 'Just tell me what your menu is so I can make sure not to repeat it.' And she said, 'I have no idea yet.' Said, 'I've never fixed an Easter dinner in my life; how would *I* know what to serve?' "

"Ham, maybe?" Morris suggested, flicking his turn signal on. "I believe that's customary for Easter."

"I hate tomatoes," Robby piped up from the backseat.

"I know you do, honey," Lily said. "Just eat your way around them." She glanced down at the bowl she was holding, although it was covered with foil and she couldn't see the contents. "At least my salad doesn't have ham in it," she said.

They merged onto the Baltimore Beltway, where traffic was surprisingly heavy. Lily had assumed everybody would still be in church at this hour. "I hope we're not going to be late," she said. "Alice wants all of us to get there before David does. She wants a kind of, like, welcoming committee."

"We're fine," Morris said. "David has to deal with traffic too, remember."

Morris was her rock. She could always count on him to set her mind at rest.

"Does it have mushrooms?" Robby asked suddenly.

"Does what have mushrooms?" she said.

"Does your salad have mushrooms?"

"Do you not know me at *all*?" Lily asked, and she turned to send him a look of mock indignation. "Would I do such a thing?"

He didn't laugh. He pushed his glasses higher on his nose—a sign of nervousness, with him. "Also," he said, "I don't like when the grown-ups say 'Robby the Boy.' "

"They have to say 'Robby the Boy' so as not to confuse you with Robby the Girl," she told him. "You wouldn't want to be mistaken for a girl, now, would you?"

"Why can't Robby the Girl have her own name?"

"Well," Lily said, "in actual fact, it *is* her own name. She had it before you did, even."

"It should really belong to a boy, though, because Robin is Pop-Pop's name."

Exactly what Lily had pointed out, during her family's first visit after she'd given birth. Alice had accused Lily of being a copycat; and Lily had said, "But *my* baby's a boy, so he has a better right to the name."

"Robin is not just a boy's name," Alice had said. "In fact, it's more often a girl's name."

"In this case, though, our father's a Robin!"

"And besides," Alice said, "I'm older."

"What has that got to do with it?"

"The oldest sibling is the one who gets dibs on the family names."

"That's news to *me*," Lily told her, and then Mercy had broken in to say, "Goodness! Listen to you two! I'm the one who should feel hurt. Two different grandchildren named for your father and none for me."

"Well, I can hardly be blamed for not naming my son Mercy," Lily told her, but they did break off their argument.

Why *hadn't* Alice used the name Mercy? Well, maybe she just didn't like it. But now Lily wondered if their mother really had felt hurt. Although she'd sounded perfectly cheerful when she brought it up.

Morris took a left onto Garden Gate Garth, a curving street of long, low ranch houses on treeless lawns. At Alice's driveway, halfway down the block, he started to turn in, but Lily said, "Wait, let's park on the street. We don't want people pulling up behind us."

"Right; we may need to make a quick getaway," Morris said with a chuckle, but he backed out again and parked alongside the curb. When he had cut the engine, he looked across at Lily. "Ready?" he asked her.

"I'm ready."

She turned to give Robby an encouraging smile, but he was already climbing out of the car. He always looked forward to seeing his cousins.

It was Kevin who opened the door to them. "Happy Easter!" he said. He was a clean-cut blond man, suntanned even in April, wearing khakis and a pink polo shirt. "Hey there, bud," he told Robby.

"Hi," Robby said shyly.

"Much traffic on the Beltway?" Kevin asked Morris.

"Fair amount," Morris said, and they followed Kevin into the living room. Robby the Girl and Eddie were kneeling beside the coffee table, working a giant jigsaw puzzle. Robby the Girl barely glanced up when Lily's Robby came to stand beside them, but Eddie said, "Hi, Robby. Want to help with our puzzle?"

Robby said, "Okay."

Eddie was only nine, but he was dressed in the same golfer style his father favored. Robby the Boy's clothes, on the other hand, were as baggy as he could get them. (He claimed he was allergic to seams.)

At times like these, Lily loved her child so much that she felt it like a physical wound.

"Alice is out in the kitchen," Kevin told her, and she said, "Thanks," and headed toward the rear of the house with her salad.

The dining-room table, she saw, was extended to its fullest length, draped with Kevin's mother's heirloom tablecloth and displaying a row of pink and lavender hyacinths all down the center. "Pretty flowers," she told Alice as she entered the kitchen.

Alice was bending over the open oven door, doing something to a large piece of meat. "Hmm? Oh, thanks," she said, and she closed the oven and straightened up to shuck off her quilted mitts. She wore a formal tailored pantsuit, navy blue, and her hair had recently been "highlighted," as Lily believed it was called. "You can just set the salad over there," she said, gesturing with her chin. "Did you bring the dressing with you, or do you need to mix it here?"

"Oh, it's dressed already," Lily said.

"Dressed already!"

"I did it at home."

Alice gave her a look.

"What," Lily said.

"Nothing!" Alice said, in an airy tone. "We're having lamb, I decided."

"Oh, good," Lily said. She was glad it wasn't a ham.

"And I asked Mom to bring one of her desserts."

"Good thinking."

"Plus, we've got a couple bottles of champagne chilling, just in case. I mean, if David makes an announcement or something."

"Did he say anything when you called him?" Lily asked. "I mean, anything about Greta?"

"Not a word. I told him we'd be doing this at my house and he said, 'Fine.' I said, 'We're looking forward to meeting Greta!' but he just said, 'What's the name of your street, again?'"

"Typical," Lily said.

"He's such a . . . brick wall!"

"Oh, well: guys," Lily said.

But she promised herself that her Robby would never turn out that way. Not if she could help it.

Alice was taking a small china bowl from the fridge. "I made my own mint jelly from scratch," she said.

"Gosh! Wasn't that a lot of work?"

"Well, I wanted this to be special."

"I guess it's just as well Mom opted out of the cooking," Lily said. "It certainly would not have been special."

"Heavens, no," Alice said. She gazed down into the bowl with a pleased expression.

"Remember?" Lily asked. "Whenever we complained about a meal she'd tell us, 'Well, your *father* has never complained.' And then she'd go into this long description of how much he loved—"

"Her salmon patties!" Alice finished for her.

"Loaf," Lily said.

"What?"

"Her salmon *loaf*."

"Oh. Right," Alice said. "Ha! Salmon loaf, for the very first meal of their marriage. Their actual wedding supper, in that little apartment on Hickory Avenue, and what does she serve him? Salmon loaf, made from canned salmon." She shook her head. "And with bottled mayonnaise, no doubt," she added.

"Well. No doubt," Lily said, uneasily. (Was bottled mayonnaise not a good thing?)

The doorbell rang. They looked at each other. Then they made a beeline for the front of the house.

But it was only their parents. Kevin was just leading them into the living room. "How was traffic?" he was asking Robin.

"Oh, not too bad," Robin said. He'd made an effort—nice plaid shirt, clean corduroys—but he wasn't dressed up. It took a lot to make Robin dress up. Mercy, on the other hand, wore a ruffled white blouse and a good wool skirt and heels. She passed Alice a brown paper bag and said, "Ice cream."

"Oh!" Alice said. She sent a sidelong glance toward Lily.

"They're not here yet?"

"Not yet," Alice said, and she went off to the kitchen with the ice cream.

"How do, kids?" Robin asked his three grandchildren. They glanced up from their puzzle and murmured their hellos, but only Robby the Girl got to her feet to give him a hug. "Hi, Pop-Pop," she said.

"Hey there, honey."

"Hi, Grandmom." She hugged Mercy, who kissed the top of her head. The two of them looked alike, in fact—both with that gilded kind of blond hair that had skipped Mercy's daughters, unfortunately.

"Little spot of congestion on the JFX—" Robin was telling Morris, and then Robby the Girl said, "They're here, I think."

They all looked toward the picture window, which was veiled with a sheer white curtain so they had only the mistiest impression of the view. But it revealed enough that Morris could tell Lily, "I see *they've* parked at the curb, too," and he sent her a mischievous look.

One, two, three blurry figures, coming up the front walk.

"Three?" Alice asked. Unnoticed, she'd returned from the kitchen. "Who is it they've got with them?"

It was a child. Somebody small, in a skirt.

They all exchanged glances.

"Men!" Alice said.

The doorbell rang.

Kevin and Alice, together, moved toward the foyer. "Hello!" the others heard Kevin say, and Alice said, "Welcome!" and then, in the confiding tone she would use for a child, "Well, hi there!"

Murmur, murmur. A woman's voice, briefly, and then David saying, "Hope we're not late."

"No, no . . ." and they entered the living room, David leading.

Lily's first sight of David never failed to startle her. Mentally, she had him fixed at some point in his late teens—his hair still golden, his face still unformed and tentative. But his hair was a darker blond now, straight and floppy and a bit rough-edged, as if he'd waited just a week or two past the time when it should be cut, and his face had taken on a squarer shape. Today he wore faded jeans and a flannel shirt fraying at the cuffs. That was the teacher in him, she supposed. Teachers were notoriously shabby dressers.

The woman who followed him was several years his senior—easily ten years, and maybe more. She was holding the hand of a little girl aged perhaps five or six, and the two of them wore identical expressions: serious, focused, on the very edge of frowning. Kevin and Alice trailed after them. Alice's own expression was a study.

"Hi, all," David said. "Like you to meet Greta Thornton and her daughter, Emily. Greta, these are my parents, Robin and Mercy; my sister Lily . . ."

Greta had light-brown hair, short and crinkly and standing up from her forehead, and she wore a fitted brown wool dress that could have come straight from the 1940s. Emily's hair was paler, pulled into braids so tight that they stretched the skin at her temples. Her clothes, too, seemed out of date—a dark print dress with long sleeves, and stiff tie shoes and knee socks.

"How do you do?" Greta asked, extending her hand to Robin. She went around the group shaking hands with everyone, even the children, who scrambled to their feet looking embarrassed. Emily didn't shake hands, but she carried herself with such dignity, following close behind her mother and giving each person an unblinking stare, that she might as well have.

"It's nice to meet you, Greta," Mercy said, and Robin said, "Much traffic on I-95, son?"

"Pretty brisk," David said offhandedly. "Emily, would you like to help with the jigsaw puzzle? Emily's a whiz at puzzles," he told the other children. Robin the Girl sat back down on the rug and patted the space next to her invitingly, but Emily circled the coffee table and took a seat on the couch, perching on just the first few inches of it with her back perfectly straight. She reached for a puzzle piece, an edge piece that was nothing but blue sky, and studied it intently and then transferred her gaze to the puzzle.

The men were discussing the absurdity of closing down a whole traffic lane on a holiday. Mercy was asking Greta if she'd ever been to Baltimore. Alice was edging out of the room as unobtrusively as possible—heading off to set an extra place at the table, Lily surmised.

Greta had not, in fact, ever been to Baltimore. "I come originally from Minnesota," she told Mercy. The way she spoke was not exactly foreign, but it was very stiff and precise, and she pronounced the *t* in "Minnesota" as sharply as somebody English might.

"And you teach at David's school?" Lily asked.

Greta transferred her gaze to Lily. Her eyes were a light-filled gray, and they gave an impression of extreme serenity—of imperviousness, almost. "I am the school nurse," she said. No contraction.

"Oh, a nurse!"

"I have been there a year."

"So you've known David a year."

"Yes."

Greta continued gazing at Lily calmly. There was a brief silence, during which a clatter of china and silver could be heard from the dining room.

"Greta, may I offer you a sherry?" Kevin asked suddenly.

Lily and her mother exchanged a startled glance. Cocktails, in the daytime? And sherry! Did Kevin and Alice even *own* a bottle of sherry?

Greta said, "No, thank you."

Another silence. Kevin didn't ask if anyone else wanted sherry. He seemed to have abandoned the whole idea.

"I told Greta that on our trip home we ought to swing by downtown so she could see Harborplace," David said.

"Oh, yes, you should definitely show her Harborplace!" Mercy said. "Baltimore's *very* proud of Harborplace," she told Greta. Although Lily knew for a fact that Mercy considered Harborplace a glorified shopping mall.

“They have fireworks there on the Fourth of July,” Robin the Girl chimed in, and both of the boys nodded enthusiastically.

Emily leaned forward a couple of inches and laid down her puzzle piece, neatly joining two long strips of sky.

“I’m not sure you want to mess with Harborplace traffic on a holiday,” Morris told David.

“Oh, well. We’ll just have to take our chances,” David said.

There was something different about him, Lily thought. He seemed more relaxed than usual. And he might have put on a few pounds. He’d always been on the thin side.

Alice appeared in the dining-room doorway. “Lunch is on!” she announced.

There was a general loosening of the atmosphere, a sense of relief. Everyone stood up and headed toward the table. For the first time, Lily noticed that Greta walked with the faintest hitch to her gait. She appeared to hesitate slightly after setting her right foot down, which made her seem even older than she was—not only too old for David but too old to have such a young child. Lily couldn’t figure the woman out, to tell the truth.

The lamb had been set at the head of the table, in front of Kevin, on a platter garnished with parsley and tiny red pepper-looking things, and there were side dishes in abundance, including Lily’s salad. Alice said, “Greta, I’m putting you at Kevin’s right. Mom, you’re on his left—”

“I think this must be why I’ve never much cared for Easter,” Mercy said. She was looking at the row of hyacinths. “Pink and lavender, together. Who thought *that* up, I wonder.”

“Emily, honey, you’re down at the end next to Eddie,” Alice forged on.

“I have no choice?” Emily asked in a small, chilly voice. She was addressing her mother; she had her eyes fixed on her mother’s face.

“You have no choice,” Greta told her firmly.

Alice said, "Greta, if you'd prefer to have her beside you—"

But Greta said, "She will be fine," and Emily sat down next to Eddie and folded her hands in her lap.

Lily tried to think whether she'd ever heard a child word the question that way before: "I have no choice?"

Her son would have asked, "Do I have to?"

She herself was assigned a seat next to Robby. She could press her upper arm very lightly against his sweatshirt sleeve, unbeknownst to him. He was chuckling at a story Robby the Girl was telling. The children were grouped together at the foot of the table, and the three cousins had begun to chatter among themselves while Emily looked on silently. Robby the Girl was talking about her very fat music teacher. Why did children find obesity so funny?

Or most children, at least. Not Emily.

Lily's father was shaking out his napkin, which had been folded into a sort of winglike shape. "What's that she's made? Roast beef?" he asked Lily in a low voice.

"Lamb," she told him.

"Hmm."

To Robin, even lamb was exotic.

Because Lily and Greta were on the same side of the table, Lily couldn't study Greta further during the meal. She did have a good view of David, though, diagonally across from her. She saw how he kept sending glances in Greta's direction, even while he was listening to Morris's assessment of the current housing market. And she saw how his expression eased when Greta laughed at something Kevin said. Clearly he was anxious for her to feel comfortable here.

There wasn't a chance, Lily realized, that Greta was only a friend.

On the other hand, neither were any announcements made that

required a champagne toast. Most of the conversation amounted to a general catching up: Kevin reporting a proposal he'd made to develop a shopping center near Towson; Mercy announcing that Koffee Kafé had agreed to show four of her paintings. "Mom paints house portraits," David told Greta, because much of the catching up was for Greta's benefit, really. A "Here's who we are" exhibit, so to speak. At regular intervals, though, some form of "And who are *you*?" would pop up. "Tell me, Greta," Alice said, putting on an alert expression, "have you always been a school nurse?" and Greta responded in kind—equally alert, graciously forthcoming. "No, I worked in an emergency room until the time Emily was born."

"Oh, yes, I imagine emergency-room hours would be difficult with a young child," Alice said.

"Very difficult," Greta said.

There was a pause. Then Alice said, "And is her father—?"

"We are divorced," Greta said.

"Ah."

Another pause.

"So!" Morris said loudly. "You still driving that VW, David?"

"Absolutely," David said. "Going to keep it running forever, if I can."

"I have to say I envy you," Morris told him. "If it weren't for company policy I'd buy a Beetle myself, first thing tomorrow. I'm in real estate," he added in an aside to Greta. "We have to have big cars for driving clients around." And so they were back once again to "Here's who we are."

David, for his part, said that his drama students were putting on a play he'd written for Graduation Day. And Robin (in answer to a question from David) said no, he wasn't thinking of retirement any time soon. "I barely work as it is," he said, "now that I have Lily. Lily is my manager," he told Greta.

"That must be very nice," Greta said.

Lily felt that this meal was going to last forever.

Mercy's ice cream was chocolate. A half-gallon carton of house-brand chocolate ice cream. It seemed she'd deliberately chosen the most humdrum dessert she could think of. In fact, she came right out and said so. "I know how you all hate fancy food," she told them while Alice was dishing it out.

Alice gave one of her nonlaughs. "*Ma*-ha-hahm! We don't hate it; we just have fairly . . . standard tastes, in this family."

"Exactly," Mercy said, and then, to Greta, "I once took a course in French confectionery, back before I was married."

"Really!" Greta said politely.

"It turned out to be all for nothing, though."

"Oh, surely not."

Meanwhile, the children were digging happily into their ice cream—except for Emily, who had barely touched her meal and sat listening now to the other children's banter, gazing first into one face and then another with a faint hint of a smile at the corners of her mouth. She made Lily's Robby seem positively outgoing by comparison.

When Alice suggested they have their coffee in the living room, Lily rose and started clearing the dishes, but Alice said, "Oh, never mind those!" Greta, on the other hand, simply stood up and limped out without the slightest move toward clearing. This was noticed. Or Lily and Alice noticed, at least, and exchanged a brief glance, deadpan.

In the living room, Robin sank onto the couch and said, "Don't know whether to sit down or *lie* down, after all that food," but David and Greta remained standing. "We should probably hit the road," David told Alice.

"What! Now?" she said. "You haven't had coffee!"

"We've got a long drive ahead of us, and if we want to swing by Harborplace . . ."

The others had been seating themselves also—returning to the same spots they'd occupied earlier, as they tended to do—but now they stood up again, and there was a general air of uncertainty and some milling about. "Emily," Greta said. "Time to go." Emily, who had settled again beside the jigsaw puzzle, rose immediately and went to stand close to her mother. "Can you say thank you?" Greta asked her.

"Thank you for my lunch," Emily told Alice in a ritual singsong.

"Oh, you're welcome, honey," Alice said.

"You have been very kind," Greta said formally, and then she looked at David and he said, "Yes, great dinner, Alice! Good seeing you all," and he gave them a wave and turned toward the foyer, with Kevin following to fetch their coats.

Granted, they were not a particularly touchy-feely family. But ordinarily David would have hugged his mother and sisters goodbye, at least, and clapped his brothers-in-law on the back.

It was Greta's fault, Lily felt. She knew she was leaping to conclusions, but she couldn't help feeling that David was under Greta's *influence,* in some way.

Not that she said this aloud. When the door had shut behind the three of them, she just said, "Well!" at the same time that Kevin, returning from the foyer, said, "Well, now!" and rubbed his hands together briskly.

"Well, *that* was interesting," Alice said.

But then Morris, dear Morris, said, "Isn't it great he's found somebody! And wasn't that little girl polite."

Everybody gave him a look, even Robin.

Then Alice went off to the kitchen for the coffee, and Lily

followed to fetch the cups, and when they returned it seemed the others had found their tongues again. "How *old* was Greta?" Kevin was asking, and Robin the Girl, looking up from the jigsaw puzzle, said, "I thought Emily was kind of weird-acting, didn't you-all?"

"Aw, now," Morris said.

Mercy said, "Well, I personally do not fault Greta and Emily. We don't even know them. We didn't get the least little sense of them. And why is that? That's David's fault. It's purely David. Oh, what makes him act so standoffish? Is he mad at us about something?"

"He's mad about the summer of the plumber," Robin said suddenly.

Morris said, "Excuse me?" but the others didn't react, having heard this story before.

"The summer after he graduated from high school, I'm talking about," Robin told Morris. "Before he started college. He wanted to volunteer with this theater group, downtown theater group, but I told him he should get a paying job. That college wasn't cheap! And it's true we could swing the tuition fees, on account of some money Mercy's dad had left her, but I'm talking about the principle of the thing. You know? I mean, larking about with this theater bunch like some rich kid, then heading to college in the fall all expenses paid and not a care in the world. I said, '*No*, sir. No, you're going to have to do something this summer to pull your own weight,' I said. 'Take on some kind of work that at least will foot your incidentals.' And I still believe I was right about that. How else was he going to learn, I ask you. How else would he ever learn how the actual world operates?"

"Good point," Morris said.

"So I got him a job with this friend of mine who was a plumber. A *real* job, that is, wrestling pipes and digging ditches, serving his time like ordinary folk. And he did do it; he did go through with it. But acting put-upon the whole while. Wouldn't say two words to me; wouldn't answer my questions. 'So how was your day?' I'd ask, and he'd say, 'How do you *think* it was?'"

"How *did* you think it was?" Mercy asked. She was sitting in the rocking chair across the room; she rocked forward so sharply that her cup clinked in its saucer. "What did you *expect* him to say?"

"Then come September," Robin went on, as if she hadn't spoken, "he left for college. Stayed away till Christmas, and then again till spring break. Around spring break I said, 'What're your plans when school is out, son?' and he said, 'Well, I'm not about to sign up for another summer of the plumber, that's for sure.' And after his exams he just stayed on in Islington, did something with a playhouse there, and never once came down to visit before sophomore year began. Never came again, in fact, for any more than a couple days."

"Now, that's not true," Mercy said. "He came longer than that for Christmas vacations! Christmas vacations he would come for a whole week or so."

Robin merely raised his eyebrows at Morris, as if she had proven his point.

"Well," Morris said, "but it's true that different folks are cut out for different jobs."

"You think Paul *Dee* loved snaking drains?" Robin asked.

"Who?"

"The guy I sent him to work for? You think he craved to go to some stranger's basement and wade through their backed-up sewage?"

"Well, but, clerking in a bookstore, maybe—"

"Paul *Dee*? I'm not even sure he could read."

This made the others laugh, but Morris pressed on doggedly.

"David, I meant," he told Robin. "David could have found some job that was more compatible, maybe. Different types of people favor different types of work, is all I'm saying."

"Huh."

"Like this one guy I went to high school with," Morris said, "he ended up trimming trees for a living. Forty feet high in every kind of weather, sprinting from branch to branch. I said one time, I said, 'Richie, how can you stand doing that?' and he said, 'Are you kidding? I'm outdoors all day!' he said. 'I'm not slaving away in some office, or sweet-talking some asshole looking to buy a house. How can *you* stand it?' he asks."

"But the thing I was trying to teach David," Robin said, "is sometimes a man has to set his teeth and do what he has to do. Never mind if it's not 'compatible,' so-called. Never mind what 'type' he is. He just has to go *against* his type, and make up his mind to get on with it."

"I see," Morris said.

"Did I do wrong? Are you thinking I did wrong?"

It was the whole room, now, that he seemed to be asking, but Morris was the one who answered. "No, no. I understand," he said gently. And none of the others said anything at all.

"*I* don't blame David's plumbing job," Alice told Lily that evening on the phone. "I mean, look at how he worded it: 'summer of the plumber.' Kind of joking. Kind of flip. I know he hated the job—who wouldn't?—but he survived it. You can stand anything for three months. No, I blame Mom. I blame her moving out."

"Oh, for heaven's sake, David was already gone by then," Lily said. "What did *he* care where she lived?"

"You know what they say, though, about parents getting divorced the minute a kid leaves home. They say it's every bit as traumatic as if they'd done it earlier, or maybe even worse, because the kid has the added guilt of thinking it was *his* fault; he shouldn't have left them alone."

"That's ridiculous," Lily told her. "First of all, Mom and Dad aren't divorced. And second, I'm not sure David even *knows* she moved out, even after all this time. He hardly ever comes home, after all. And is so self-centered besides; let's face it."

"Self-centered!"

Of course Alice would take offense at that. She'd always shown a special fondness for David; she'd been one of those officious big sisters who act like a second mother, almost a *competition* mother. Whereas Lily, who'd been eight when he was born, had viewed him as kind of a nuisance.

"Self-centered now and self-centered before," she told Alice. "Close-mouthed, secretive . . . Did he ever give us the slightest inkling who his friends were, or his girlfriends?"

"That's just because he's a guy," Alice said. "Guys don't like to chitchat."

"Even when they're little? Robby likes to chitchat."

"Well, so did David, back when he was little," Alice said. "Remember?" There was a smile in her voice now. "Remember that mouse joke he loved?"

"No."

"This mouse and this elephant happen to meet in the jungle, and the mouse looks up at the elephant and says, 'My, you're big!'" (Alice made her voice go tiny.) "And the elephant says"—in booming tones—"'My, you're little!' Then the mouse says"—tiny voice again—"'Well, I been sick.'"

There was a silence.

"Get it?" Alice asked.

"Yes, sure, I *get* it," Lily said, "but—"

"He would totally crack himself up every time he told that

joke. And he told it a *lot,* to everybody. But think about it: the point was what a lame, self-serving excuse that little mouse made. Don't you find it kind of surprising that a five-year-old would understand that?"

"He was five?" Lily asked.

"He was five. Still in kindergarten."

"So what are you saying: he understands now that his family's not worth talking to?"

"*No*-ho-ho. Lily."

"He understands that a divorcée who-knows-how-much older than him is the woman he wants to marry?"

"He didn't say a word about marriage!"

"Tell me you really believe that Greta's only a friend," Lily said.

"Well, who can say? Maybe she is," Alice said.

Then she changed the subject to what Mercy had brought for dessert.

Neither Lily nor Morris thought to ask Robby *his* opinion of Greta, but at supper the next evening he said, "Mama, is Emily's mother going to marry Uncle David?"

"We don't know, hon," Lily said. "What makes you ask?"

"Because Daddy said she was Uncle David's girlfriend but Emily said she wasn't."

"Oh, really?" Lily said. She and Morris looked at each other. "Well, then!" she said.

"Emily's already got a dad in Minnesota, is why."

"Oh," Lily said.

"She went to visit him at Christmastime, all by herself."

"I see."

Robby dragged an upside-down spoonful of mashed potatoes over his tongue, thoughtfully. Then he said, "When you and Daddy got married, did your family approve the intended?"

Lily laughed, mostly out of surprise. She never knew what Robby would retain in that head of his. "They certainly did," she said. "First your aunt Alice met him and then Pop-Pop and Grandmom, and everybody loved him."

"Well, I wouldn't go *that* far," Morris said. He reached for a biscuit. "I had to have an extremely difficult conversation with your pop-pop," he told Robby. "I was nervous as all get-out."

"What'd you have a conversation about?"

"Oh . . ." Morris said.

"Roofs," Lily said.

Morris said, "Huh?"

"You had a conversation about whether our house should have a slate roof."

"Oh, that was later," Morris said. He told Robby, "First I told your pop-pop how very, very serious I was about your mom. I told him how the first time I laid eyes on her, she showed up for work with this letter box, this official-looking black-and-white speckled letter box, and she set it on her desk and unlatched it and took out a little jar of hand cream, and a teeny cactus plant in a clay pot, and a framed photo of her cat, who happened to have died, by the way; it was a photo of her *dead* cat—"

"Heavens, Morris," Lily said, at the same time that Robby said, "What'd he die of?"

"It was a she," Lily said, "and she died of old age."

"Was she dead in the picture?"

"*No,* she wasn't dead in the picture. Good grief," Lily said.

"So after your pop-pop heard *that,*" Morris told Robby, "he said, 'Okay, then! Okay!'" And here Morris turned his palms up in a gesture of defeat. "'Go ahead, then!' he said."

"Ha!" Robby said. "You won, Daddy!"

"I certainly did," Morris said, and then he and Lily smiled across the table at each other.

There was a lot he'd left out of that story. For instance, his months-long, starry-eyed worship of her after that first sighting, which made him a joke to the whole office and which she herself shrugged off. And the random conversations they started having by and by in the lunchroom. And her gradual realization that this was a very likable man, in fact; very kind and sympathetic. Though not her type, of course. Until he was, all of a sudden.

She'd been terrified, once she suspected she was pregnant. All her years of risky behavior, she saw, had been based upon the assumption that she could have a do-over any time she liked, but that turned out not to be so. This was irreversible; it was real. An actual, real pregnancy, in the days before legal abortion. A very-much-married man—*unbreakably* married, she had sensed, as longtime childless couples often were. Which was why she had told him the news as a statement, not a question: "I'm pregnant but I don't expect a thing from you; I'm dealing with this on my own."

This was after she had been fired (a little issue with chronic lateness), and she couldn't imagine what she was going to do for money. But she just kept putting off the problem. Something would come along.

Then one night she was awakened by her doorbell, and she stumbled to the foyer and squinted through the peephole and saw Morris's white, set face, his glasses looming owlishly. When she opened the door he said, "I have to be here. I can't not be," and he walked in and set down an absurdly small vinyl suitcase. "Please don't send me away," he told her.

It was the "please" that touched her heart. Not that it had crossed her mind to send him away, in any event.

She knew her family made fun of him. Or found him amusing, at least. She knew he came across as stuffy and too earnest, prone to telling the entire plots of movies and to making a low, place-holding humming noise any time he paused to search for words; and he was going to have one of those tacked-on-looking bellies if he didn't cut back on those biscuits. What a contrast to the men in her past! her family must be thinking—those dashing, handsome, edgy men she had always favored. (B.J. in his motorcycle jacket, so debonair and courtly until they married and he all at once started viewing her as his ball and chain.) But she was no longer remotely tempted by such men. She was sobered—she was shattered—by her three months of terror, and she vowed that she would never be that vulnerable again.

Now Morris gave a sudden nod to himself, as if he'd come to some private conclusion. "You know," he told her, "maybe Greta was just as nervous yesterday as I was that time with your dad. Maybe she's the kind who acts sort of cold when she's unsure of herself, and we'll like her better when she gets to know us better and starts to feeling accepted."

Lily said, "Oh, honey, you are such a dear."

And she reached across the table and laid her hand on top of his, for a moment.

"Well," Robby said finally, "*I* would approve Greta."

"Would you, buddy?" Morris said.

"And then Emily could be my friend."

"Oh. Emily." Morris chuckled. "Well, Emily could be your friend even if they *don't* get married, in fact."

"She could?"

"Absolutely," Morris said, and Robby said, "Oh, good," and dug his spoon into his potatoes again.

Except they did get married.

It was Alice who broke the news. She telephoned that Friday evening, when Lily was watching *The Incredible Hulk* with Morris and Robby. Lily said, "Hello?" and Alice said, "Well, they're married."

"What?"

"David and Greta. They're married."

"Oh, my heavens," Lily said, and Morris sent her a questioning look. "Let me change phones," she told Alice. She handed Morris the receiver and went out to the kitchen to lift the extension. "Got it," she said, and then, as soon as she heard Morris hang up, "Tell me from the beginning."

"There's not much to tell," Alice said. "This thank-you note came from Greta saying—hold on." There was a brief fumbling sound at the other end of the line. "Saying, 'Dear Alice, Thank you for the delicious Easter dinner. I enjoyed meeting all of you.' New paragraph. 'David and I would like you to know that after school yesterday, we were married. Emily was our only guest, because we did not want a fuss. I hope you will wish us happiness. Sincerely, Greta Thornton Garrett.'"

"That's *it*?"

"That's it."

"Well, okay," Lily said after a pause. "I guess they had a right to do this the way they wanted."

"No forewarning," Alice said, "no prior announcement. What, were they worried we'd crash the wedding? And then who is it who tells us, finally? Greta! Not even David! *Greta* tells us! I feel like I've just gotten word of his death."

"Oh, Alice!"

"I haven't told Mom and Dad yet. I haven't even told Kevin. It's like I'm thinking if I don't say it aloud, it didn't happen."

"Did you call David?"

"David?"

"Did you call to congratulate him?"

"Are you *nuts*? Honestly, Lily. I know you're not as invested as I am; you were always jealous of him because up till he came along you'd been the youngest. But don't you see how hurtful this is? I don't know if I'll ever again feel the same way about him."

"I wasn't jealous!" Lily said.

"Oh, now she's going to get all prickly," Alice said, no doubt addressing the ceiling.

"I was *fine* with him being the youngest! I mean . . . Look, Alice, think of what Morris said. Shouldn't we just feel happy that David's found somebody?"

"That he's found a divorcée three times his age who could barely be troubled to speak to us?"

Lily started laughing.

"What," Alice said.

"The poor woman has one foot in the grave, to hear you tell it," Lily said. "She can't be *that* old."

"She's ancient. And I honestly do not know where she comes from."

"She comes from Minnesota," Lily said.

"But what is her story? How did she end up here?"

"She had an unfortunate first marriage of some kind and they divorced and she moved east with her daughter. Period," Lily said. "I don't see the problem."

"You're just saying that because you want to look more open-minded than me," Alice told her.

"I *am* more open-minded than you."

"While I, on the other hand, am concerned about David's happiness."

Lily said, "All I'm saying is, Morris thinks—"

"Morris thinks our family is narrow and unfriendly and judgmental; I know," Alice said. "I've heard all about it."

"No," Lily said, "Morris thinks maybe Greta was acting like she did because she was feeling nervous. He says maybe she's someone we'll like, by and by."

And then she said, "If you insist on finishing my sentences for me, couldn't you at least finish them *right*?"

She slammed the phone down. She smoothed her hair and tucked her shirt in and went back to the TV room.

She waited for a commercial break before she told Morris. She said, "Guess what Alice had to say."

"She's leaving Kevin?" Morris suggested.

"No, silly."

"They're moving to a row house in Govans?"

"Very funny."

"Ssh!" Robby told them, because he liked to pay rapt attention even to the commercials.

"David and Greta got married," Lily said.

Robby swiveled his head to stare at her. Morris said, "Really!"

"Greta wrote Alice a thank-you note and just happened to mention the fact."

"But they didn't invite *us*!" Robby wailed.

"Well, it wasn't a *wedding* wedding, sounds like. Still," Lily said to Morris, "they must have known they were going to get married when they were here for Easter. Why didn't they at least tell us?"

"They probably didn't want a scene," Morris said.

"We wouldn't have made a scene!"

"No," he said, "but maybe David worried one of you would say something that sounded . . . unwelcoming."

"We'd have been *very* welcoming! We even had the champagne ready!"

"You did?" Morris blinked.

"We're not cold sticks, you know."

"Hey! *You*-all!" Robby protested, because the Hulk was on the screen again.

Lily stood up and went back out to the kitchen. The quiet there was a relief, after the blare of the TV. She sat down at the table and reached for the address book that dangled on a string from the wall phone.

Didn't it say it all, that she didn't know her own brother's number! She looked it up and dialed it, and then she sat back in her chair and listened to the ringing at the other end of the line.

If Greta answered, she planned to be downright effusive. A regular cheerleader type. "Greta!" she would say. "This is your new sister!" Or no, maybe not. That might be going too far. "Hello, Greta, I'm so pleased to hear—"

But it was David who answered. "Hello?" he said.

"Hi, David."

"Hi, Lily."

"So you're married."

"Right."

"Well, congratulations."

"Thank you."

He seemed to be waiting for something more.

"It was such a surprise!" she said. "I didn't know till I heard it from Alice."

"Yeah, well, I was planning to tell you. I was going to write Mom and Dad first, though."

"I see," she said. "Well. Anyhow. I just wanted to say I'm happy for you."

"Thanks," he said, but he still seemed to be waiting for something.

"I thought Greta seemed very nice," she offered finally.

"Oh, she *is*," he said. "She's just . . . remarkable! She hasn't had an easy life, you know. She comes from these immigrant parents who struggled to make a living; she had polio as a child; she worked her way through school as a waitress and a caretaker for old people and a dishwasher in a diner—"

Lily couldn't remember when she'd last heard David utter so many words at one time. It was a river of words, a torrent. "Her husband was this total cad," he was saying, "an orthopedist; he left her for his secretary a month after Emily was born but now he thinks he's this *father* type; he's always angling for custody when at first he purely resented her, wouldn't give her so much as a—"

"Oh, and Emily seems like a sweetie," Lily said.

"She is the child of my heart," David said.

Lily was struck dumb.

"She's such a—she's no ordinary kid, you know. I just love watching how her mind works! Oh, I tell you, Lily, I never in this world gave a thought to having children. I really couldn't imagine I'd be able to *connect* with children. But over Christmas, when Emily had to fly alone to visit her father, I was way more worried than Greta was. We were seeing her off in the airport and I said, 'Emily,' I said, 'let's say someone starts acting pushy or talking to you too much. Let's say you start feeling uncomfortable. What you should do is just—here,' I said. 'I want you to look around you right now and choose a person you would go to for help. Someone you think you could trust.' And then Greta laughs and says, 'David,' she says. 'She has her very own assigned stewardess,' she says. 'She has an ID tag pinned to her front. She is labeled like a parcel. She will be *fine*!' she says, but meanwhile Emily's begun looking all around and she says, 'Well, um, I don't know; I could trust *that* person, maybe?' and wouldn't you know she has singled out this totally inappropriate teenage boy bopping about with his Walkman. Ha!"

Lily almost couldn't believe that this was really David. And David must have sensed it, because he stopped speaking all at once and cleared his throat. "Well, listen to me go on!" he said. And then, more quietly, "Greta still teases me about that. When we first discussed getting married, she gave me a nudge in the ribs and said, 'Tell me the truth, now, is it a wife you would like or a daughter?' And I said, 'Both! I want you both! I want the entire package!' I wanted to have a family; I never thought I did but I do, it turns out. And I'll be good at this, Lily; I know I will."

"Well, of course you will," Lily said.

There was a whole lot more she could have said. "Why, David!" she could have said. "*There* you are! I thought you were gone!" But she didn't want to scare him off, so all she did was tell him again, meaning it this time, that she was very happy for him, and he thanked her again and they said their goodbyes and hung up. After that she sat at the table awhile, gazing into space.

She really didn't remember David's mouse joke. Maybe he'd never told it to her, although that seemed unlikely. Or maybe, at age thirteen, she'd been too caught up in her own concerns to listen. At any rate, it had rung no bells when Alice reminded her. Now, though, she could hear his small voice so distinctly; she could hear him singing out the punch line. "I been sick!" he said, and that curly chortle of his traveled across the years to her from long, long ago when they were still a family.

5

ROBIN AND MERCY'S fiftieth anniversary happened to fall on a Thursday. Specifically, Thursday, the fifth of July, 1990. At first, Robin felt this was unfortunate. Who throws a party on a Thursday? Particularly a daytime party. And it should definitely be a daytime party, because young children were involved.

But then he saw a solution. He wanted this party to be a surprise, and if he scheduled it *before* their anniversary—say on the Sunday before, since Sundays were the most wide-open day of the week for everyone—Mercy was all the more likely to be taken unawares.

Oh, things were shaping up nicely, he felt.

He started with Lily; he approached her at work. Theoretically he was retired by now, but he tended to drop by the store fairly often, because what else did he have to do? He would take his time over breakfast, most days, and putter a bit afterward, but then he would start feeling itchy. He would wander the house; he would tackle some minor yardwork out back that was over with way too soon; he would find himself in front of the fridge, forking cold spaghetti directly from the dish even though he wasn't hungry. (All his pants were getting snug around the middle. Who'd have thought he would be the type to put on weight?) And so eventually he would show up at the store just to nose around a bit, as Lily put it. "What are *you* doing nosing around?" she would ask, but playfully, teasingly. "You're supposed to be lolling at home!"

"Oh, I don't know," he would say. "I'm not much of a one for lolling."

Today he found her in the office. She was sitting at his desk with the phone pressed to her ear, but he could tell she was on hold; she was idly twining her fingers in and out of the spiraled telephone cord. (And yes, in his mind it was still "his" desk; still a small shock to see a woman there, even a nonfussy woman like Lily with her straight blond ponytail and practical khaki pants.)

He knocked on the door frame and mouthed, "You busy?" and she untwined her fingers in order to give him a little wave. "Hi, Dad," she said in a normal tone of voice.

"I've got a proposition," he told her.

"Oh? What's that?" she asked.

"Thinking of throwing a little party."

"A party!"

"Party for your mom. For our fiftieth anniversary."

"Well, so, wait," she said. "What—?" and then "Hello?" into the receiver. "Yes, I'm here. Yes, it's Lily Drew, at Wellington's Plumbing Supply."

He backed out of the office and left her to her job. Drifted over to where two men in pinstriped coveralls were debating a sink-spray attachment, but they didn't look at him when he drew near so he decided not to offer his input. He continued toward the next display.

"So," Lily said, coming out of the office a few minutes later. "A golden anniversary party."

"Right," he said.

"Well, gosh, Dad. What does Mom think of that?"

"She doesn't know. And I don't want her to know; I want this to be a surprise."

"Uh-oh," Lily said. "I don't think Mom is the kind who likes surprises, to be honest."

"But if I tell her ahead, you see, she'll think I'm asking her to help with it. To clean the house and cook the meal and all. It would just wear her out. Plus, she's so busy with her painting, don't you know."

"Couldn't you tell her you're *not* asking that? Tell her it's going to happen but not to worry, you'll be the one in charge?"

"She would expect me to do it all wrong, though," he said.

"Well . . ."

He knew what Lily was thinking. He could read her like a book. She was thinking he probably *would* do it all wrong. "I was hoping you and your sister could advise me," he told her. "I mean, not help me with the meal or such; I have my own ideas on that; just advise me on the etiquette of how a golden anniversary works, exactly."

"But things like the guest list," Lily said. "You know she'd have all kinds of opinions about the guest list."

"The guest list is our family," he said. "How could she argue with that?"

"Oh."

"Now, for instance," he said, cannily, "you girls might have some notion about the proper time of day for this. A Sunday, I'm thinking—Sunday, July the first—but would we want it to be in the evening? Bear in mind we'll have the little 'uns."

"Oh, not in the evening! Not if the children are coming!"

He pretended to think this over. "Well, you're right," he said at last.

"We should make it an early lunch," she said, "and that way David and them can drive back before it gets dark. It could be at our house, if you like."

"No, I want it at our house," Robin said.

"At your house. Okay."

And he had her. It was just that easy.

The greatest accomplishment of Robin's life was: not a single one of his children guessed that Mercy wasn't living at home anymore.

Oh, they knew they should try her studio first if they wanted to get in touch with her. Or the girls knew, at least. (There was no telling what David knew, since he wasn't much in touch with any of them.) And they never seemed surprised if they dropped by the house for some reason and found Robin on his own. But that could be explained by her work, her dedication to her work. Artists! They were all crazy. In a good way, of course.

And his greatest fear was: Mercy might come right out someday and tell them the truth. "Your father and I live separately, needless to say," she might tell them—letting it drop just offhandedly, just by the by, as if she assumed they already knew. It would kill them. They would be devastated. Just the thought of her doing that could almost make him mad at her, although in fact she'd never spilled a word on the subject. He had nothing to be mad at her for.

His great-aunt had disapproved of Mercy. She hadn't actually said so; she'd merely spoken against marriage in general. "I just want to warn you," she'd said, "that the quality you marry a person for will end up being what you hate them for, most often."

Robin knew she was referring to Mercy's "high-class manner," as she called it, but that was not what he was marrying her for. What did he care about class? No, it was Mercy's quiet dignity that first attracted him—her upright posture and her composure as she stood behind the counter. She was so different from the clingy, flirtatious, giggly girls he was used to. It was Aunt Alice—a lifelong cannery employee—who was concerned with questions of class.

He had lived with Aunt Alice since the age of fourteen, after his mother died of cancer. Although really, Aunt Alice said, she had died of a broken heart. "If it wasn't for that father of yours, she'd be alive and well to this day," she told him. His father was a long-haul trucker who met some woman up in New Jersey and filed for divorce when Robin was six years old. "Divorce"—a word like a knife, in Robin's opinion: hard and sharp and vicious, the cause of his mother's eternal mute, damp misery. She went to work after that for a dry cleaner, doing alterations, but when Robin thought of her now he pictured her endlessly at home, endlessly slumped in a comma shape on the living-room sofa. Possibly, he allowed, there were some factors—physical cruelty, for instance—that could justify divorce, but otherwise, no. Couples who divorced were shirkers. They were simply not grown up. He had said as much to Mercy when he proposed. "I tell you this," he had said. "If you can imagine us ever, ever divorcing, then I don't want you to accept." And she had known to take him seriously. She had squared her shoulders and looked him in the eye and said, "I promise you, Robin. That will never happen."

But who could say what quality had attracted Mercy to *him*? He still marveled, after all these years, that she'd given him the time of day. He knew he was nothing much to look at, short of stature and socially awkward, forever doing the wrong thing and then groaning at his mistake, shaking his head at himself for hours afterward. A neighbor might call out a greeting, for instance, and Robin would answer, "Well, hey!" and wave an arm like a fool, only to realize a second later that the neighbor had meant the greeting for somebody farther down the street. Or a cashier at the store would tell him, "Enjoy your lunch," as Robin left for his noontime break, and he would say, "You too," and then wince and clap a hand to his forehead once he was outside, because *she* wasn't going to lunch! She was just *back* from her lunch, for God's sake!

Even the simplest interaction racked him with anxiety. He was always missing cues, it seemed. And yet Mercy loved him. He had never asked her why; he was afraid that if she reflected too deeply, she would realize her mistake. He just kept the thought close to his chest, and polished it and cherished it as he had since the day she had said yes to him: Mercy loves me.

Alice phoned. "So," she said. "I hear you're planning to throw an anniversary party."

"Right," he said. He nudged his bowl of chili away and sat back in his chair. Alice routinely called during his supper hour, five-ish, to keep him company while he ate. In fact Robin didn't believe in doing two things at once, and so he always stopped eating until she said goodbye, but Alice didn't know that.

"I would just like to say," she told him, "that in my opinion, surprise parties are never, ever, under any condition whatsoever, a good idea."

"Okay," he said agreeably.

"So will you just tell Mom right now what it is you're planning?"

"Oh, I think not, hon," he said.

There was a pause at the other end of the line. No doubt she was rolling her eyes despairingly at Kevin.

"Also," she said, "it's really *us* who should be doing this. The three of us; your three offspring."

"Well, that's nice of you to offer," he said. (Although she hadn't, actually.) "But I've got this, thanks. I've got it all planned out."

"Dad—"

"However!" he said brightly. "I did want to ask a favor."

"What's that?"

"Could you phone David for me and make sure he comes? Twelve o'clock noon on Sunday week, the first of July. Tell him it really matters that they be here. You know best how to talk to him."

"Well . . . but he may be tied up," Alice said.

"Even if he *is* tied up! Tell him it's important. Say they're welcome to spend the night, if they like."

"He's not going to want to spend the night," Alice said.

"Just try, though, hear? You've got a way with him."

"Well . . ." she said. And then, "Okay."

He allowed himself a little smile of self-congratulation.

"Now, about the menu," she said.

"I've got the menu."

"What? What are you serving?"

"It's all, all under control," he said soothingly.

"But I could make my—"

"I've got it. Thanks, hon. Bye."

And he hung up and drew his chili bowl close again.

Everyone could come except the two Robbys. (Robby the Girl had a camp-counseling job in Rehoboth this summer. Robby the Boy was off in Spain with his college's study-abroad program.) Even David and his family could come. Alice didn't mention if she'd had any trouble persuading him, and Robin didn't ask. She did say he'd declined to spend the night.

Robin hired his next-door neighbor's cleaning lady to clean the house. It took her a full day, and that was just the downstairs. After that he was very careful not to let the place get cluttered again.

He ordered a cake from the supermarket, because he'd have had to be out of his mind to try baking his own, especially for Mercy. And he laid in all the groceries he'd need—simple stuff; his cooking skills weren't up to much—and mowed the lawn and cut back the wisteria where it was taking over the porch.

Did people give each other gifts for their anniversaries? Yes, he was sure they did, although he and Mercy never had. But what would he give her? "Golden," this one was called; that probably meant the gift should be made of gold. Mercy didn't wear jewelry, though. Even her wedding ring, thin as a wire, generally lived in the soap dish on the back of the kitchen sink. Besides, she would not, of course, be giving *him* a gift, so why embarrass her? That was what he told himself.

"What is your plan?" Lily asked him, the Friday before the party. He had stopped by the store to say hello, but only briefly; he didn't have a lot of time these days. "How can you be sure Mom's going to be available for this?"

"Oh," he said, "I'm going to wait till the actual day and then call her and say David is here."

"David," Lily said.

"I'll phone her at the studio and say they just happened to stop by while they were heading someplace else and so why doesn't she come over and say hello."

"Okay," Lily said.

"It's a Sunday," he said. "No chance she'd be off seeing a customer or some such."

"Okay," she said again, and then she sighed; he wasn't sure why.

. . .

On Sunday, the weather was perfect. Sunny and hot, but not *too* hot, not as hot as it had been all the past week; and anyhow, Mercy enjoyed the heat. Like most women Robin knew, she was forever complaining that she was feeling a draft.

He opened all the windows and doors and cranked down the awning out back. He had asked the cleaning lady to set the table while she was there, even though it meant the dining room would be more or less out of commission for the next few days, and now he put out all the food that didn't need refrigerating—the rolls and butter and the cucumber slices dowsed in Mazola and vinegar. After that he filled the cooler with ice and soft drinks, plus a few cans of beer for the guys.

Although Kevin, of course, was bound to bring champagne. The man was obsessed with champagne. Any possible occasion—birthdays, holidays, graduations—he had to show up with his "bubbly," as he called it. Always the expensive kind, highway robbery in Robin's opinion. Robin was more inclined to beer or Dr Pepper. He suspected the others felt the same, although they were polite about it. "Thanks, Kevin," they would murmur, and "Cheers, everybody!" and "Isn't this delicious." Then they'd take one small sip before setting their glasses down and forgetting to pick them up again, or wandering out to the kitchen with them and returning empty-handed.

Oh, the lengths this family would go to so as not to spoil the picture of how things were supposed to be!

So here came Kevin with his special insulated carrier, the very first to arrive, charging through the back door and heading straight for the fridge while the rest of his family trailed some distance behind—Alice, Eddie, and little Candle, carrying the sleepy-doll she never traveled without. And right on their heels, Lily and Morris with Serena. Candle and Serena were barely a year apart in age—kindergartners or thereabouts—and they eyed each other bashfully while the grown-ups milled in the kitchen and made forays into the dining room to check on the preparations. "Nice flowers, Dad," Alice said, and Robin said, "Thanks, I got them at the Giant."

"Mind if I rearrange them a bit?"

"No, go ahead," he said, although he'd been thinking he had done a not-too-bad job. They were tulips, bright red, and they'd started out as tight cylinders but the cashier had assured him that by Sunday they'd have opened up just fine, and she was right.

Now he was starting to feel nervous. "It's awful darn hard to gauge how long it will take to drive from Philly," he said. "I hope David and them won't be late."

"Don't worry. In my experience it's invariably a two-hour trip," Morris told him. "Could be a totally empty highway or it could be bumper-to-bumper; two hours flat, either way."

Morris was good like that, always doing his best to put a person at ease.

The three grandchildren trooped outside again—first Eddie, scooping up the ancient basketball on the back porch as he went, and then the two little girls, who thought Eddie hung the moon. (He was kind of a favorite of Robin's, too; he was the only one who liked building things.) Alice started cutting the bottoms off the tulip stems at the kitchen sink, and Kevin opened the fridge again to admire his champagne bottles. "Maybe we should go sit in the living room," Robin said, but then above the sound of the bouncing ball out back he heard the crunch of car tires. He went to the screen door to check and sure enough, there was David's little blue Beetle pulling up next to Kevin's BMW. Eddie called, "David's here!" and started dribbling his ball toward the Beetle.

David stepped out of the car and held one hand up for the ball, and meanwhile Greta emerged from the passenger seat and folded it forward so that Emily and little Nicholas could scramble out from the rear. Emily had grown a good foot, it looked like to Robin. She was in her early teens by now, tall and slim, with a very adult-looking bun low on the nape of her neck. She followed her mother toward the house, but young Nicholas—just seven or so—hung back to watch his father sink the basketball from an impressive distance.

"Hi, all!" Robin called from the doorway. Instead of following the others outside, though, he returned to the kitchen and dialed Mercy's number on the wall phone.

"Hello?" she said.

"Hey, hon."

"Hi, sweetheart. How's your day going?"

"Oh, okay," he said. "But you'll never guess: David and them are here."

"David!"

"They stopped by on their way to, they're on some kind of road trip and they happened to stop by, and—"

"What on earth!"

"Yes, and I thought you'd like to come say hello."

"Well, naturally! I'll be right over."

"You want a lift?"

"No, no, I can walk."

"Don't take too long!" He practically sang it. He hung up and then headed out back to join the others.

Most of the grown-ups—all except David—stood talking among the parked cars. Emily was with them, standing very close to her mother as if she felt shy, and Greta was holding an exotic white orchid-looking flower in a ceramic pot. "Hello, Robin," she said when she saw him. "Happy anniversary. This is for the two of you."

She walked over to him and placed the pot in his hands. As usual, she was wearing an outdated-looking dress, a navy print with a belt and short cuffed sleeves. (Emily, though, had joined the modern age; she was in jeans and a white peasant blouse.) "I believe this will not require much care," Greta said, and Robin said, "Well, thank you." The flower smelled like rainwater, pure and fresh rather than perfumey. He took a deep breath of it and then asked, "How was traffic?"

Instead of answering, she turned to Emily. "Say happy anniversary to Robin," she told her, and Emily took a precise step forward and said, "Happy anniversary, Robin." It had been suggested on several occasions that she call Robin and Mercy "Pop-Pop" and "Grandmom," but she never had, and Robin wasn't going to push it. (She still called David "David," after all, though it was obvious she doted on him.) "Thanks, honey," he said, and then, to the others, "It isn't our actual anniversary yet. That won't be till Thursday."

"The day after Independence Day," Kevin said in a musing tone.

"Yes, well, it was the first date in July that the pastor had available. Mercy held out for July, you see, because she thought June weddings were commonplace."

This made Alice and Lily laugh, but Greta nodded solemnly and said, "Yes. That is like her."

Robin knew his daughters weren't much taken with Greta. Alice referred to her as an "icicle." But at least you never had to wonder where you stood with her. She said things straight out; she was what she was; she was never nicey-nice, as he called it.

Ha! He hadn't thought of it till now, but she was something like his aunt Alice.

He recollected himself and turned to his daughters. "We have to go inside," he told them. "Your mom's on her way from the studio, and she'll be coming through the front."

Lily said, "Okay, into the house, everybody! Grandmom's coming."

David dunked the ball one last time and then snagged it and tossed it toward the children. "Where's your apron, Dad?" he asked as he approached. "I hear you're in charge of the cooking."

"My whole outfit was my apron," Robin said. "Till I shed it about an hour ago and chucked everything in the hamper. Though I maybe should have burned it instead."

He looked past David to Nicholas, who was chasing after the basketball rather than coming along with the rest of them. But once he got hold of it he did start dribbling it toward the house. He resembled David at the same age, it struck Robin—blond and skinny and knobby-kneed, except with Greta's pale-gray eyes.

As they entered the kitchen Alice asked, "What are you serving, anyhow?" but Robin said, "Oh, this and that," because he'd be darned if he would let her take things over at this stage. He set the potted plant on a counter, and they passed on through the dining room and into the living room. Eddie said, "Are we supposed to hide and then pop out when Grandmom gets here?" but Robin said, "Oh, no, I think just sit around like normal. Just minding our own business, and looking up real casual-like when she walks in and then we tell her, 'Happy anniversary.'"

They all found seats around the room, although Nicholas had to get up again and take the basketball out back when his mother told him to. Robin, though, remained standing. He went over to the front window and stood looking out at the shady sidewalk, the row of parked cars along the curb, a young couple passing by with a child in a stroller. Then he spotted Mercy heading down the street from the left. She was carrying a bulky white sack—no, a pillowcase, stuffed with her laundry. Her skirt was fluttering around her shins because even at age seventy, she walked as briskly as a young girl. "She's here," he said.

Everyone got quiet.

Robin stepped back from the window so as not to be seen. He heard the click of her shoes when she turned up their front walk; he heard her climbing the porch steps. The screen door twanged open and she crossed the foyer and came to a stop in the living-room doorway.

Oh, maybe they should have hidden themselves after all. Because what Robin had not foreseen was that the sight of them sitting so motionless, completely silent, hands very still in their laps, seemed to distress her. She opened her mouth to say something, but said nothing. Neither did they, for some reason. Were they waiting for Robin? He drew in a breath to speak, but then Greta said, calmly, "Happy anniversary, Mercy."

Mercy said, "Pardon?"

Then they all found their tongues. "Happy anniversary, Mom!" they cried, and "Happy anniversary, Grandmom!" and they stood up and came thronging around her, but Robin was the first to reach her. He took her laundry from her and set it on the floor, and then he said, "It's been fifty years, hon."

Even then, she looked puzzled. "What has?" she asked.

"It's our golden anniversary."

"It is?"

"July fifth, 1940, coming up this Thursday. I just thought a Sunday would be a better day for a party."

"Well, my goodness," she said, and by now her face had cleared, and she started hugging the others and kissing them and telling Nicholas how he'd grown. "Well, goodness, I just—" she kept saying, and "Well, I just don't—"

"Are you surprised?" they asked her. "Did you guess? Did you wonder if we'd remember?"

"Why would I wonder that, if I didn't remember myself?" she asked.

"Good point," Morris said, and Alice said, "Oh, Mom, how could you not remember? Fifty years, can you believe it?"

"No, actually," Mercy said.

Then she gave David another hug, although she'd already hugged him once, and she said, "Look at you, Emily! You're a young woman now."

"Dad planned this every bit," Alice said. "The date, the invitations, the menu—"

"Oh, I wish I'd known," Mercy said. "I could have been looking forward to it all this time!"

This caused the tiniest little hitch in the conversation. Everyone paused to glance at Robin. "Oh," he said.

But then here came Kevin from the kitchen, holding up two champagne bottles. "Toasts all around!" he said, and he sent Eddie and Emily to the dining room for glasses. Then he made a big production over the popping of the first cork, and looked resigned the way he always did once the glasses arrived, because they were the dish-shaped kind handed down from Mercy's grandmother. Kevin had mentioned several times that flutes were what people used nowadays.

The toasts were brief, thank goodness—just "Happy anniversary" several times over and "Here's to another fifty years!" (from Morris). Robin wasn't sure whether he should drink when he was one of the toastees, so to speak, but he saw Mercy first wait a beat and then smile and nod and take a sip, and so he did the same. Stuff was so fizzy it tickled his nose. He said, "Oops, better check the oven," and took his glass off to the kitchen.

Alice, of course, followed close behind with her own glass. "What can I do for you?" she asked him.

"Oh, pour the water, maybe?"

"Sure thing."

He emptied the plastic container of potato salad into a bowl and took it to the dining room, and then he returned to the kitchen and grabbed some pot holders so he could remove the two loaf pans from the oven. "What's that you've got?" Alice asked, re-entering with her pitcher.

"Salmon loaf," he told her.

"Salmon loaf," she repeated.

She came up next to him and peered down at the loaves. The tops had browned nicely, he saw, and puffed above the rims of the pans in a very attractive way. But something in Alice's tone worried him, and he raised his eyes to check her expression. "Is that okay?" he asked her.

"Oh! It's fine," she said.

And then she kissed him on the cheek, so he must have been wrong to wonder.

Somehow, it still didn't seem that Mercy had grasped the surprise-party concept. As she was taking her seat at the far end of the table, she asked David, "Where were you all on your way to, honey?"

"Excuse me?" he said.

"When you stopped by to visit, I mean. Your dad said you were on a road trip somewhere and just happened to stop by."

"No, I—" Robin broke in, because David was looking baffled. "No, that was just something I made up, hon, to get you here for lunch."

"They aren't on a road trip?"

"This lunch was a surprise, you see, and they drove down for it especially, but I didn't want you to know that."

"But I would *like* to know it," she said.

Which made Robin feel sort of frustrated, because how hard could this be, for heaven's sake? Which part did she not understand?

"To know ahead, he means," Alice explained. "If he'd told

you ahead they were coming for lunch, you might guess he was throwing a party."

"Well, I'd have to know sooner or later," Mercy said. "I know *now,* after all. Right?" She searched the others' faces. They were all looking confused too. "Am I right?" she asked them.

"He was afraid you might say no," Greta told her, a bit too loudly.

Mercy focused on her.

"He was afraid you might not want to celebrate your marriage."

"Oh," Mercy said finally.

And that seemed to satisfy her, although Robin felt slightly unsettled by the whole exchange.

Later, though, she returned to the subject. People had branched out by then into several different conversations—Alice and Lily discussing Robby the Boy's latest letter, and the little girls competing to entertain Emily (whom they found even more alluring than Eddie, evidently), and Morris telling Kevin and David one of his long-winded real-estate stories, overexplaining as always and detouring pointlessly and doubling back to insert some detail he should have mentioned to begin with. Then out of nowhere, Mercy said, "When I walked in and saw you all sitting around the living room, I thought somebody had died."

"Died!" several people said, and Alice asked, "Who?"

"David, maybe?"

"David!"

"Well, right off I saw I was wrong," she said. "But you were all so quiet!"

"We were quiet because you looked scared," Morris said.

Robin glanced at him in surprise.

"I was scared because I thought someone had died," Mercy said.

Well, this was getting them nowhere. Robin pushed back his

chair and stood up. He cleared his throat. "I'm not much of a one for speeches," he said.

He had their attention. He plowed ahead. "But I wanted to tell about this salmon loaf."

"It is delicious," Greta said.

He paused to say, "Well, thank you."

"I would like the recipe."

"I got it from this church cookbook my great-aunt gave us for our wedding," he said. "I'll copy it out for you." He went back to his original line of thought. "We'd been going on all these dates, you see. I'd taken Mercy to all these restaurants, trying to make an impression. Just about pauperized myself!" Soft chuckles around the table. "Crab Imperial in white china seashells, chickens wearing leg ruffles, this dessert they set on fire, one place—"

"Cherries Jubilee," Mercy murmured.

"*Crazy* foods! So then we got married. We didn't take a honeymoon; couldn't afford to. All those pricey restaurants, I guess." More chuckles. "First night in our own apartment, then, that little place in Hampden; you girls remember that place. First meal of our marriage. Mercy goes out to the kitchen and starts to fix our supper. I stay sitting in the living room reading the evening paper. It feels like I'm acting in a play or something. I'm wondering what she'll feed me; I'm hoping it's not something French. I'm thinking I don't care if I never see another French dinner in my life. Then she calls me to the table. I fold up my paper; I go out to the kitchen . . . In front of my plate there's this salmon loaf, waiting for me to serve it. This loaf pan of salmon with a toasty brown top, and it looked so . . ."

He swallowed. His eyes were filling with tears; he hoped nobody noticed. "It looked so cozy," he whispered. "It looked to me like home. Like I finally had a home."

He had planned to say more, but he stopped. He sat down.

From her place at the other end of the table, Mercy said, "Thank you, sweetheart."

He raised his eyes to her and found her smiling at him. That made it all worthwhile.

The cake was a big success, especially with the young ones. Of course it was only a sheet cake, because they'd told him at the Giant that that would be the most practical for such a crowd, but "Happy 50th Anniversary" was written in flawless cursive across the top and there was a yellow sugar rose at each corner. Alice asked, "Shall I do the honors?" and Mercy said, "Yes, please," and waved a hand. So Alice started slicing the cake and passing it around. Even before she was finished the two little girls were ready for seconds, so the people at the Giant had been right.

Greta, meanwhile, went out to the kitchen and fixed a pot of coffee without being asked, which was something of a surprise. While it was brewing she retrieved her plant from the kitchen counter and carried it into the dining room and set it in front of Mercy. "This is what we brought you," she said in that blunt way of hers.

"Oh, how pretty!" Mercy said, and then, "Robin, did you see?"

"Yes, very nice," he said.

"I think we should put it in a south-facing window," she said. "Right, Greta?"

"The light there would be too strong," Greta said.

"Oh, I guess east would be better, then. Say the east window in the living room," Mercy told Robin.

"Okay," he said.

He was grateful she had spoken as if she still lived here.

That little Candle! Such a live wire. She had polished off her second piece of cake now and she wanted all her cousins to come outside with her again, even though they were still eating. "Please? Please?" she said, and she and Serena nagged Emily into laying down her fork. In no time all the young ones were gone, and their section of the table was silent but somehow still raucous-seeming, with the messy plates they'd left behind and the balled-up napkins and crumb-littered tablecloth.

Morris was telling Mercy how his clients admired her paintings. (He had two of them hanging in his office.) "I always say, 'Well, her card's in there with your paperwork,'" he told her, and Mercy said, "Aren't you nice." Alice was quizzing David about his classes; it seemed he was teaching a summer-school course in improv. And now Greta brought the coffeepot in from the kitchen, walking with that little hitch of hers and looking a bit weary.

Robin had asked Mercy, once, "How old is she, do you think?" (This was back when they first heard that Greta was pregnant with Nicholas.) "Forty-two," Mercy said promptly. "I asked her." Eleven years older than David, therefore. Well, it could have been worse. And they did seem happy. Although who knew, really? How did anyone know what was really going in their kids' lives?

He had long ago accepted that his experience of fatherhood was not what he used to envision. The girls and he got along, thank heaven, but girls were more a mother's business and so he couldn't take much credit for that. David, on the other hand . . . For some reason, he and David had never seemed quite in step with each other. He couldn't put his finger on it. He had certainly tried his best. It would have helped, maybe, if David worked with his hands. That would have given them something to talk about. But he didn't. Which was okay! Better than okay! Robin was fine with that. He was proud of David's profession, in fact, and somewhere he still had a news clipping about a play of his that a local theater group had staged.

The women were beginning to bestir themselves—reaching for plates, stacking them, collecting silverware. Even Greta had risen to help. "Oh, don't fuss with those," Robin told them, but he didn't mean it. How could he ever have dealt with such a mess on his own? Alice said, "You and Mom just go settle yourselves in the living room," and so they did, along with David and the sons-in-law. But instead of sitting down with the others, Robin went to the TV and squatted on his haunches.

"What are you doing?" Mercy asked, instantly alert. (She always objected when the men watched a game instead of conversing, although Robin had explained several times that watching a game *was* conversing, in a way.)

But he said, "You'll see!" and proceeded to load a tape into the VCR.

"What *is* that?" she asked.

"A movie," he said. "Home movie."

"What?"

"Remember those movies your dad used to make?"

"Yes . . ."

"I had them converted."

This caused the sons-in-law to perk up. They were always game for a little tech talk. "Is that so!" Kevin said, and Morris said, "They can do that?"

"Oh, yes," David told him. "Any place that develops photos can do that, just about."

Robin said, "Mercy's dad bought a movie camera back in . . . what year would you say, hon?"

"Well, sometime in the late forties," Mercy said. "I know the girls were still small."

"I do remember Grandpa with a movie camera," David said, "but I'm not sure I ever got to see the results."

"No, well, showing a movie was such a production in those

days," Mercy said. "Special screen, special projector, all the shades drawn . . ."

"And now look," Robin said happily. "Just a click of a button and we're rolling."

The TV stood next to the fireplace, angled slightly away from the wall so as not to reflect the windows. This house—Mercy's parents' house, once—had been built before the advent of TV rooms. Ordinarily that was a drawback, or it used to be before the young folks left home. Now, though, Robin was glad, because your average TV room would have been too cramped for this size crowd. The women drifting in from the kitchen, once the dishes were done, the children summoned from the backyard . . . In fact some of the children, the two little girls, had to sit on the floor. The children were flushed and sweaty but they came without much urging; they could always be lured into watching something on a TV screen. "Now, this is a movie about the olden days," Alice told Candle in an instructive tone. "About our family when we kids were growing up. Does it go all the way to our teens?" she asked, turning to Mercy. "I don't remember. I know I must have seen this, but it was so long ago."

"Well, *your* teens, at least," Mercy said. "Your grandpa lived till 1956. You would have been fourteen by then."

"But once he'd died," Robin said, "sayonara to the movie-making. I don't think we even took the camera out of its case after that."

"Although I'm sure we still have it somewhere," Mercy said, because she was always shaking her head about all the old junk this house held.

Robin pressed the Play button and retreated to his recliner. A few random numbers flashed across the screen. Then a too-brightly dressed little group was standing on a lawn, *their* lawn, under a dogwood tree in full bloom that had died some twenty years ago. A very young man and a very young woman with two little girls, the smaller astride the young woman's hip. The sight of those children shocked him. They were back! They'd returned! He'd forgotten they'd ever existed, but all at once they'd rematerialized. And Mercy: look at her frilly sleeveless dress, nothing like the kind of thing she would wear nowadays.

Robin himself was an embarrassment—a bony, gawky fellow with a way-too-short haircut that exposed his scrawny neck, his smile so forced and toothy that he cringed to see it. But everyone said "Aww!" Even the little girls: "Aww!" Then flash again, and here was a slightly older Alice in a puffy pink sunsuit. Did they even make such things as sunsuits anymore? She was standing beside a bicycle with a pink bow tied to the handlebar. Then Alice and Lily together, squinting against the sunlight.

It seemed that Grandpa Wellington hadn't fully grasped what motion pictures were all about, because every one of these scenes was almost motion-free, posed as if for a portrait. But then by 1952 (an infant David in Mercy's arms, was how Robin could tell the date), Lily at least was a blur of activity, turning cartwheels across the screen and showing her underwear. Wasn't it surprising how the sight of Lily brought little Candle to Robin's mind! And yet Candle was Alice's daughter, not Lily's. It almost seemed his two granddaughters had been issued to the wrong mothers—impish Candle to staid Alice, docile Serena to Lily, who had always been such a handful. And then Alice's Eddie, son of Mr. Country Club, as Robin liked to call Kevin, had turned out to be the one grandkid who enjoyed helping Robin with his carpentry projects. So maybe parenthood was meant to be educational, Robin thought—a lesson for the parents on totally other styles of being. And now he smiled to see Alice picking strawberries in some field who-knows-where and depositing them in a Crisco tin. Even without a sound track he could summon up that bossy voice of hers. "One for the bucket, *one* for me; one for the bucket, *one* for me," as she popped every other berry into her mouth.

Oh, and now a new addition: Grandpa Wellington in person, glaring disapprovingly downward at a very small David, who was clinging to his grandfather's trouser leg as if that were all that kept him upright. And a new voice in Robin's head, Grandpa Wellington's own, finding fault every Sunday afternoon when Robin stopped by to report on the past week's sales. By then the old man was housebound, forbidden after his first heart attack to so much as climb the stairs or take a walk around the block and reduced to holding court in this very recliner, where he chain-smoked Lucky Strikes while peppering Robin with what-about-this and you-should-have-done-that and "What were you *thinking,* for God's sake?"

Who had filmed this scene? Robin wondered. Not Mercy, because here she came, tripping across the grass to link arms with her father and smile down at little David. So it could only have been Robin himself, although he had trouble believing he'd been entrusted with the precious camera. "Oh, Lord, would you look at me?" Mercy cried from across the room. "My hairdo's like a . . . floral arrangement!" And Robin shifted his gaze to where she sat and discovered that she had grown old. Still pretty, even now, but her hair had faded to an ivory color while all these years he had been seeing it as blond, and it was no longer a piled-up tumble of curls but a knot on the back of her head.

Had there been some kind of limit, in those days, on how long a scene could last? Each one was so brief. Here's so-and-so! And then *pouf,* here's such-and-such! *Pouf*—and then goodbye. Goodbye to all of it, in fact. It was over in a matter of minutes. Darn, he'd have liked to see more. Lily dressed up for a prom, maybe, looking like a princess with Jump Watkins standing next to her.

Or David tussling on the floor with their good old dog, Cap. Especially, he'd have enjoyed some footage of that nice week at Deep Creek Lake. It had flown by way too fast, he thought as the screen went blank. And he didn't mean only the movie.

"Well!" Kevin said. "Very interesting!" And Morris said, "What'd you think, kids?" and there was a general stirring—the children released to mill about again, the women gathering purses and cast-off sneakers and asking where Candle's sleepy-doll was. No, it emerged, David would not change his mind about staying over. No, none of them wanted the last of the cake, or the potato salad, or the tulips from the dining-room table. And just like that, they were gone.

But Mercy wouldn't leave too, would she? He didn't think he could bear it if she left. He stood next to her on the back porch, after they'd seen the last car off, and he felt almost scared to look over at her. He did, though, finally. He found her smiling at him. "You were very sweet to do that," she told him.

"Oh, good," he said, letting out his breath.

"But promise me something," she said.

"I know."

"What do you know?"

"You don't want any more surprises."

"Never, ever again," she agreed.

"I promise," he told her.

"But if you already knew that," she said, "then why did you do it?"

"I don't *know* why," he said. "It was a miscalculation."

Although it occurred to him, after the fact, that he did know why. Greta had had it right: he'd worried that Mercy would say no to celebrating their marriage.

She was still smiling at him, though.

And when he said, "Shall we go inside?" she didn't say anything about needing to get back to her studio.

The women had cleaned the kitchen to a fare-thee-well, he saw. All the counters were wiped down, and the dishwasher was humming. In the dining room, the tulips had started hanging their heads over the rim of their vase as if they were admiring their own reflections in the polished tabletop.

When he and Mercy reached the living room, he headed toward the couch rather than his recliner. He was hoping Mercy would sit down next to him. But instead she crossed to the foyer doorway and bent for her pillowcase of laundry. "Do you have any whites in the hamper?" she asked him, and he said, "No, no," even though he did. She went off to the rear of the house with her pillowcase, and he heard her a moment later descending the basement stairs.

From his place on the couch he gazed around him at the empty chairs, the dented cushions, an almost-full champagne glass abandoned on the mantel—all those signs of vanished life. The VCR was still on, he noticed; he could see a red dot glowing, but he made no move to rise and turn it off.

He heard Mercy climbing the basement stairs and then pausing in the kitchen. He worried she had found something to distract her, but no, she appeared now in the dining-room doorway. Crossed to the couch. And sat next to him, finally.

"You're running low on Tide," she told him.

"Oh, okay."

"I put it on your grocery list."

"Thanks," he said.

A silence. He had thought she might want to say a little more about the party, but she didn't. So finally he asked, "Can you believe it, hon? Can you believe it's been fifty years?"

"In one way, no, I can't," she said. "But in another way, it seems like forever."

"I know what you mean," he said.

"We were just kids, in those movies!"

"You want to watch again?" he asked, sitting forward.

"Not really," she said.

He sank back in his seat.

"They made me kind of sad, to tell the truth," she said.

"Oh, yes, me too," he said hastily.

"I guess it's just as well there's no movie of our wedding day."

"But we do have photographs," he said hopefully. "In the album."

She was pursuing her own train of thought, though. She said, "And yet I didn't *feel* like a kid, at the time. Remember how Daddy wanted us to wait a year? 'Wait!' I told him. 'That makes no sense! I'm already twenty,' I told him. 'I'm a grown-up.'"

"Well, *I* didn't feel grown up," Robin said. "Not on the actual day. I remember when I was all dressed and ready, I looked in the mirror and saw I'd missed a spot shaving. I didn't even know how to shave right, I thought, so what business did I have marrying? How would I know what to *do* with a wife?"

"You knew enough, though," Mercy told him, and she gave him a mischievous little dig in the ribs with her elbow.

"Oh," he said, "I'm not so sure about that."

"Now, now, don't be modest."

He made a chuckly sound.

She said, "At first I thought, Will he know *how*? Because *I* surely didn't. And it did seem you were slow to start, somewhat."

"That was Reverend Ailey's doing," Robin said.

"Pardon?"

"In our counseling session. Remember how he had us each meet separately with him before he'd marry us? And what he told me was, I should be 'considerate.' I wasn't sure what he meant by that. 'Considerate how?' I asked, and he said, 'The groom should know not to rush into things on the wedding night. The bride might be feeling timid,' he said. Said, 'I always counsel the groom to view that first night as just a chance to get to know each other better. You don't want to put her off,' he said."

Mercy laughed. She said, "You never told me that!"

"So there I was, quick-quick scrambling into my pajamas while you were changing in the bathroom. New pajamas I'd bought specially. I ducked under the covers; I folded my hands across my chest . . . And then you came out of the bathroom in your slinky white satin nightie."

"And you looked away," Mercy said. "You looked off toward the bedroom window."

"I was trying to get control of myself," he said.

"So I slipped into bed next to you, and I lay on my back and waited. And after a while I said, 'Well! Here we are!' And you said, 'Mm-hmm,' and went on looking out the window."

"I was trying to figure out what Reverend Ailey meant about getting to know you better. Did he mean, like, conversationally? I should ask you about your interests or something? Or did he mean more like in a physical way, I mean a sort of working-up-to-the-main-event kind of way."

"And that's when I turned to you and started unbuttoning your pajamas," Mercy said.

Now he was laughing too. He said, "You were shameless!"

"Well, I had waited so long, you see," she said. "Up to then, I'd been so well-behaved."

She was speaking into the crook of his neck now. She was nestling closer against him. He bent his head to kiss her, and he had started to slide one hand up her thigh when she pulled slightly away to whisper, "You want to go upstairs?"

"Okay," he said.

In the old days, they would never have managed to wait till they got upstairs.

When he woke up, it was late afternoon. He could tell by the deep-yellow dust filming the windowpanes. Mercy's side of the bed was empty, and her tossed-back sheet had a hardened look, as if she'd been gone for hours.

But then he heard footsteps downstairs, and he took heart. He got up and put on his bathrobe and his terry-cloth mules, and he padded down to the dining room. Mercy was folding clothes from a laundry basket she'd set on the table. Her hair was neatly reknotted and she was fully dressed. "Hi, sleepyhead!" she told him.

"I was out like a light," he said. "How long have you been up?"

"Ages," she said, waving toward the laundry as proof.

He didn't often manage to fall asleep in the daytime. No doubt it was due to relief, he thought—the relief of having the party over and done with—and he considered telling her that but then decided not to. It might sound like a complaint. Still, the fact was that he'd been sort of tense the past couple of weeks, and now he could safely say that the whole thing had gone off without a hitch.

He sat down at the table and watched her shake out a slip and fold it into a square. "I dreamt about the Hampden apartment," he told her.

"You did!"

"I guess it was all that talk about the past. I dreamt I was closing up the couch we used to sleep on after the girls were born, that old hide-a-bed. I was lifting up that metal bar at the foot of the mattress; I was doing that dip thing, that dipping motion where you kind of tuck the mattress down and then back till it's folded into the couch again."

He knew he was going into way too much detail. He hated when other people did that; he hated when they discussed their dreams at all, in fact. But it seemed important, for some reason, that Mercy should envision this scene as concretely as he had himself. "The whole motion of it came back to me," he said. "Do you remember that motion?" and she nodded and said, "I remember," and drew a blouse from the basket.

"And then Alice was there. Alice about three years old or so. She had that square kind of Dutch-boy haircut she used to wear back then, and she said, 'Guess what, Daddy, we're having busketty tonight.'"

Mercy looked up from her folding. "Oh," she said softly. "Busketty."

"You remember?"

"Busketty and meatballs," she said.

"It wasn't so much a dream as a kind of time trip," Robin said. "It felt a whole lot realer than a dream."

"She was a cutie, wasn't she?" Mercy said. "Weren't they all? Oh, that was so long ago!"

"We're getting old, Mercy," he said.

"It's true. We are."

She was taking another blouse from the basket, but she folded it in slow motion. And she gave it a sort of caress before she laid it on top of the other clothes.

"So," he said, "do you think you might want to move back to the house now?"

"Oh," she said.

"Nothing would change! You could still paint your pictures! You just wouldn't paint in your studio. Or maybe you could retire! *I'm* retired! You and me: we could loaf around together, take it easy, spend more time with the grandchildren or even travel a little, if that's the kind of thing you . . ."

Once again, he was talking too much. And too fast. He was watching her take the very last item from the basket—a pillowcase—and shake it out and then carefully slide the stack of folded laundry inside it. She gave the pillowcase a gentle shake to settle the contents, and then she lifted it with both hands and turned to smile at him. "Oh, honey," she said. "You hate to travel!"

He could have argued. He could have said that maybe he would learn to like it, or—more to the point—that travel was only the tiniest part of what he had just proposed. But he didn't. All he said was, "Do you want Greta's plant?"

"No, thank you," she said.

"I could carry it for you."

"It would be too much to take care of," she said.

"Okay."

He followed her to the foyer, but since he was still in his bathrobe he didn't come out on the porch with her; just accepted her kiss on his cheek and then held the screen door open for her to pass through.

After that he went upstairs and got dressed, because there was nothing more pathetic than an old guy wearing a bathrobe in broad daylight. Then he went to the kitchen to rustle up some supper. Not that he was the least bit hungry after that big lunch, but it was past five o'clock by now and another pathetic thing was when old people started skipping meals and grazing on junk food and developing what Dr. Fish used to call tea-and-toast syndrome. No, indeedy: here was this nice potato salad the women had packed into Tupperware. He took it out of the fridge and set it on the kitchen table, along with a half-cup or so of cucumber slices grown only slightly translucent in their dressing. And a third of a salmon loaf, just about, still in its baking tin. He took that out too and carried it over to the silverware drawer so he could get himself a fork. Still standing at the drawer, he stuck the fork into the edge of the loaf and took a sample mouthful. Delicious. And then another. And then he sank onto a kitchen chair with the loaf pan cradled in his left arm and forked up mouthful after mouthful, each bigger and more hastily shoveled in than the one before, and all the while he was thinking, Why not? And, Who's going to stop me? And, I have a right to this, goddammit!

In the end he finished it, every last crumb, and scraped the last crusty bits from the rim. Then he placed the empty pan on the table and laid the fork down beside it and sat staring straight ahead of him, while outside the screen door the birds were still singing and the sun was still brightly shining.

6

ON CANDLE LAINEY'S twelfth birthday—January 8th, 1997—she announced that she was instituting some changes in her life. Those were her exact words. "I am instituting some changes in my life," she told her mother when she walked into the kitchen that morning.

"Oh?" Alice said, and then she planted a kiss on Candle's forehead and asked what she would like for her birthday breakfast. So, basically implying that whatever those changes might be, they wouldn't much matter.

"First," Candle said, "I'm getting my hair cut. Ponytails are for kids. I'm thinking a kind of feathered look, a kind of winged look at the sides."

"Isn't that a little passé now?" Alice asked.

"Second, I'm getting my ears pierced. You *said* I could; you've been saying for years that I could do it when I turned twelve."

"I said *maybe* when you turned twelve."

"And third, I want to be called by my actual name from now on. Kendall."

"That's fine with me," Alice said. "You were the one who started pronouncing it 'Candle.'"

"Only because I was too little then to say it right," Candle told her. "Now I'm changing it back."

"Fine," Alice said. And then she asked again what she would like for breakfast.

Candle did get her hair cut that Saturday, not exactly with wings but with kind of a swept-back look at the sides, stopping just above her collar. And she got her ears pierced immediately afterward at a jewelry store in the same mall. But nobody made the slightest effort to go along with her name change. "Nice haircut, Candle girl!" her father said when she got home. She gave him a flat-eyed stare, and he said, "What?"

"She wants to be called Kendall," Alice reminded him. But then she herself, not two minutes later, addressed her as "Candle."

Candle was the baby of the family, was why. The last one left at home. Nobody took her seriously.

Even her friends, at her birthday slumber party that night, kept slipping and calling her Candle. They did try to remember. They did say "Oops!" when she corrected them. But on Monday morning they were back to Candle this and Candle that, and her teachers didn't even make an effort.

Eventually, she became Candle again even to herself. It was as if the change had never happened. When she wrote "Kendall" on her test papers—which she'd been doing all along; it was the name in her official school records—she would give it a wistful glance now, remembering that brief moment when she had imagined it was possible to become a whole new person. She had to admit, though, that the name had never really felt as if it were hers.

And her hair grew out again, because she led a crazy-busy life these days and there just wasn't enough time for beauty-parlor appointments. And then softball season started and it was easiest just to yank her hair back in a rubber band before she fitted her catcher's mask on.

The pierced ears, though, remained, and gradually she accumulated quite a collection of earrings—mostly studs, because dangly earrings of any kind were not allowed by her coach.

She figured that when she turned thirteen, she'd campaign for a whole row of piercings running up the outer rim of each ear. Then she'd fit a tiny hoop into each and every one, so that the edges of her ears would resemble the spine of a spiral notebook. She'd seen that style on a girl in McDonald's, an extremely I-don't-care-looking girl with raccoon-eye makeup and black lipstick. The kids at school would fall over! They would practically not know her; that was how different she would look.

That summer, she went to the sleepaway camp in Maine that she had attended every year since she was eight. Three of her school friends went too, and she already knew a number of the other campers from previous summers, so it wasn't all that adventurous but she liked it well enough and it was better than staying home. This year, though, there was a new art counselor. Tomorrow, her name was. (Tomorrow!) She was younger than the previous art counselor, and hipper; had a bumblebee tattooed on her wrist. Right away she and Candle hit it off. For one thing, she said she really loved the name Candle, and when she learned how it had come about she confided that her name too had been adapted from the original. "It started out Tamar," she said. "I changed it when I hit my teens. You were well ahead of me, changing yours when you were so young." This made Candle feel glad, all at once, that her family had paid no attention when she'd tried to change it back again.

More important, though: Tomorrow thought Candle had talent. She showed the other girls the still life Candle painted—the same still life they'd all painted, a bowl of fruit and a pitcher of Kool-Aid set up on one of the picnic tables—and she said, "See how Candle has put her own special twist on things? She didn't *copy* the pitcher; she exaggerated it. She narrowed the neck and she ballooned the base. That is what makes it art, folks."

Candle hardly knew where to look. She had always "exaggerated" her pictures, if that was what it was called. Drawing a fairy-tale princess, as she liked to do when she was little, she had swooped the skirt of the ballgown out to the very edges of the paper; she had elongated the torso; she had made the princess's arms as curvy as the scrolls on the front of a violin. But no one had said she had talent. The artist her friends at school admired was Melanie Brooks, in eighth grade. Melanie drew fashion models so polished-looking that they could have been in a magazine.

Eventually, the other campers moved on to pottery making, lanyard braiding, and basket weaving, but Candle was allowed to stick with painting. And when her parents came to pick her up, at the end of her six weeks, they were treated to an entire show of her paintings thumbtacked around the art cabin. "I'd love to see what she could do with oils," Tomorrow told them. "The camp limits us to just watercolors for easier cleanup, but she might want to branch out into other mediums."

"My mother works in acrylics, as it happens," Alice said.

"Oh? Your mother's an artist?"

"In a way," Alice said.

"Maybe Candle could pick up some tips from her," Tomorrow said.

Alice looked uncertain, but she said, "Well. Maybe."

Candle's paintings were forgotten once she was home again. Or forgotten by her parents, at least, because the house was all abuzz now with her sister's wedding plans. Robby was marrying her longtime boyfriend in the fall. Carlton, his name was. He was a dental student with a receding hairline; so, big whoop. Candle couldn't figure out what all the fuss was about.

Candle herself, though, did not forget her paintings. There were six long weeks before school began, and she had nothing in the world to do. All her friends were away on summer vacation, but Candle's parents had already taken their vacation while she was at camp. So one day she asked her mother if they could go to a crafts store and buy a few supplies, and although it took several days for that to happen, they did go eventually. Except Candle didn't know what exactly she needed. She'd been thinking she would just pick up a ready-made set of oil paints, but oils didn't seem to come in sets; they came in expensive single tubes. Acrylics came in sets, though. "Well, I'm not sure," she told her mother. "I mean, acrylics don't sound so professional as oils."

Her mother said, "I don't know why you say that. Your grandmom uses nothing but, and *she's* a professional, supposedly." Then she said, "Tell you what: let's arrange a time for you to visit her studio and ask her all about it. Bring along some of your pictures from camp and maybe she'll have an opinion as to what kind of paints would work best for you."

So that was the plan. Alice phoned Mercy as soon as they got home, and they settled on an afternoon two days from then.

"Now, one thing you should bear in mind," Alice said as she was driving Candle into town, "is you shouldn't get your feelings hurt if Grandmom says something critical about your pictures. She might not be as complimentary as Today, or whatever her name was."

There was no way on earth Alice could have forgotten what Tomorrow's name was. She was just being snooty, as usual. She just liked to sound all amused by people.

She didn't go into the studio with Candle when she dropped

her off. "Tell her I'll say hello when I come to pick you up," she said. "In an hour or so; hour and a half tops." She was heading to a mother-of-the-bride-dress fitting, up in Towson.

The studio was above a garage in somebody's backyard. Candle had to climb a rickety outside staircase that shivered with every step she took, so her grandmother knew to expect her and already had the door open by the time Candle reached the landing. "Kendall!" she said. "It's so nice to see you!"

Until that moment, Candle had forgotten that her grandmother, at least, had been calling her Kendall all along. She felt a rush of gratitude. She said, "Thank you, Grandmom," and gave her a little hug, although ordinarily she wouldn't have bothered.

Mercy was more interesting-looking than most old ladies—still thin, with a flyaway bun and a small, pointy face. She was wearing a man's shirt as a smock, probably Pop-Pop's, long enough so it almost covered her skirt, and she had a slightly bitter smell, like tea. Her studio was the kind of place Candle approved of but knew she could never manage for herself, because her room at home was chronically messy whereas here, all the surfaces were bare and everything had been put away. She stepped inside and looked around appreciatively, and then she handed over the folder containing her work. "Mom says to tell you she'll stop in when she picks me up," she said, and Mercy nodded, but absently, because she was already opening the folder and looking at the top painting.

"They're not very good, I'm afraid," Candle said.

Mercy glanced over at her. "*Never* tell people that," she said. "Rule One."

"Okay, but I mean, they're just stuff I did at camp."

Mercy started laying the pictures in a row across the table, moving aside several paint tubes to make room. "Hmm," she said as she examined each one. "Mm-hmm. Mm-hmm."

First the fruit bowl and the Kool-Aid. Then a tree by the lake at camp with huge plates of white fungus sticking out from its trunk like CDs when you hit the Eject button. And then a portrait: Ditsy Brown from cabin 8. Ditsy's plump left shin, crossed over her right knee, was the largest object in the picture because it happened to be closest to the viewer. The effect was cartoonish, Candle saw now. It was not what she'd been aiming for at all. She started to say so but stopped herself, and they moved on to a picture of a rowboat.

One of Mercy's paintings, half finished, lay on the other side of the table. It showed somebody's front porch. Candle knew it was only half finished because it was nothing but a vague smear of floorboards and Adirondack chairs, with no part detailed. All of Mercy's paintings featured one tiny portion that was super-detailed. She must find Candle's paintings childish; they were so ordinary and same-all-over.

"I know they're not like yours," Candle told her, and Mercy said, "Well, I should hope not. They shouldn't be like anyone's." Then she gathered the paintings up again and slipped them back into their folder. "But I can see why you'd want to try a different medium," she said, "because your style relies upon line. You'd find linear painting easier with oils or acrylics. Would you like to try my acrylics?"

"Yes!" Candle said.

"Let me set you up, then, and you see what you think."

She tore a piece of paper off a pad and laid it in front of Candle, along with a couple of pencils. Candle sat down at the table and slid a finger testingly across the surface of the paper, which had a woven feeling, like cloth.

"Now for your subject matter . . ." Mercy said, and she went to the kitchen area and started rustling around. When she returned she had a cantaloupe, a bottle of apple juice, and a wooden-handled string dish mop. "Pay no mind to the weird assemblage," she told Candle as she positioned them on the table. "I wanted to give you a variety of textures. Just experiment; try using different-size brushes. I'll leave you to it."

And then she crossed the room to the daybed, where she settled herself with a flounce of her shirttails and reached over to turn on the radio. WLIF, it sounded like; an old-people station. From behind one of the couch cushions—the big one, which was really a bed pillow—she pulled a library book covered in clear plastic and opened it and started reading, meanwhile wagging her feet back and forth in time to something waltzy on the radio. She was small enough that her feet stuck straight out in front of her on the daybed, like a child's.

At first Candle felt lost. Shouldn't she be getting some sort of instruction, here? But eventually she drew a few tentative lines to indicate the three objects, and then she picked up a tube of yellow paint and squirted a blob onto the palette. It was just as well, she realized, that she'd been left to her own devices, with no one to wince and suck in a sharp breath if she happened to do something wrong.

She tried a round-tipped brush and then a slant-edged one, dipping each first in the jar of water next to Mercy's vase of brushes. She tried mixing a little white with the yellow to make it paler; she was working on the apple juice. Mercy was humming along with the radio now, but only off and on—a measure or two under her breath as she turned a page. Candle's mother claimed Mercy read junk. English whodunnits, mostly, she said. "I personally," she often added, "have never been able to care who done it, myself."

Candle started in on the dish mop. She liked painting the gray strands of string. She learned to use less water for adding fine black lines on top of the gray, and much more water for painting the swash of gray Formica tabletop.

By the time Alice knocked on the studio door, Candle was stippling in the pores of the cantaloupe and Mercy had tucked her book away and was fixing iced tea at the kitchen counter. Not once had she so much as glanced at Candle's painting. She went to open the door for Alice, who instantly asked, "How'd it go?" as if she'd spent this whole time in suspense.

"Hmm? Oh, fine," Mercy said, and she crossed to turn off the radio. "Want a glass of iced tea?"

"No, we really should be—what do you think of acrylics, sweetie?" Alice asked Candle.

"I like them," Candle said.

"Really? Should we get some?"

"Yes!"

"Mom? What do *you* think?"

"Why not?" Mercy said airily.

"Okay, well . . . and what do you think about her work? Do you think it's worth her while to pursue this?"

"I like her work very much," Mercy said, "but only she can tell you whether it's worth her while."

Alice turned toward Candle expectantly, but Candle chose not to say a word, for some reason. She just sent her mother a blank smile and then got very busy gathering her brushes together to wash them.

She did get her own set of acrylics, along with a selection of brushes and a pad of the woven paper. But at home, it turned out, she couldn't paint in private. She had to work in the kitchen because that was the only room without a carpet, and it was ridiculous how often her mother kept passing through and peering over Candle's shoulder but ostentatiously making no comment, which seemed a comment in itself. "Things went better at Grandmom's," Candle told her. What she meant was, it was better not to have anyone breathing down her neck; but Alice, misunderstanding, said, "Shall I phone your Grandmom and ask if you could come back, then, and she can give you some helpful tips?" And Candle didn't correct her.

So she started painting in Mercy's studio once a week or so. It wasn't at a certain set time, although Alice would have preferred that. "I *said* to her," Alice told Candle, "I said, 'If we could make it, like, every Monday afternoon . . .' but your grandmom said, 'I can't always be sure if my Mondays will be free or not.' I said, 'Well, is there a day you *can* be sure about?' and she said, 'Not really.' What does the woman do with herself? I'd like to know. What could possibly keep her so busy? It's not as if she has scads of customers beating down her door."

So Candle went to the studio on a Monday one week but a Thursday the next, and so on. And then the new school year began and weekdays were no longer an option; Saturdays and Sundays were her only free times. Alice said, "Well, you know what your grandmom will say to *that*. 'Oh, I just can't commit,' she'll say." And here Alice used an old-lady voice, even though Mercy's voice wasn't old-lady at all.

But this time Candle herself called Mercy, and things went more smoothly. "Poor you," was all Mercy said. "Back to the grindstone! Yes, fine; either day, provided it's afternoon."

This was because Mercy liked to sleep late, Candle discovered. It wasn't that customers were beating down her door in the mornings, or even that she necessarily painted then. It was just that she lived this lackadaisical, unplanned life, this suit-herself life that Candle would have *loved* to live. "Grandmom," she said on one of their afternoons, "when I grow up I'm going to follow your schedule exactly."

"What schedule would that be?" Mercy asked, looking amused.

"Well, your nonschedule, I mean. I'm going to do what I want when I want to, and nobody's going to order me around."

"It does have its pleasures," Mercy said. "And will you have children?"

"Well . . ."

She had kind of assumed she'd have children, actually. But she could see this might complicate things.

"Sometimes people live first one life and then another life," her grandmother said. "First a family life and then later a whole other kind of life. That's what I'm doing."

And she flashed Candle a tucked smile, an almost mischievous smile, and went back to humming along with the radio. "Moon River," she was humming, while she worked a crossword puzzle in *The Baltimore Sun.*

Candle painted pictures of a couple dancing together, and a boy running down a hill, and a little girl walking alone in the woods—all completely made up. Once she tried painting her grandmother, but real things were less fun, she decided. With real things you were confined to the facts—the finicky details of hair straggling out of a bun and wrinkles in the bend of a neck. An impossibly tall tree looming above a tiny lone child in the woods had more pizzazz, somehow.

When she was satisfied with a painting, she would offer to show it to Mercy. "Want to see how it turned out?" she would ask, and Mercy would say, "Why, of course," and hop off the daybed and come look. She grew very serious when she was examining a painting. She studied it first from close up and then from several steps away; she cocked her head; she narrowed her eyes. Then she would say, "I like it." Period. Would she have said if she *didn't* like it? Candle thought she probably would have, even though that never happened.

One time Mercy greeted her at the door with "I've just been

given a commission, so today we'll both be working," and then she returned to her own painting. Not at the kitchen table, though; she had moved her materials to the counter. So Candle sensed she shouldn't peek, and she unpacked her supplies quietly and resumed work on a picture she had started the week before. The only sounds in the studio were the whiskery strokes of their two brushes. She'd grown used to hearing old-people music, but evidently Mercy preferred to work in silence, and Candle saw her point. Silence made what she was doing seem more important, somehow—more purposeful, almost like praying. There wasn't a single word spoken till her mother arrived to pick her up an hour and a half later.

For her sister's wedding, Candle and her cousin Serena were bridesmaids while the maid-of-honor position went to Mary Ann Locke, Robby's old college roommate. This was fine with Candle; she was so much younger than Robby that they'd never been that close. Nor did she feel close to Serena, for that matter, since these days they hardly saw each other. All they'd ever had in common, anyhow, was that they were their family's "littlies," as opposed to the "biggies."

"What happened there?" Candle had once asked her mother. "Aunt Lily heard I'd been born and decided to have another one too, just to keep you company?"

"Ha!" her mother had said. "You think that sister of mine ever *decided* about a pregnancy?"

Because not only were there littlies and biggies in this family; there were the sensible ones and the wacko ones. Or—as Aunt Lily put it—the difficult ones and the easy ones. According to Aunt Lily, Alice was a difficult one while Lily herself was easy, meaning carefree and relaxed.

The good ones versus the bad ones, was what they were secretly talking about. By which each of them meant something different.

Candle's grandmother was a bad one, in Candle's mother's opinion. "Oh, not that I don't love her dearly," she said. "But face it: the woman should not have had children." Then she went into the whole long spiel about how their dining-room table had always been covered with paint tubes and brushes; how they'd never once in their lives been fed a balanced meal; how at one point, hearing that ordinary citizens might someday be invited to set up a colony on Mars, Mercy had said, "I would go! I would go in a flash!"

"And this was back in the sixties!" Alice said. "This was when she still had one of her children at home!"

"She meant after all her children were gone," Candle explained patiently. "When she was leading her next life."

"But even to think of it! Even to have it cross her mind!"

"Well, it's not as if she was actually invited, for gosh sakes, so why make such a fuss about it?"

"No need to take that tone with *me*, missy," Alice said.

Hard to believe that Candle's mother considered herself to be one of the sensible ones.

It was at Robby's wedding reception that Mercy asked Candle if she'd like to go to New York with her. "To where?" Candle said. This was coming out of the blue.

"My old friend Magda Schwartz is having an art show," Mercy said. "I'm thinking of going to see it." She and Pop-Pop were on the point of leaving the reception; they'd already said their good-byes, but now she told Candle, "If you're interested, I'll phone your mother tomorrow and see if she'll let you come along."

"Yes! I'm interested!" Candle said.

She had never been to New York. It was a straight-shot three-hour train ride but she'd never once set foot there.

"It's going to be a grown-up event, though," Mercy said. "I just want to warn you. We'll arrive in time for lunch, meet Magda at this little restaurant she knows—I told her I'd take her out to celebrate—and then go look at her paintings and hop on a train back home. We can't afford to spend the night; not for what a New York hotel costs."

"That's okay," Candle said. "But can we get a Nathan's hot dog?"

"A what? Oh. Yes, why not. You can do that before we get back on the train."

"Goody," Candle said. A girl on her softball team was always raving about Nathan's hot dogs.

She didn't mention the invitation to her parents; she figured Mercy could be more persuasive. They were too busy, anyhow, during the reception, and then the reception was all they talked about on the drive home. The next day, though, she grew very alert every time the phone rang, just in case it was Mercy. The phone rang a lot, unfortunately. Everyone had to weigh in on what a lovely wedding it had been, how beautiful the bride had looked and how sweet the groom seemed, blah blah blah. Late in the afternoon, though, Candle heard her mother answer the phone with "Hello? . . . Oh, hi, Mom." Candle put aside the funny pages and went to stand in the kitchen doorway. "Yes, I thought so too," Alice was saying. "I'm glad it's over, though." Then she listened for a moment. "New York?" she said. "What for?" More listening. "Well, I don't . . . But would she be interested, do you think? . . . What?" She turned to glance toward Candle, who pressed her palms together pleadingly. "So you already spoke to *her* about this? Well, I really wish you had—" Another spell of listening. "All right, let me see what Kevin says. I'll get back to you, okay? What was the date again?"

When she hung up, she told Candle, "I wish you had let me know she was planning to do this."

"I didn't have a chance to," Candle said.

"Right."

"So can I go? Please, please?"

"What makes you so sure you'd enjoy it?" her mother asked. "Long, crowded train ride; see a few paintings; long, crowded train ride home again—"

"But it's New York! I've never been!"

"Well, New York is overrated, if you want my honest opinion. It's packed with pushy people and it's dirty; take my word for it."

"Shouldn't I be allowed to find that out for myself?"

"Also," her mother said, "I'm not entirely comfortable with your grandmom having sole charge of you."

"Why not? She raised *you* three, didn't she?"

"Exactly," her mother said mysteriously.

"And we two get along so good. I like seeing what her life is like."

"So *well*, you mean," her mother said. "Oh, my. I guess it's true what they say about how you have to skip a generation to appreciate some of your relatives."

Candle thought there was a lot more to it than that. Her cousin Serena had skipped a generation too, but you didn't notice *her* having much to do with their grandmom.

Her dad saw no harm in her going, as long as it was only a day trip. "But tell your grandmother I'll drive you both to the station and pick you up after," he added. He had this theory that Mercy was a terrible driver, just because she had once backed into her friend Bridey—Bridey herself, not Bridey's car—and poked her head out her side window to apologize even though luckily Bridey had not been knocked down, and then pulled her head back in and resumed backing up and *did* knock Bridey down, that time. Most people in the family thought this story was hilarious, although in Candle's opinion it was more about

Bridey than about Mercy. How come Bridey hadn't just moved out of the way, for gosh sake, after she'd been hit the first time? But Kevin himself failed to see the humor. He was always saying that Mercy ought to have her license revoked.

So anyhow, on a warm Saturday morning in late October he drove Candle into town, stopped for Mercy at her studio, and delivered them both to Penn Station. Candle wore an actual skirt, in case the restaurant they went to was fancy. Mercy wore a skirt too but just her normal, everyday kind, with an everyday cardigan draped over her arm in case the train was too air-conditioned. She had reserved their tickets ahead of time so all they had to do was pick them up at the window, after which they walked through the station and directly down to the tracks, not waiting till their train was announced, because Mercy had made this trip often and already knew how things worked. She knew to take a position some distance up the track, for instance, because the front cars would have fewer passengers. And sure enough, when their train arrived and they boarded she easily found them a pair of seats together. She gestured for Candle to slide in first, and then she sat down herself and pulled a paperback from her purse and started reading, as much at ease as if she were sitting on her daybed at home.

Candle had brought a book too, in her knapsack, but she didn't so much as open it during the whole train ride. She was too busy staring out the window, and eyeing the other passengers, and eavesdropping on a young couple sitting just behind them who were arguing about whether to get a dog or not. When she grew bored, she drew invisible pictures with her index finger. This was a new habit of hers and it drove her mother crazy, but Candle kept her hand tucked at her side and her grandmother didn't notice. And probably wouldn't have minded even if she *had* noticed, Candle thought.

At a certain point Candle's eyes drooped shut—she'd been up

since crack of dawn—and when she woke they were traveling through New Jersey, where the stations stood close to the tracks and the passengers waited in clusters, sometimes whole families of them. Shortly afterward people in their car began stirring, assembling their belongings, rising to lift bags down from the luggage racks. The train entered a tunnel and the car grew dim. Candle's heart was beating faster but her grandmother went on reading, even in the poor lighting.

"Penn Station!" the conductor announced, which was odd when you thought about it because Penn Station was where they had left from. But this one was totally different; there was no comparison. When Candle and Mercy arrived at the top of the escalator—Mercy having closed her book at the very last minute and risen unhurriedly from her seat—they entered an impossibly large, looming space that made Candle feel tiny, with a blur of people shoving past and uniformed men pushing luggage carts. "This way," Mercy said, and she led Candle through the crowd and up another escalator, out onto a street that smelled like warm scrub water, and from there into a taxicab, only then bothering to slip her book back into her purse. "So," she said, after telling the driver their destination. (Which was not a street address but the name of a restaurant, as if naturally he would recognize it, which, in fact, he seemed to.) "So, what do you think of New York?"

"Well . . . it's tall, okay," Candle said, peering out her side window. "But not any taller than parts of Baltimore. I was thinking I would maybe, like, have to look up and up and up till I accidentally fell over backwards, you know?"

"Oh, that could still happen," her grandmother said, and then she smiled and gazed out her own window. There seemed to be a great many food carts on the sidewalks, Candle noticed. And a great many people stopping to buy hot dogs, but none were Nathan's hot dogs.

In front of the restaurant—small, with an awning—Mercy handed the driver some bills and said, "No change required," as if she did this every day of her life, and then she opened the door and stepped out onto the sidewalk and Candle followed.

Mercy's friend was already waiting, seated at a small table. She was a bony, vivid woman—long straight black hair contrasting oddly with her old-looking face; slash of dark-red lipstick; glaringly bright geometric-print tunic hanging off her sharp shoulders. "Merce!" she cried, half standing, and she kissed Mercy on both cheeks and then sat back down.

"And this is my granddaughter Kendall," Mercy said.

Candle smiled, tongue-tied, and slid into the chair to Magda's left. "How nice to meet you, Kendall," Magda said. "Your grandma tells me you're a painter yourself; is that right?"

"Well, kind of," Candle said. She looked around at the other diners—all seated at white-draped tables, all super–New Yorkish and glamorous. Mercy was wearing her cardigan now, and it was pretty obvious that she was only from Baltimore.

The two women ordered after barely glancing at their menus—an Asian salad for Magda, the roasted scallops for Mercy, with a glass of iced tea for each—but Candle had trouble making up her mind. Partly she wanted something new and exciting, but she hoped it wouldn't be *too* exciting. She settled finally on a shrimp salad sandwich and a Diet Coke, and as the waiter wrote it down he said, "Excellent," which she found reassuring.

Magda, meanwhile, was telling Mercy about her opening, which a lot of people had attended, including someone named Bruce whom they both apparently knew from long ago. "Naturally he bought one of your paintings," Mercy said, in a tone that suggested that naturally he had not; and Magda said, "Wouldn't *that* be the day, and of course he had to criticize the refreshments they were serving."

"He didn't!"

"'My dear young woman,' he said to the waitress, 'please don't tell me there is no red wine on offer.'"

"Oh, I just love it when people behave in character," Mercy said.

"Me too, especially when it's in bad character. And do you know what I really love?"

"What's that?"

"I love it that for once it's not *me* behaving badly."

Then they both dissolved in giggles, putting their heads together like schoolgirls, while Candle watched, smiling shyly.

By the time their food arrived, the talk had moved on to Mercy's own paintings. Was she still doing her house portraits? Was there much of a market for them? "Oh, no," Mercy said dismissively. "Just, you know, a few commissions here and there, most of them fairly humdrum, although every now and then I'll come across *something* intriguing, some place with real personality."

To Candle, this sounded both modest and a little bit boastful, because it wasn't really a few here and there; it was more like one or two, with months and months in between when Mercy's paintings were only for herself. But she was glad her grandmom was putting on a good show. She didn't want Magda to feel sorry for her.

Candle's sandwich had potato chips alongside, but high-class ones, cut thicker than usual, with rims of brown peel left on. They could have used a little more salt, though. And there were weird dots of pickly things mixed in with the shrimp salad. But Mercy said her scallops were delicious. "I never order scallops back home," she said. "They're so often overcooked. Really you have to come to New York if you don't want leathery scallops." Then she gave Magda a playful nudge and said, "Robin claims the reason he hates to travel is, the food never tastes the same as it does in Baltimore. You just never can be sure what you might be getting, he says."

They both started giggling again.

"Oh, my," Magda said finally, shaking her head. "Darling Robin."

"When our grandson left for his study year abroad," Mercy said, "his parents gave him one of those watches with two faces, one face set to foreign time and the other to home time. And Robin said—" here she knotted her eyebrows, putting on a perplexed look. "Said, 'Really? I would have thought,' he said, 'that a person would just always somehow *know* what time it was at home.' "

This made Magda laugh again, and Mercy looked pleased. "Right?" she asked Candle.

Candle, who had no memory of that conversation, smiled but didn't answer. She hadn't even remembered that a grandson had studied abroad. (Could it have been her brother, Eddie, even? He was the one who liked learning new languages.) Oh, she was just too much younger than the others; that was the problem. She was hopelessly young, and out of step and inexperienced. But she was doing her best to catch up.

Say the word "gallery" to Candle and she pictured the National Portrait Gallery over in DC, where she'd gone once on a school field trip. A double row of columns, massive wings at either side . . . So when they arrived at Magda's gallery, a few blocks from the restaurant, she was disappointed to find a tiny storefront with a single mullioned window. Mercy, though, had the opposite reaction. "Why, Mags!" she said. "This is very classy!"

"Ah, yes," Magda said. "I seem to be moving up in the world." Then she told Candle, "My last show was in a framing shop."

Candle liked her for admitting that.

They went inside, and a young woman seated behind a desk stood up immediately. "Ms. Schwartz," she said. "How nice to see you."

"Hello, Virginia," Magda said. "Is Mr. Phillips in?"

"No, he's at lunch, I'm sorry to say."

"Well, never mind. I'm just bringing my friends by to see the exhibit. Mercy here is an artist from Baltimore. We went to school together. And this is her granddaughter, Kendall."

"How do you do," Virginia said, and she made a little bobbing motion that was almost a curtsy. She wore a fascinating outfit, a black knit top that had a ruffle at the bottom too long to be mere trim but too short to be a skirt, with nothing below but black tights and black ballet shoes. Candle took careful note, wondering if her mother would allow *her* to wear such an outfit. Meanwhile, Magda had clasped Mercy's elbow and was leading her toward the first painting. "This is the one I was telling you about," she said. Candle followed, two steps behind. "I still can't decide if it's finished or not. What do you think? Should I have held it back until I felt more certain?"

"No, you should not have held it back," Mercy told her firmly. "You know what Mr. LaSalle always said: 'The worst thing you can do to a painting is overwork it.'"

"Oh, yes, he did say that," Magda said. "You're right."

Candle, though, wasn't so sure. The painting was a glossy white rectangle, some two feet by three feet, with a single black curve like a Nike swoosh in the lower-left-hand corner. Had Mr. LaSalle ever felt that a painting could be *under*worked?

The next painting had more going on—five green V shapes, floating here and there on a matte beige background. You could almost imagine the Vs were a flock of birds. Although maybe, Candle thought, it was wrong to try and turn such a painting into something recognizable. Probably you were supposed to appreciate the Vs for themselves. She narrowed her eyes and concentrated on appreciating.

It wasn't as if she had never seen abstract paintings before. At her grandparents' house there was an oversize art book with scribbled drips by Jackson Pollock and linoleum squares by Mondrian. But these were the first she'd actively struggled to understand, frowning intently at each as she followed the two women around the perimeter of the room. "Oh, Magda, so many red dots!" her grandmother said, and Candle thought, Many? because at the moment she was studying a large white square with only one red dot set slightly off-center. But Magda said, "Yes, sales have not been bad, I have to say," and Candle realized what Mercy had been referring to. She stopped following them and took a little detour to the front of the gallery, where a sheet of paper was tacked to the wall just inside the front door. Red dot, red dot, red dot, next to the list of titles and prices, all of the prices in the thousands. Four thousand, five thousand. Seven thousand, in one case. She turned away and went to catch up with Mercy, who was continuing the circuit on her own now because Magda had gone over to speak again with Virginia. "What do you think?" Mercy asked Candle, and Candle said, "They're really . . . interesting."

Then she winced, because she was reminded of what her pop-pop always said when he was served some dish he wasn't used to. "Very . . . *inner*-esting," he would pronounce, and the family members around the table would exchange knowing smiles.

Mercy, though, just patted Candle's arm reassuringly and said, "What I find interesting is, I like to look at paintings like these and imagine how it must feel to finish one. I mean, you'd lay down your brush, you'd take a step back, you'd say, 'Yes, that's what I had in mind, all right.' And when I think about it that way, I can see that it really must be a great satisfaction. Not to overstate things, I mean; not to feel the need to spell everything out. To be capable of such . . . restraint. *I'm* not capable of it, but I have to say I admire it. Oh, isn't it amazing, all the different ways that different artists' minds can work?"

"Okay," Candle said, "but how about the prices?"

"How about them?"

"These things cost thousands of dollars! It's not fair!"

"Fair?" Mercy asked.

"You put *way* more work into *your* paintings, I bet."

Her grandmother laughed. "Oh, hon," she said, "it's never wise to look over your shoulder."

"Huh?"

"Just run the race on your own, I say. Don't fret about the others."

This didn't make sense, for a moment, but then it did. Candle felt as if she'd had some burden lifted from her, and she gave Mercy a grateful smile and Mercy smiled back.

All the same, her grandmom did seem unusually quiet after that—distracted in some way, focusing on some private concern—because Magda had to ask twice if she'd like to get a drink down the street once they'd finished touring the gallery. "Drink?" she said vaguely, and Magda asked, "How much longer before your train?"

"Train? What? Oh!" Mercy said, and she checked her watch and said, "We should get to the station!"

So Magda hailed a cab for them, raising her right arm in a queenlike gesture, and they parted in a flurry of hugs and thanks and must-do-this-again-soons. "Goodness," Mercy told Candle once they were settled in the cab. "I should have—I wish I'd reserved a later—I just didn't know everything would take so long!"

"Can we still get a Nathan's?" Candle asked her.

"A what, hon?"

"A Nathan's hot dog?"

"Oh, I . . . The part I hadn't planned on, you see, was the walk to the gallery. That was a *long* walk. It took way more time than I'd allowed for."

Really the walk had not been long at all; it was just that Mercy was old. Candle heaved what she hoped was a noticeable sigh, but then she gave up and faced forward to focus on the traffic. Luckily it was an easy ride, and when they drew up in front of Penn Station, Mercy said, "See there?" as if she'd never had a moment of anxiety. "*Plenty* of time," she said as she paid the fare.

But when they went to the information board to see when their train would arrive, she said, "Oh! It's already here!" And then, "But we were going to get you a hot dog!" just as if this were the very first time the subject had come up. Candle said, "Never mind," and Mercy looked relieved and turned immediately to lead the way to the escalator.

They descended to a dim underworld where their train sat quietly humming, its windows filled with bowed heads as if all the passengers were seriously thinking things over, although probably they were just reading. Mercy charged into the first car they came to, and when Candle, following, asked, "Shouldn't we go to a car up front?" Mercy tossed back, "I just want to find two seats together."

Which was exactly Candle's point, because this car was almost full and no adjoining seats were available. So they had to walk forward anyhow, and it took a whole lot longer than if they'd walked forward on the platform.

Eventually, though, they found two empty seats side by side, and her grandmom slid in and plopped down and said, "Whew!" Then she turned to Candle, who was just getting settled herself, and said, “Oh, Kendall. Oh, hon,” in a low, stricken-sounding voice.

“What,” Candle said.

“Didn't you want to buy a hot dog?”

“What?” Candle asked, and then, “That's okay, Grandmom.”

“I'm so sorry! You should have reminded me!”

“I'm too full from lunch, anyhow,” Candle said.

And this was the truth, she realized. Besides which, she was starting to get a worried feeling. Worry always caused a sort of lump in her stomach.

The train gave a lurch, by and by, and glided out of the darkness and into the afternoon light, and a man's voice on the loudspeaker welcomed them aboard and listed the cities they'd be traveling to. Not till he mentioned Baltimore did Candle fully relax. And eventually Mercy caught her breath and seemed more like herself, and when the conductor came by she promptly produced their tickets. “Well!” she said to Candle after he'd moved on. She took a flowered cloth hankie from her purse and blotted her face. “That was quite the foofaraw, wasn't it?” she said.

Candle said, “It sure was,” because even though she'd never heard the word “foofaraw” before, it was easy enough to figure out its meaning.

The train had reached full speed by now. Other passengers were talking together quietly—all Baltimoreans, it seemed to Candle; all faded and soft and rumpled and relieved to be heading home. Her grandmother, though, was silent, and when Candle glanced toward her some time later she found her sound asleep, her head tilted against the window.

This time, Mercy hadn't offered Candle the window seat. On the way up, she'd made such a point of it. Candle could see plenty from where she sat, but even so, she couldn't help feeling a little bit neglected. I'm too young for this! she found herself thinking. She should be taking better care of me!

Mercy slept on, her handkerchief gradually uncurling itself on her lap.

They stopped at various towns in New Jersey; they stopped in Philadelphia; they stopped in Wilmington, Delaware. Candle hadn't been to a restroom since lunch, but she figured she could wait. She gazed out the window at passing trees, most of them still fully leafed and not even starting to turn, and she traced their shapes invisibly on her seat cushion with her finger. She watched a woman diagonally across from her examine her face in her compact on three separate occasions, as if maybe she felt anxious about whoever was meeting her train.

"Baltimore next," a conductor finally called—not over the loudspeaker but in person, standing at the front of the car. He began making his way closer, plucking ticket stubs from above certain seats as he approached.

Candle turned toward Mercy. "Grandmom?" she said. "Time to wake up."

Her grandmom slept on. Candle gave her a light tap on the wrist. "We're coming into the station, Grandmom."

Still no response. Candle bent closer and started to speak again, but what she saw made her draw back sharply. Mercy's eyes were just the slightest bit open. There was the narrowest slit of glassy shine beneath each lid.

Candle jumped up and into the aisle, bruising her thigh where it hit against the arm of her seat. She stumbled forward to intercept the conductor, who was reaching for a ticket stub above the mirror woman's head. He was a large, slow-moving man with warm brown skin; she had a feeling she could rely on him. "Mister Conductor?" she said.

"Yes'm?" he said. He had one of those deep, furry, comforting voices.

"I can't get my grandmom to wake up."

He didn't seem to find this alarming. He just said, "*Well,* now.

Let's see what we can do about that," and she turned to indicate her grandmother.

Mercy was still leaning her head against the window. Wouldn't it have been wonderful if they'd found her sitting up by then, calmly returning her handkerchief to her purse! Wouldn't Candle have felt foolish; oh, wouldn't she have *loved* to feel foolish! Instead she stood aside to make room for the conductor, and he leaned forward—still not appearing alarmed—and picked up Mercy's wrist and thought a moment. "So," he said finally. Then he said, "So, tell you what, little lady. You come up front with me till she's feeling a mite livelier."

"What's wrong with her?" Candle asked.

"Why, she is plumb wore out, looks like to me," he said. "New York'll do that to a person."

"N'Yawk" was how he pronounced it. He made the city sound kinder-hearted than she thought it probably was.

"But is she going to be okay?" she asked him.

"*Oh,* yes. *Oh,* yes. You just come on with me."

So she followed him, feeling glad beyond words to get away from her grandmom but also guilty about feeling glad. He led her into the next car forward, where he stopped at the first seat on the right and motioned her into it. Beside her were someone's belongings, maybe his—a canvas zip bag and a lunchbox. "You just settle yourself here," he said. "I won't be any time a-tall."

Then he left. Watching his back as he lumbered on toward the front of the car, she already missed him.

After that there was some confusion. Partly this was because they entered a tunnel, which she knew meant they were nearing their stop, and the windows grew dark and people started standing up and fetching down their luggage. Then the conductor came back and asked her who would be meeting her upstairs in the station. Or no, maybe first the train came to a halt, still inside the tunnel, and *then* he came back to ask who'd be meeting her. "My dad, I think," she said, and he said, "What's your dad's name, honey?" and she said, "Kevin Lainey," and he went away again. But now that she thought about it, "Kevin Lainey" didn't sound quite right. It was like when you repeat a word too many times and it begins to sound foreign. *Was* her dad's name Kevin Lainey? The train was too quiet, lacking not only the hum of the tracks but the rush of the air conditioner, and the car began to grow hot. Then a man came on the loudspeaker—not her conductor but somebody else—to say they would be approaching the station momentarily. People were murmuring; people were restless, and they went on standing in the aisle. A baby started fussing in an itchy, chafing way. Finally the train began moving again and the AC began blowing and they slid out into the light, the lovely late-afternoon light, and the train slowed to a stop and the people in the aisle pressed forward. But the loudspeaker came back on and said the doors wouldn't be opening quite yet. There would be a brief delay. More murmurs. Now some people did sit back down, but most remained standing, one so close to Candle's seat that the sleeve of his folded raincoat kept brushing against the side of her head. She thought that if she couldn't get off the train this instant she would snap like a branch that had been bent and bent and bent; she couldn't endure it anymore. But then, oh! Her conductor. Her dear, dear conductor, squeezing past the people in the aisle and plodding toward her. "All right, little lady?" he asked her.

"What about my grandmom?"

"They're seeing to her right now," he said, "and she is fine and dandy. You just come with me and we'll get you out of here."

She should have reminded him that the doors were still shut, but she didn't want to. She wanted to believe that the two of them could approach the nearest door and it would magically open only for them. And that is what happened. They went out to the space between cars and they turned toward the door to the platform and just like that, it slid open and she stepped straight off the train and into her father's arms.

He told her things were all right now and they would go find their car now and the two of them would head home now to tell her mom. She didn't ask what it was they were going to tell her. She somehow knew. She walked beside him toward the stairs without saying a word, without shedding a tear until he said, "I am so, so sorry you had to go through this, Candle girl."

And then she just somehow crumpled up. He had to grab her arm or she might have fallen, and she turned and buried her face in his chest and started crying so hard that she got his shirt wet, and he kept saying, "There, now. I know. You've had a terrible shock. I am so, so sorry."

But it wasn't the shock she was crying about. She was crying because she'd just walked out on the only person in her world who called her Kendall.

7

BY THE SUMMER OF 2014, the only members of the Garrett family still living in Baltimore were Lily and Eddie. Not under the same roof, of course. Lily was still in the Cedarcroft house, although she'd lost Morris to cancer the previous winter. And Eddie owned a row house in Hampden, which the family found ironic in light of the fact that Robin and Mercy had forsaken Hampden some sixty years before. Nowadays, however, the neighborhood was considered hip. Residents often had to park their cars several blocks from home because their streets were full of outsiders dining at trendy new restaurants and shopping for funky jewelry.

Both Robin and Mercy were dead now—Robin less than a year after Mercy, as if he had seen no point in carrying on without her—and Alice and Kevin had retired to Florida, where Kevin could golf year-round while Alice audited courses at the local college. In theory Lily was also retired, but like her father before her she had a tendency to drop by the store from time to time purely to keep her hand in, as she put it. Eddie always welcomed her and brought her up-to-date on her favorite longtime customers and the newest line of products. ("Bidets!" she said. "What next! Who in all of Baltimore even knows what a bidet *is*?") Eddie had been working at Wellington's since his teens. Of all the Garrett grandchildren only he had inherited Robin's fondness for tools, and his interest in how things worked and what might make them work better. It seemed only right that he should take over the business. Originally there'd been talk of his signing on with his father's firm instead, but he had zero enthusiasm for malls and suburban developments. Really the talk had been all on Kevin's side, not his.

Outside of the store, though, Lily and Eddie didn't mingle much. She had her friends; he had his. They led very separate lives.

So he was mildly surprised when she phoned him at home one Sunday morning and invited him to lunch. "Lunch?" he said. "You mean today?"

"I know it's short notice," she said, "but I've been packing up my belongings, and before I call the Salvation Army I want to find out if there's anything here you might like."

"Why are you packing up your belongings?"

"I'm moving to Asheville, North Carolina, to help Serena with the baby."

"What! You're moving for good?"

"Right."

"You're selling your house? You're buying a new one?"

"Well, not buying a new one. I don't need to. Serena and Jeff have an in-law apartment on their third floor."

He was taken aback. He stood holding the kitchen phone and gazing blankly at his wall calendar, a pair of pruning shears dangling from his left hand.

"Serena is going *crazy*!" Lily said. She sounded pleased, for some reason. "She was crying so hard when she called that I couldn't make out a word she was saying, but eventually I managed to gather that motherhood is turning out to be a whole lot harder than she was expecting."

"Well, maybe . . . how old is her baby, again?"

"Four and a half weeks," Lily said.

He couldn't remember the baby's name. Or even its sex, for that matter. Avoiding all pronouns, he said, "Could the baby just be temporarily colicky or something?"

"What's that got to do with it? It's Serena who's crying, not Peter."

Peter. Okay.

"All I meant was," Eddie said, "maybe this is just a difficult stage, and pretty soon she'll get the hang of it, so you don't have to move there permanently."

"Well, of course it's just a stage! She'll get the hang of it in no time, if I know Serena. So I have to go right now, quick-quick, before she finds out she doesn't need me after all."

Eddie started laughing.

"What's so funny?" she asked.

"I advise you not to put your house up for sale yet, is all," he said.

"Too late!" she said. "I've already listed it with Dodd, Goldman. Morris's old firm."

"Oh," Eddie said.

"So can you come for lunch, or not?"

"Yeah, sure," he said. "I'll be happy to come."

He figured he'd take a few items off her hands just to be polite and then return them when she came back. Because she *would* come back, he was sure of it. Serena would prove more than adequate to the challenges of motherhood. And Lily was a Baltimore girl, born and bred. She'd go out of her mind in Asheville.

. . .

When they'd settled on what time he was expected for lunch (one p.m., which meant he'd be starving, having awakened at six), he hung up and went back outside to finish pruning. Claude was still seated at the patio table, reading the Sunday paper and drinking coffee. He was not an early riser himself, or a gardener, either. You could sense that just by the look of him—his comfortable, barrel-shaped body and slouched posture, his unkempt frizzy brown beard and smudged spectacles. When he saw Eddie he raised his eyebrows inquiringly, and Eddie said, "That was my aunt Lily."

"How's she doing?" Claude asked.

"She says she's moving. She's going to Asheville to help with her grandbaby; she wants me to come to lunch so she can show me the stuff she's leaving behind in case I can use any of it."

"When, today?" Claude asked.

"Yup."

"Well, see if she's got any lamps she wants to get rid of."

Claude was always complaining that they didn't have any good reading lamps.

"I'll keep an eye out," Eddie said, "but I bet you anything she'll be back here inside of a year, wondering where they've gotten to."

Claude snorted. He didn't point out that he had no grounds for betting on Aunt Lily's behavior one way or another, never having met her.

Claude was much more forthcoming than Eddie. He had introduced Eddie to his parents years ago, and Eddie and Claude had had a standing date with them ever since for Sunday supper. But Eddie's own family had never laid eyes on Claude. In fact they didn't even know he existed.

Fortunately, though, Claude was also one of those rare people who could accept a loved one's failings with a philosophical shrug and say no more. When Eddie told him, now, "Sorry to duck out on brunch," Claude just said, "That's okay," and turned a page of his paper. And after a brief hesitation, Eddie went back to pruning the nandina.

"You think I'm being hasty," were Lily's first words when he arrived. He wasn't even properly through the front door yet. "You think I'm going to regret giving up my house. But I'm not, Eddie; believe me. I know what I'm doing."

He had brought a bottle of wine, and he had dressed for a social occasion—at least to the extent that he ever did dress. Although he still resembled his father physically, he had long ago exchanged Kevin's dapper clothing style for one more suited to his workplace: T-shirts and baggy khakis. Today, though, his shirt had a collar and it buttoned down the front, and his khakis were fresh from the dryer. Lily, on the other hand, looked prepared for serious labor. She wore faded jeans and a tank top that exposed her withered arms, and her gray-blond ponytail was doubled back through its elastic to keep it out of the way. "Wine!" she said. "How nice of you. But don't let me overindulge, because we've got some heavy lifting to do." Then, continuing with her original train of thought as she led him through the living room, "Do you have the remotest notion what it's like to be Serena's mother? She's always been so darn competent. More like *your* mother. Sorry. And at first I thought the baby hadn't changed that. I went down there for the birth and she was all radiant and Madonna-like and, well, serene. But that was when Peter was brand-new and still sleeping all the time. A couple weeks later, after I have gone back home and he has gotten his little personality together, is when she calls me."

Lily's living room looked the same as ever, the furniture where it had always been and the rug lying flat on the floor. But when they passed through the dining room, Eddie saw that the entire table was covered with stemware and china and decorative objects. Lunch had been set out on the kitchen table instead: grilled cheese sandwiches on two plates, with paper napkins alongside. "Could you fetch wineglasses from the dining room?" Lily asked him, and then, raising her voice as he left the kitchen, "So when she stops crying long enough for me to make out what she's saying, she tells me that all that day as she was taking care of the baby she'd had this nagging feeling there was something she'd needed to do. 'What *was* it?' she kept saying to herself. 'I know it was *something*,' and then along about five p.m. she said, 'Oh, *now* I remember. I meant to comb my hair.'"

Eddie clucked sympathetically and set the wineglasses on the kitchen table.

"I told her, I said, 'Oh, honey. It's not always going to be this way. You just don't have things organized yet,' I told her. 'You've always been so good at organizing.'"

"Where is . . . Jeff? Where is her husband in all this?" Eddie asked.

"She says he's useless. Worse than useless. She says he's *scared* of babies. Well, that's what she gets for marrying a weird scientist type."

Eddie clucked again and pulled out his chair to sit down.

"So I am thinking now is my chance," Lily said, settling across from him. "When am I ever, ever again going to get to step in and take charge? Hee hee!"

Throughout his life Eddie had heard his mother talk about how wild and scatty her sister was, but this was his first in-person experience of it. (Had Morris been a calming influence, maybe?) Lily's face was stretched tight with excitement; her eyes seemed to give off light. "Lily to the rescue!" she crowed. "Well, face it: I'll never have this chance with my *other* grandchildren. That wife of Robby's is Madame Know-It-All, and besides which, they're off there on the Eastern Shore with her own family close by. Oh, it's true what people say about daughters-in-law."

Eddie had no idea what people said about daughters-in-law. (His own mother had only sons-in-law, Robby the Girl's husband and Candle's, both in other parts of the country.) He said, "Yeah, I can see why you'd want to help out. And I know Serena'd be glad to have you. But still: are you sure you should be selling your house yet? Don't you want to change your mind about listing it?"

"No, I do not," Lily said, and she took a big swig of wine and set her glass back down decisively. "I'll have a lovely third-floor apartment that I won't even need to furnish, because it's already filled with tasteful antiques from Jeff's side of the family. Say, maybe *you'd* like to buy my house! Just think: it would come completely stocked."

Eddie smiled and said, "Thanks anyway." He could just imagine Claude's reaction if he proposed they move to Cedarcroft.

Lily did have a nice set of dishes—a complete set, not just mismatched odds and ends like Eddie's. And two of her frying pans were cast iron, seasoned to a rich glow, and she also owned a Crock-Pot big enough to feed an army. Every time Eddie remarked upon something, not even saying for sure that he would take it, Lily made one of her crowing sounds and reached for a cardboard carton. She had a whole stack of them, the professional movers' kind, heaped flat in one corner of the dining room alongside a stack of fresh newsprint. Each piece of china had to be wrapped in its own sheet of newsprint, which meant that one carton was quickly filled and they had to start in on another.

"Hold on, there," Eddie protested at one point. "My car's a subcompact, may I remind you."

"So? You can make several trips," Lily told him.

He declined any furniture. "I'm overfurnished as it is," he told her, "what with all that Mom and Dad passed on to me when they moved. Oh! But do you have any spare lamps?"

"Do I have lamps!" she said. "Do I! Just come with me, my boy," and she led him into the living room, where one lamp, a craneneck, appeared to be perfect for reading, although the other two were more ornamental.

It was then that Eddie happened to notice the recliner. "I remember this," he said. "It used to be Pop-Pop's."

"Right, and Grandpa Wellington's before that," Lily said. She stroked the back of it affectionately—the slightly arched curve of worn brown leather. "A genuine family heirloom. You *need* this, I tell you."

"But wouldn't one of your kids want it? Robby, maybe, seeing as he's a papa now?"

"Robby! His wife would throw a fit. She's big on that chrome-and-glass style. And I already asked Serena, but she said, 'Please, I beg of you, don't bring me any more *objects.*'"

Eddie sat down in the recliner and tipped it back. Pretty comfortable, all right. Although it wasn't his own comfort he was thinking of; it was Claude's. He could see Claude reclining in it happily every evening, the crane-necked lamp lighting the term papers he was grading.

"Morris used to claim this chair was better than a sleeping pill," Lily said, still stroking the leather. "He'd settle into it after supper and *whoops!* Next thing you knew, he'd be snoring."

"I almost think I've *seen* him sleeping here," Eddie said, half to himself.

"You probably did," she said. "Dear, dear Morris. You know,

sometimes I imagine how it would be if he came back. He'd walk in the door looking all shy and sheepish, not wanting me to make a fuss, and I would say, 'Oh, sweetheart, I have so much to tell you!' That's what I feel saddest about: everything he's missed, just in the little time he's been gone. 'Robby's got his own byline now; can you believe it?' I'd say. 'Serena named her baby Peter Morris Hayes. And Joan and Mel across the street are getting a divorce—the last couple you'd expect it of.'"

"Maybe he already knows," Eddie said. He didn't actually think that, but it seemed to be something people said to the bereaved.

But Lily was having none of it. "I certainly hope he does *not* know," she said, "because can you think of any worse hell than to look down from heaven and see your loved ones suffering without you?"

"You've got a point," Eddie said.

"So you'll take the recliner?" she asked.

"Well . . ." He stood up and looked down at it, considering. "I'm not sure how I'd transport it, though."

"I can do that! I can put it in my hatchback and follow you home." And then, perhaps believing she had worn down his defenses by now, "You should take the albums, too."

"What albums?"

"The family photo albums."

"Oh. No, thanks. I'm not much of a one for memorabilia," Eddie said.

"Darn. I know my kids don't want them; I've already asked."

"One of my sisters, maybe?"

"I can try," Lily said, sounding doubtful. "If not, I could send them to David."

"David!"

"Just to remind him he does have a family," she said with a wry chuckle. "Yes, I think that's what I'll do: wrap them up and mail them to David. He can dispose of them as he likes. Probably *will* dispose of them, straight into the wastebasket. Oh, what does that man have against us?"

Eddie shrugged. He had heard the subject rehashed too often to find it interesting.

"Just watch," she told him. "It'll turn out to be something tiny, like 'I always got the smallest piece of cake.' Or 'You made me mow the lawn every week and my sisters never had to.' I mean, nothing big. Nothing like . . . he was molested, or locked in the basement or something."

"Oh, well," Eddie said. "Maybe he just doesn't like us; ever thought of that?"

"Not like us!" She looked thunderstruck.

"So, were you serious about your hatchback?" he asked. "Not to put you to any trouble, but—"

"Absolutely," Lily said, and then she wiped her palms on the seat of her jeans in a businesslike way and stepped forward to seize one end of the recliner.

"Oh, I didn't mean right this minute," Eddie told her.

"What better time?" she asked. "I'm only going to get busier from here on out."

So he gave up and bent to lift the other end.

He knew he shouldn't text while driving. He contemplated pulling over to the side of the road for a moment—"Bringing aunt home want to warn you" was all he would need to say—but then Lily might get to the house before he did. So he kept going. If Claude saw them coming, he figured, or heard them (if Eddie spoke extra loudly as they entered), he would know enough to duck out of sight; no problem.

But *would* he duck out of sight?

Sometimes Eddie wondered if Claude fully understood Eddie's

situation. It was easy for Claude, after all. He had parents who'd always accepted him just the way he was. Well, and he had *known* who he was; that was another difference. Eddie, on the other hand . . . Eddie had been sort of clueless, up until eighth grade. Eighth grade was when he developed a crush on Karen Small, the most popular girl in his class. (And therefore unattainable, he saw now. No danger of her reciprocating.) But Karen was going steady with Jem Buford, and so Eddie had closely studied Jem Buford in order to learn what was so great about him. He took note of Jem's lopsided smile, and the single quirky cowlick standing up on the crown of his head, and his habit of keeping a fountain pen cartridge jutting from between his teeth like an unlit cigarette. And finally . . . Wait, Eddie had thought, is it *Jem* I have a crush on?

He turned onto his own street and glanced down the block. By some miracle, there was a parking space free directly in front of his house. He pulled up next to it and checked his rearview mirror. Above the row of cartons looming in his backseat he could just make out Lily's Toyota slowing to a stop behind him. He shifted to neutral and got out to speak with her, and Lily rolled down her window as he approached and looked up at him expectantly.

"You take this space here," he told her, "and I'll look for something up ahead."

"Okay," she said, and she closed her window again while he returned to his car.

But up ahead he found nothing—not in his own block or in the next one. He had to turn down a side street, where he parked clumsily and too far from the curb because he was in such a rush to get back to the house. By that time, he'd kept Lily waiting so long that he didn't even bother unloading a couple of cartons to take with him before he hurried to meet her.

She was no longer in her car, though. The driver's seat was

empty. And when he peered through the rear window he found that the recliner was gone.

He glanced up at his front porch and saw the inner door standing open. He climbed the steps two at a time, already calling "Hello?" as he entered.

Lily was in the living room. She was shoving the recliner a few inches right, a few inches left as she positioned it in a corner. And Claude was dragging away the rocking chair that had stood in that corner till now.

"Oh," Eddie said. "Well, hi, Claude! How *are* you?"

"What do you think?" Lily asked, straightening up and brushing her palms off. "Is this the right place for it?"

"Sure! It's great! Aunt Lily, this is Claude Evers. Claude, this is—"

"Oh, yes, we two are bosom buddies," Lily said. "We've just lugged a recliner up an entire set of porch steps together." She laughed and turned to Claude. "You've got dust all across your front," she told him. "I guess my housekeeping's showing."

"That might actually be from the rocker," Claude said. He looked ruefully down at his T-shirt.

"I'm sorry it took me so long to park," Eddie told Lily.

"That's quite all right!" she said, and she picked up her purse from the seat of the recliner and gave him a kiss on the cheek. "Okay, buddy, I'm off. I'll call to say goodbye before I leave for good, though. It won't be for another week or so."

"Okay . . . well . . . thanks again for all the stuff, Aunt Lily. And for lunch."

"My pleasure!" she said. "Thank *you* for that lovely wine." She trilled her fingers at Claude. "Bye, Claude."

"Bye, Lily. Nice meeting you."

Eddie walked her to the front door, and he stood watching till she got into her car. Then he returned to the living room. "What happened?" he asked Claude.

"What do you mean, what happened?" Claude said. He had hold of the rocking chair again and was sliding it toward the stairs.

"How come you two ran into each other?" Eddie asked.

"She just told you how. I look out the front window; I see this woman trying to haul this huge recliner out of her car; what am I supposed to do? You can't expect me to let her struggle with it on her own."

"Well, that is just . . . transparent," Eddie said.

"Excuse me?"

"You must have at least suspected who she was, and yet you fall all over yourself rushing out to be seen."

"I'm thinking we could put the rocker up in the guest room," Claude said.

"And how did you explain your presence?" Eddie demanded.

Claude released the rocker and turned to look at him. He said, "Why should I have to explain my presence?"

Eddie didn't even have words for this. He just flung his hands out helplessly. There was a silence.

Then Claude said, "Oh, babe. She knows."

Eddie dropped his hands.

"She knew all along," Claude said.

And he resumed sliding the rocker across the room. When he reached the stairs, he picked it up by both arms and began trudging upward as Eddie watched.

A slow bloom was coming over him, a flush that warmed his face. Of course she knew. He saw that now. And it wasn't only Lily who knew, because here he was, forty-one years old, and yet no one in his family had ever asked him whether he had a girlfriend. No one had said, at weddings, "Your turn next, Eddie!" And he remembered how his cousin Robby the Boy, watching TV with him years ago, had abruptly switched channels when somebody onscreen called somebody else a faggot.

You would think this realization would come as a relief to him. And it did, in part. He felt a rush of love for his whole family, whom it seemed he had underestimated. He had thought that guarding his secret was a kindness to them; he was protecting them from knowledge that would hurt them. But now he saw that not telling them had been more hurtful, and it was they who had been kind.

He stood gazing up the stairs in a sort of trance, overwhelmed with regret for all the time he had wasted.

8

DAVID GARRETT retired from teaching when he was sixty-eight years old. He had planned to work longer, but halfway through spring semester of 2020 the pandemic struck and all his classes switched to Zoom. It turned out he wasn't much good at Zoom. He winced at the sight of his own face on the screen; he deplored the artificial tone of his voice; he felt he was shortchanging his students. Not only that, but the senior class play, which he had directed for the past forty-odd years, abruptly folded in the middle of rehearsals. In fact, drama classes in general were a thing of the past now, along with art, chorus, and orchestra—all the subjects that made school worthwhile, in David's opinion. He had never enjoyed his English classes half as much as drama. So at the end of the semester he handed in his notice: he would not be returning next fall. And of course there would be no summer school this year.

Greta had retired some time ago, so she was accustomed by now to the stay-at-home life. David, though, found sheltering in place more of an adjustment than he had expected. "You know how when the electricity fails, you marvel that you could ever have taken it for granted," he told her. "Well, that's how I feel now when I remember that the world was wide open, once upon a time. We used to come and go at will, remember? Hit the grocery store, head out to the mall, have dinner at a restaurant whenever we got the urge . . ."

Greta smiled at this. "Not that we really did, so much," she said. "I had to pry you out of your study with a crowbar, as I recall."

"Well, you just watch what happens once things get back to normal," he told her.

Privately he thought, *If* they get back. But he didn't say that aloud.

What was easier to adjust to—shockingly easy, really—was their sudden lack of a social life. In the past they had gathered now and then with a few choice friends, people from the school or from his theater projects, and yet often he had been conscious, as he sat conversing with them, of a renegade thought so insistent that he had worried he might blurt it out by accident: I like you very much, but do we really have to *see* each other? Now it emerged that they did not. They were not supposed to. They could exchange regretful emails or even, in Greta's case, talk on the telephone, but mostly it was just the two of them. David didn't mind this in the least. It might have been overstating to say that he found it a relief, but . . . well, it *was* a relief, to be honest. If only they'd had their children nearby, he would have felt perfectly contented.

Then Nicholas phoned.

Nicholas lived in New York City with his wife, Juana, who was a gastroenterologist, and their five-year-old son, Benny. They hadn't visited since the pandemic started, and David worried they wouldn't again for months or even years. But what Nicholas said now was, "How would you feel about Benny and me coming to stay for a while?"

"Are you serious?" David asked. He was the one who'd answered the phone—made a grab for it the instant he saw the caller ID. He raised his eyebrows meaningfully at Greta, who was standing next to him waiting for her turn to talk.

"Would it worry you?" Nicholas was asking. "We'd self-quarantine for two weeks ahead of time, needless to say, and get tested before we set out. We do know you're both at risk, at your ages."

"We're not at risk! We're healthy as horses!"

"What? What?" Greta was asking, so David covered the receiver long enough to tell her, "He wants to come stay here awhile with Benny."

Greta clasped her hands under her chin and nodded vigorously.

"Your mother's already heading out front to watch for your car," David told Nicholas. And then, "No Juana?"

"No, here's the thing: Juana is on the front lines now. They've transferred her to Infectious Diseases because we're getting slammed in this city; I don't know if you've heard. So she hardly comes home at all anymore, and even when she does, it's not safe for her to stay in the same room with us. And since our nanny's gone home to *her* family, that leaves me in sole charge of Benny. I was wondering if maybe you and Mom could help me with childcare."

"Lord, yes," David said. "Of course we'll help. And forget about the self-quarantine; start packing up this minute."

"No, no, we don't want to take any chances. We'll isolate here first and then see you in—"

But David didn't hear the rest of that, because Greta seized the phone from him. "Nicholas?" she said. "You must come right away. There is no need to self-quarantine."

David retreated to a kitchen chair to let her handle this; she still had the nurse's air of authority about her. And she was right to argue, because in fact they were not at all at risk. Or only a little, maybe. They certainly didn't resemble the people you pictured when you saw those DON'T KILL MEE-MAW signs urging masks and social distancing. David's hair was not so much white as merely a washed-out blond, and Greta had that smooth, tan, firm kind of skin that showed only a few deep crevices around her eyes.

But he'd forgotten that doctors outweigh nurses, because now Greta was saying, "Yes, I do realize Juana's the expert . . . Yes, of course I see her point . . ."

So David resigned himself. Okay, two more weeks. But then finally, at long last, they'd have a child under this roof again.

What nobody understood about David, with the possible exception of Greta, was that he had suffered a very serious loss in his life. Two losses, in fact. Two very dear children: Emily and Nicholas. It was true that these days there happened to be two very dear grown-ups who were also named Emily and Nicholas, but they weren't the same people. It was just as if those children had died. He'd been in mourning ever since.

And now he felt a surge of hope, a sort of inner effervescence, and even before Greta got off the line he began to make plans for their time with Benny.

They started preparing immediately—ordering an inflatable wading pool from Amazon, for instance, and a badminton-like game that didn't require a net. It was decided that Benny would sleep in Nicholas's old room, which still had glow-in-the-dark constellations plastered to the ceiling, and Nicholas in Emily's room. (No chance that Emily herself would be needing it, sad to say. She lived in Wisconsin, where she was an emergency-room physician and therefore in the thick of things. But don't think about that, David told himself. Don't let your mind go there.)

His study, which opened off the kitchen, could serve as Nicholas's work space. Nicholas earned his living by marketing his inventions: a roll-up pallet arrangement called a Naptress, for example, that small children could bring to daycare with them, and a beehive-like system of fiberglass sleeping pods called GoWings for use in airports. David wasn't sure what the current enterprise was, but he knew it was bound to involve quite a few business meetings—all online now, of course—and the study had the least glitchy Wi-Fi connection.

Another preparation, one that David made on his own, was to start a small vegetable garden. This required taking some shortcuts, since two weeks was not enough time to grow anything from scratch. He paid their lawn-mowing people to come in with a rototiller, and he ordered a variety of young plants to be delivered from a nursery. "But would this really interest a child?" Greta asked. "It won't be so exciting as watching new shoots poke up from seeds."

"Well, at least it's something he and I can do together," David said. "Pull weeds together, and pick the vegetables once they're ready."

He had given it a good deal of thought, because they would have to find ways of keeping Benny occupied. When Nicholas was Benny's age it hadn't been a problem; there'd been dozens of neighborhood children to play with. But nowadays, that was forbidden. David cast his mind back to his own childhood: what had he and his father done together? Not a lot, really; his father had worked such long hours. David did recall a carpentry project they'd once embarked on, a wooden birdhouse they had planned to hang in a tree. But it hadn't gone well. David had never been good with tools, whereas Robin couldn't get enough of them.

(Toward the end of his life, Robin's idea of bliss had been cruising the aisles of the twenty-four-hour Home Depot whenever he couldn't sleep.) He had taken over the birdhouse project and finished it on his own, as best as David could recollect.

David was counting the days now; both he and Greta were. Yet as time grew short, he found himself feeling uneasy. He became distracted and inattentive, in a way that he hadn't experienced even during the earliest, most unsettling days of the pandemic. He couldn't seem to read anymore or focus on TV, and at night anxious dreams skittered jerkily through his sleep. He would wake and lie staring into the darkness, trying to make his muscles relax. Beside him Greta slept peacefully, her breathing as soft as flour sifting, and he wondered how she could be so oblivious when there was so much to worry about. The world was collapsing, people were dying, they were losing their jobs and starving, the planet was racing toward extinction, and this country was turning against itself. And Emily: would she manage to stay safe? Was she taking proper precautions? Plus, why was she still alone? She kept mentioning new men's names, but then somehow no more was heard of them. And then Juana: how could Juana think of choosing her work over her family? What would it do to Benny? What would this whole pandemic do to Benny? He needed playmates; he needed real school; he was missing a stage of his development! As were all children everywhere; good Lord. The little ones who should be making friends, the older ones who should be gaining some distance from their parents, the young adults who should be living on their own right now and finding their true loves.

When he had lain awake so long that he thought he might go crazy, he would rise and pad downstairs and turn on the TV. (The people in old-time movies stood so close to each other! Unmasked! He flinched at the sight.) Eventually he would fall asleep sitting upright on the couch, and wake only when Greta discovered him there in the morning.

"I think I know what's wrong with you," she told him over breakfast one day.

"What do you mean, wrong with me?"

"Why you are so edgy lately."

"Well, that's not exactly a mystery," he said. "I don't know if you've happened to notice that everything's falling apart."

"You were like this once before," she said, as if he hadn't spoken. "Before Nicholas was born."

"I was?"

"You started worrying it had been a mistake to decide on a second child. 'We were doing fine with just Emily,' you said. 'What if this new one's not a good fit? What if we're not compatible?' 'Compatible!' I said. 'This is our very own baby! Of course he'll be compatible!' But you said, 'No "of course" about it. We can never be sure of such things. And why did you say "he"?' you asked. 'Are you thinking this is a boy? But I'm not used to boys!' you said. 'I wouldn't know how to raise one!' "

"I don't remember that," David said.

"Yet you see how it all turned out. You were a wonderful father."

"I don't remember a word of that," David said. Although it did have a vaguely familiar ring, now that he thought about it.

"I heard what you asked Emily on the phone yesterday," Greta told him, and she flashed him a triumphant glance that he couldn't interpret. "You asked her about Benny. How well did she know him, you were asking, and what was he like, exactly, and when was the last time she'd seen him?"

"So?" David said. "Your point is?"

She started laughing. "So," she said, "you're anxious because you're expecting again. In a manner of speaking. Expecting another child and worrying you'll fail him somehow."

"Well, that's ridiculous," David said. But he was smiling now.

Greta often knew best, he had learned.

He was aware that some people had been surprised when they heard he'd married her. Well, he'd been surprised himself, for that matter. At first he'd barely registered her existence. She was peripheral at the school, not a teacher but the school nurse, a slightly older woman with a hint of a foreign accent and a limp. But then one day she and Lillian Washington, the college counselor, had brought their sandwiches to the faculty lounge while he was brewing himself some coffee. He started complaining about the new coffee maker, which required a fresh filter every time it was used. (David's role at the school was Lovable Curmudgeon; he fell into it naturally, surrounded as he was by motherly middle-aged women, for the most part.) "Why must they keep *changing* things?" he was grumbling. "It's my considered opinion," he said, "that all change is for the worse."

He wasn't expecting a response—or at least, no more than a sympathetic chuckle—but Greta made a tsking sound. "You say that to me," she told him, "who could have used the Salk vaccine, and Lillian here, who is Black."

That made him turn to look at her. She was surveying him with a cool, challenging gaze—a woman more handsome than pretty, with a strong face and short, crinkly hair streaked like woodgrain, brown and light brown mingled. He'd been planning to make some flip retort ("Okay, well, not *all* change, but just tell me what was so bad about our old-style percolator") when something caused him to truly notice her. And she, it seemed, noticed him, because her lips all at once parted and she took on a startled expression.

They were married six months later. Even that seemed to him a very long time to wait, because by then he had met Emily, and he couldn't have borne it if Greta's ex-husband had followed through with his threat to wrest Emily away from her.

. . .

Nicholas pulled up at the curb on a Wednesday afternoon in early June. David and Greta had been keeping an eye out, and they emerged from the house immediately—Greta flying down the front walk while David followed at a more dignified pace. While Nicholas was still unfolding himself from behind the wheel, Greta was tugging the rear door open and leaning in to unlatch Benny's booster seat. But he could do that for himself, it appeared, and so she straightened and took a step back to give him room. "No hugs, remember," Nicholas warned her as he approached, but she said, "How could I not hug you?" and flung her arms around him.

With Benny, though, she was more reserved; she did know enough not to rush him. He stepped forth and stood blinking a moment—a serious-looking little boy under an upside-down bowl of straight black hair. "Say hello to Grandma and Grandpa," Nicholas told him, and Benny said, "Hi, Granna. Hi, Grappa." It made David happy to hear that Benny hadn't outgrown his toddler names for them. And he still had that snuffly, croaky little voice—adenoids, maybe, or tonsils, but David found it appealing even so.

"How was traffic?" he asked Nicholas, and Nicholas said, "There wasn't any. We could have roller-skated down the middle of the highway."

"We could?" Benny said.

"Lots of luck, though, finding your kid a bathroom nowadays."

"Oh, dear! What did you do?" Greta asked.

"Jif peanut butter jar," Nicholas told her with a shrug. "Remind me to bring it in, by and by."

He went around to the trunk to unload their belongings—just a couple of canvas duffel bags, but a considerable number of boxed games and wheeled toys—and he and David began carrying them toward the house. Greta followed with a plastic barn, and Benny walked next to her with a worn-looking plush bear. "We're going to get a dog while we're here," he told her.

"You are?"

"Now, hold on, buddy," Nicholas said, turning to give him a stern look. "We're going to *talk* about getting a dog."

"Can we?" Benny asked Greta.

"We'll talk about it," Nicholas said again, and then to David, under his breath, "*Oh,* Lord." He had a weary, rumpled look, and he seemed thinner. And now that he'd shifted his sunglasses to the top of his head, David could see the strained skin around his eyes.

"I don't think any dogs are even available right now," David told him. "Our shelter has closed for the duration, and the staff has taken home whatever animals they couldn't place."

"Yeah, but one of that staff is Julie Drumm," Nicholas said. "Remember Julie, from high school? She thinks she can line something up for us."

"Ah."

They entered the house from the front. "Pot roast!" Nicholas said, and he sniffed appreciatively.

"I thought you might like something homey," Greta told him.

"I'm *craving* something homey," he said. "It's been pretty slim pickings lately."

Then he told Benny, "I'm going to take our bags up. You can stay down here with Grandma and Grandpa." Benny said nothing, but when Nicholas started toward the stairs he followed, still carrying his bear. Clearly he was feeling a bit out of his element.

By suppertime, though, he seemed more comfortable. He had taken a tour of the garden, where David let him pluck a tiny nubbin of a green pepper, and he had tried out a badminton racquet. In the garden he'd gone so far as to confess that he was a little scared of bugs, which David treated respectfully. "Of course you are," he said. "I was scared too, once upon a time. Eventually you won't be, but for now we'll just steer clear of them." Benny reported this to his father over supper. "Grappa used to be scared of bugs too, so he says we'll just steer clear of them."

"Or power through," Nicholas suggested. "Learn to face up to them, maybe."

"No, I think steer clear," Benny said firmly, and he speared a chunk of potato. Then he told David, in a confiding tone, "I'm scared of banana threads, too."

"Banana threads. I see. Well, I can understand that," David said. He couldn't help feeling honored.

In the evening, Greta read Benny some of the picture books from Emily's and Nicholas's childhoods. Benny proved to be on the very edge of knowing how to read for himself; he pounced on random short words and called them out to her. "Cat," he said. "Dad." And then, triumphantly, "Truck!"

"That is correct," Greta said each time. She was always very formal with children. Even with her own, she had avoided the fluty voice and the cutesy phrasing that other mothers used, and children seemed to find that reassuring. When it came time for Benny to go upstairs to bed, he asked, "Can Granna tuck me in?" and Nicholas said, "Why not?"

"He misses having a woman around," he told David once they were alone. "I don't think he fully understands why he's seeing so little of Juana."

"It's hard, I imagine," David said.

"That was how come I've been talking about getting a dog, maybe—adopting one here and taking it home with us when we leave. Not a puppy, though; a grown dog. I'm not sure we could deal with a puppy, at this stage. But if you and Mom have any objection, we'll just wait till we're back in New York."

"It's fine with *me*," David said. "Greta?" he asked as she reentered the room. "Would you be okay with having a dog in the house?"

"Yes, of course," Greta said, and she sank onto the couch with a sigh. Probably she felt as tired as he did. Children took so much energy! But it was a pleasant kind of tiredness. That night, David slept better than he had in some time.

The dog that Nicholas's friend Julie arrived with, a couple of days later, was a sand-colored, short-haired mutt with one floppy ear and one upright one, which gave him a sort of quizzical look. He bounded out of her car and rushed up the front walk toward the house, where everybody stood waiting, since Julie, of course, would not be coming inside. "Wait up, boy! Slow down, boy!" she called after him, but he paid no attention and instead headed straight for Benny in a purposeful manner. Benny shrank back slightly but held his ground, and the dog stopped in front of him and sat down, panting and grinning, till Benny reached out and gave his nose a tentative pat with just the tips of his fingers.

"Did you tell the dog ahead of time it was a kid who'd be adopting him?" Nicholas asked Julie, and she said, "No, but I think he was hoping."

She was one of those young women without any airs, curly-haired and sturdy in Levi's and a tank top. A bandanna-print mask covered the lower half of her face, but David could tell by her eyes that she was smiling. "I've just been calling him 'boy,'" she told Benny, "so you'll have to come up with a name for him." And then, to Nicholas, "How you been, Nick?"

"Pretty good. And you?"

"Oh, hanging in there."

"You remember my parents, Greta and David," Nicholas said.

"And this, of course, is Benny. Julie Drumm," he reminded his family.

"Hi there," Julie said. Since all the Garretts wore masks as well, she couldn't have seen any more of them than they could see of her, but she gave them a friendly wave. "Looks to me like we've got a match, am I right?" and she tilted her head toward Benny and the dog.

"Yes, I'd say so," Nicholas said. "You like him, Ben?"

"I love him!" Benny said.

So Nicholas followed Julie down to her car for the supplies she'd brought, while Benny ventured to stroke the top of the dog's head. "What name will you give him?" Greta asked.

"I'm not sure," Benny said.

"*I* had a dog named Cap, once," David offered helpfully.

Benny gave him a pitying look. (He had tugged his mask below his chin the very instant Julie left them, so that he seemed to be wearing a little candy-stripe Amish beard.) "No," he said at last, "his name is John."

"John. Okay."

And when Nicholas returned, hugging a giant bag of dog chow and clutching a coiled leash, Benny said, "Meet John, Daddy!"

"How do you do, John," Nicholas said. And they all went into the house.

It didn't take long for them to settle into a routine. The first one up in the morning was Nicholas. David and Greta would come downstairs to find the study door closed and Nicholas murmuring behind it, probably talking to Juana, who often called very early. David would let the dog out to pee in the backyard and then feed him, after which he and Greta had breakfast. They learned not to bother offering Nicholas any breakfast; he would subsist till lunchtime on the pot of coffee he'd brewed. The last to rise was Benny. He would tumble downstairs at nine or so, calling, "John? John?" which suggested he might have stayed in bed even later if not for the lure of the dog. John, who'd clearly been just making do with David and Greta, would prick up his one erect ear and race to the bottom of the stairs to make joyful snuffling sounds while Benny hugged him. Then Greta tried to wheedle Benny into eating something, although he was far more interested in trying to place a call to his mother. (The first of many calls, every day; they had her on speed dial now, although she wasn't always free to answer.) After that, while Greta busied herself around the house, David would spend his biggest block of dedicated time with Benny. They would go out to the garden and pull a few weeds, empty the wading pool from yesterday and refill it, and then start the drip hose in the garden and take John for his walk. David, remembering his years with Cap, assumed John should walk glued to Benny's left side. However, John had his own ideas. His leash was the retractable kind that gave him a lot of leeway, and he frequently lagged behind when he came upon some intriguing smell or raced ahead when a squirrel crossed his path. Otherwise, though, he trotted along docilely enough, and David gave up trying to make him heel.

This neighborhood was a nondescript bedroom community, a modest Philadelphia suburb that had grown leafier and more established-looking as it aged. David and Greta had become less a part of it after their children left; but now, out walking with Benny, David noticed all the new young families who had moved in. Everybody was home these days, of course, out mowing the lawn or teaching a child to ride a bike or speaking to a next-door neighbor over a hedge. Although Benny wasn't supposed to play with the children he came across, they did manage to interact to a degree. Benny would pull his mask up and stay at a respectful distance, and they would eye one another in silence awhile. Then a boy might throw a soccer ball toward him and he would clumsily catch it, or a little girl might let her chihuahua stretch to the end of his leash and touch his nose to John's nose. As time went on, David hung farther and farther back—so far back that he seldom bothered pulling his own mask up—and their walks became longer. Often they didn't get home until lunch was being served. "It's our wanderers!" Nicholas would call from his seat at the table. "What's the news from the outside world?"

Surprisingly, Benny always did have news. "My friend Jason got a skateboard," he might say, or "Did you know if you stand under a trellis and press the backs of your hands to both sides of it, your arms will float up by themselves after you step away?" He serenaded them with one of those eternal-loop songs David remembered from his own childhood, the kind that kept circling back to its beginning and driving grown-ups crazy:

This is a song that never ends.
Yes, it goes on and on, my friends . . .

Years ago, when electronic devices were first becoming popular, David had read that children's age-old sidewalk games were in danger of being forgotten. Jump-rope rhymes and hopscotch and such, the experts said, were passed by word of mouth from child to child; they were never taught by grown-ups. So if just one generation of children failed to teach the younger ones, those traditions would vanish forever.

But guess what: even socially distanced, even deprived of normal playdates, Benny had somehow learned the levitating-arms trick and the song that never ends.

. . .

After lunch, Nicholas would return to the study for a couple of hours while Benny spent some time with Greta. The two of them would make things together: cookies, lemonade, child-size masks from leftover quilting fabric. For the masks, Greta taught Benny how to use her sewing machine. David worried he was too young, but in fact he did just fine, producing masks that actually functioned, although they did look a little bit messy where the machine had gotten away from him. Then along about midafternoon or so, Nicholas would re-emerge and collect Benny and the dog for another walk. David had to admit that he welcomed the break. Finally, a chance to slump in a chair, to give up acting optimistic and enthusiastic and focused! But then, bit by bit, he would begin to notice the silence. It was a *shocked* silence, almost. "What'll we do when they leave for good?" he asked Greta. "Will we have to go through that whole empty-nest thing all over again?"

"This time we might be better at it," Greta told him. "I'm hoping it's an acquired skill."

"I kind of doubt it," he said. And when they heard the dog barking out front, he was the first to jump up and fling open the door.

It wasn't till after supper that the four of them spent any length of time together. They would sit in the backyard; or rather, David and Greta would sit, while Nicholas and Benny played a haphazard game of badminton. The days were so long now that the sun was still shining and the heat was still oppressive, and eventually Nicholas would drop into a chair alongside his parents and Benny would start splashing around in the wading pool. Other families were outside as well, hidden behind their hedges. David could hear their voices, here and there. Occasionally he caught a few words, but in general, all he could make out were unintelligible murmurs. He began to appreciate the rhythms of ordinary conversation—the taking of turns, the questions, the answers, the chiming in, the soft laughter. Wasn't it amazing how *resilient* people were, how they persisted, how they kept trying to connect! When Greta announced, finally, "Off to bed with *you*, Master Benny," David half regretted leaving the voices behind.

After Benny had told Juana good night on the phone and Greta had tucked him in, the grown-ups would adjourn to the living room. Then Nicholas might report on the day's virtual meetings with his business associates. (He'd designed a kind of sleeping bag that had arms and legs, just in case any schools held outdoor classes this winter. An EduBunting, he called it.) Or he and David would exchange jokey suggestions for a Covid cure they might stumble on by accident. ("Philly cheesesteaks!" "Crystallized ginger!" "Beer! But not the pale kind.") And since Nicholas belonged to that generation that never left home without a cell phone, not even for a neighborhood walk, he usually had new photos to show them from that day's outing. Benny and a little redheaded girl sat six feet apart eating peaches on somebody's front step; Benny and the dog ran through somebody's sprinkler. "Email these to me, please," Greta would instruct him, but David studied them without speaking. He marveled that already they looked like something from the distant past, faded and nostalgic. And what a surprise to see how much of a Garrett Benny was! Since birth he had seemed entirely an *other*—not a pale beige biscuit of a person like David's people but black-haired and brown-eyed and golden-brown-skinned, small for his age and wiry. These were differences David had always been glad of, in fact. For him, Benny represented a fresh beginning. But now he noticed the child's raised shoulders as he cupped a hand to catch the peach juice, and his tucked-in chin when he ran. David's father had raised his shoulders like that whenever he was intent on some task—a man Benny had never laid eyes on. David's sisters used to run with their chins tucked, but Benny hadn't met them, either, so far as David knew. And while he realized that most children went through some sort of playacting stage, he couldn't help feeling that Benny's complicated dialogues with his bear (who seemed to have an English accent, of all things) were very like his own long-ago scenarios with his plastic veterinarians.

Last week, Benny had started coughing and then said, when he had recovered, "I swallowed down the wrong throat"—a Garrett phrase. And he wouldn't eat hard candies because, like David himself, he hated how they roughened his teeth. Also he called club soda "prickle water," the way Nicholas used to do, and cut-up orange wedges were "boats," and pocketbooks were "ladybags."

"What is the name of that braid that starts high up on little girls' heads?" David asked Greta one night when they were getting ready for bed.

"High up on their heads?"

"Emily used to have them. They would start with two skeins of hair high up near her temples, very skinny and tight, and then join in with two thicker braids lower down."

"Oh, a *French* braid," Greta said.

"That's it. And then when she undid them, her hair would still be in ripples, little leftover squiggles, for hours and hours afterward."

"Yes . . ."

"Well," David said, "that's how families work, too. You think you're free of them, but you're never *really* free; the ripples are crimped in forever."

Greta started laughing. "You are finding this out just now?" she asked.

He said, "I'm a slow learner, I guess."

. . .

His sister Alice phoned from Florida one evening during supper. Greta was the one who picked up, but after checking the caller ID she passed the receiver to David without speaking. He was surprised to see Alice's name. (The family wasn't much for casual phone conversations.) "Alice?" he said. "Everything okay?"

"More or less," she told him. "How about you?"

"We're all fine. Got Nicholas and Benny staying with us at the moment."

"Oh?" she said. "Where's, um . . . ?"

"Juana's working on the front lines."

"Ah," she said. "But none of you have been sick, right?"

"Not so far, knock on wood."

"Same down here," she said. "Which I consider a miracle, since Kevin still insists on playing golf every day with his buddies."

David clucked, and then waited.

"But why I called," she said, "I thought you'd like to hear what your *other* sister's been up to."

"What's that?"

"Well, so there she was, living on her own for the moment because Serena and Jeff have taken Petey to their mountain place for the duration and not even Lily is dumb enough to think she and Serena could stay in a tiny log cabin together without one of them strangling the other . . ." Alice took a fresh breath. "*And,*" she said, "this morning Serena gives Lily a call because she's been feeling so guilty about leaving her to fend for herself, and she asks how things are going in Asheville and Lily says, 'Oh,' she says, 'I guess I might as well tell you: I don't know how things are going in Asheville, because I happen to have gotten married a while back and moved to Winston-Salem.'"

"*What?*" David said. Across the table, Greta raised her eyebrows inquiringly, and Nicholas looked up from slicing Benny's meat for him.

"I know: right?" Alice said.

"Who'd she marry?" David asked.

"Someone named Henry something who's a retired history professor. Nobody'd heard a word about him, up till then. Serena says he was certainly not in the picture when they left, and that was only two months ago."

"Huh," David said.

"I really thought Lily had settled down some," Alice said. "I honestly thought she was past such behavior."

"Well, look at it this way," David told her. "Now Serena can quit feeling guilty about leaving her to fend for herself."

"Yes, I guess there is that," Alice said with a sigh. "And I have to admit Lily's coming up in the world. From motorcycle mechanic to real-estate agent to history professor; what next?"

"I forgot about the motorcycle mechanic," David said. "Husband number one, right?"

"Well, he was only around for about a nanosecond," Alice said.

"I did like Morris, though."

"Yes, Morris was a sweetheart," she said, and she sighed again. "Anyhow, I just thought you'd like to know," she said.

"Everyone else okay? Your kids?"

"They're fine. Robby's having to work from home, but who doesn't, nowadays. Candle's been laid off for months but Mac's got *his* job, so they're not starving, and Eddie and Claude are still hunkered down in Hampden."

"Well, tell them all hello," David said. "Give Lily my congratulations when you speak to her."

"I'm not sure I want to speak to her," Alice said. "Really: what does this family actually have to do with each other anymore?"

But David was getting that too-long-on-the-phone feeling now, and he said, "Okay, well, thanks for calling."

He passed the receiver back to Greta and she hung it up. "Lily seems to have gotten married," he told her.

"So I gathered," Greta said.

Nicholas asked, "Who'd she marry?"

"Some history professor nobody's met, and she lives in Winston-Salem now."

"Just like that!" Nicholas said in a wondering tone.

"Serena didn't even know the man existed," David said.

"But . . . Serena is Lily's daughter, right?"

"Right."

Nicholas looked at Greta. He said, "So Lily didn't inform her own daughter she was getting married?"

"Oh, well," Greta said. "This is America, remember."

"What's that have to do with it?"

"Consider the gene pool," she told him. "This country was settled by dissidents and malcontents and misfits and adventurers. *Thorny* people. They don't always follow the etiquette."

"Seems to me we're dealing here with more than a question of etiquette," Nicholas said. "To me this seems downright peculiar."

Then Benny asked, "Can I still have dessert if I don't eat my peas?" and Greta said, "Did you try a spoonful, at least?" and the subject of Lily was dropped.

It was a couple of days afterward that Nicholas emerged from the study with one of the old photo albums David had somehow fallen heir to. He had his finger on a crinkle-edged black-and-white snapshot that must have dated from the 1930s: a strikingly handsome man in a fedora. "Who's this?" he asked David.

"No idea," David said.

Nicholas turned next to a picture of a small woman wearing a dress with prominent shoulder pads. "And this?" he asked.

"Couldn't tell you."

Same for the photos on the facing page: two little girls crammed into an armchair with a puppy, and a baby whose vast bouffant christening gown seemed to be wearing *him* rather than the other way around. There were no captions. Once the subjects' identities must have seemed so obvious; it hadn't occurred to the album's creator that the time would come when no one alive remembered them. David said, "I do at least know that this is your grandmom's side of the family. I don't think my dad's people had the money for things like cameras."

"Oh, here's one I recognize," Nicholas said, because he had flipped several pages ahead and was gazing now at a photo of David himself at age six or so, wearing a short white bathrobe. A framed copy of this picture used to hang in David's parents' bedroom. David didn't comment, and Nicholas sank down on a kitchen chair and continued turning pages. "Huh," he said once or twice, and then, "This must be Lily's motorcycle mechanic." David was fairly sure it wasn't (B.J. had always made himself scarce when a camera was brought out), but he didn't glance over to check. He was thinking about that white bathrobe.

So much of his past was lost now, whole years of it. (Nearly all of junior high, for instance.) But every now and then some fragment would jump out at him vividly, viscerally. He remembered that the white bathrobe was a beach robe, in fact—the kind worn over a swimsuit. And he knew the precise summer he'd worn it: he'd been seven, not six. It was the summer before second grade, when they'd all gone to Deep Creek Lake for a week. He recalled the coarse texture of the sand underneath his bare feet, and he saw his father standing on the dock next to his new friend Bentley, a tough-faced, muscular guy who made his father look puny. He heard the explosive churning of water as Bentley's son Charlie swam past, showing off his Australian crawl. In David's memory, the droplets spattered his face even there on the shore. And his father was saying, "Come *on*, son. What's the holdup?" in a bossy voice he would never have used if the two of them had been alone. So David had untied his sash, and let his robe drop, and felt the air on his bare chest as he inched into the lake. The bottom felt like some kind of pudding; it oozed up between his toes with every step. He kept going, though, because he didn't want his father to feel ashamed in front of Bentley. Deeper and deeper he waded, holding his arms straight out at his sides to keep them dry, clenching his jaw to stop his teeth from chattering. Step after step, until—

Then there was nothing beneath his feet, all at once, and water was filling his nose and he was sputtering and choking. And he couldn't call for help because that would mean opening his mouth, so he hoped his father would just *guess* he needed help; but no, it was Bentley who guessed. "Looks like your boy could use a hand," he told Robin, and Robin glanced down at David from the dock, and he was wearing the oddest . . . he was wearing the most peculiar expression.

Nicholas said, "Could this next one be a picture of Uncle Kevin? He looks so young!"

"I couldn't tell you," David said, and he turned and walked out of the room.

By August, things in New York were getting better. Juana was returning to her own department, and the nanny was coming back to work, and Nicholas and Benny were going home. David was glad for their sakes, of course, but also he felt sad, and he could tell that Greta did too.

On Nicholas and Benny's last afternoon, Nicholas made an extra-big grocery-store run for his parents while David and Greta took Benny and the dog for a final walk. They started up Kane Street as usual, but when they reached Noble Road, where David was accustomed to turning right, Benny and John continued straight ahead. Evidently they followed a whole different route when they walked in the afternoons. Benny slowed in front of a house David had never noticed before, and an older woman cutting hydrangeas called, "Hello there, Benny!"

"Hi," Benny said. "Me and my dad are going home to see my mom tomorrow."

"You are! Well, isn't that nice!" She turned to David and Greta. "I know you'll miss them."

"We certainly will," Greta said, but by then Benny was on his way again, flinging a "Bye!" over his shoulder, so David and Greta gave the woman an apologetic wave and turned to follow him.

Approaching the next corner, Benny stopped short, and John stopped too and settled on his haunches. When David and Greta caught up, they found Benny fixated on a bumblebee that was hovering in front of his face. "Just keep walking," David advised him. "He's not going to sting you."

"I think he *is*," Benny said.

"No, he's only warning you off. See those other bees, on the rosebush? He's protecting them."

Benny didn't seem persuaded.

"Want to hear something interesting?" David asked him. "You notice how he's hanging there right in front of your eyes, right? Well, think about it. That means he knows your eyes are the part of you that will see him. He's figured out where humans' true selves are, you might say."

Benny went on standing where he was, though, and John gave a soft moan and lay down on the sidewalk.

"I did not know that!" Greta told David, clearly just making small talk.

"Oh, yes," David said, "there's a lot about insects that might surprise you." And then, gathering inspiration, "For instance, you know how sometimes you see a beetle in the middle of the sidewalk and you step around it so as not to smush it. Well, I bet you didn't realize that the beetle rushes home then to tell its friends that it's finally met up with a kindhearted human being."

Greta gave a hiss of a laugh and said, "Oh, you!" but Benny turned to ask, "It does?"

"He's joking," Greta told him.

At which Benny laughed too. "Grappa, you are *crazy,*" he said.

And then he resumed walking, the bumblebee forgotten, and the dog picked himself up and shambled after him.

When they were far enough behind so that Benny was out of earshot, Greta told David, "And here you were feeling so anxious before he got here! Remember? But you see how things turned out."

"It's been fun," David admitted.

"Did I not tell you? I said this. It was exactly this way after Nicholas was born."

"Still, though," David said, "you can never take it for granted that family members will like each other."

"Oh, David. Families love each other!"

"'Love,' well, sure. I'm talking about 'like,'" he said.

He hesitated a moment. He saw that old snapshot again in his mind: his seven-year-old self in his beach robe on the shore of Deep Creek Lake.

He said, "My father didn't like *me,* for instance."

"Excuse me?"

"Children know these things," he said. "It's a matter of survival. They have to be able to gauge their parents' minutest reactions, decode the least change in their voices."

"So," Greta told him, "then surely you know that your father thought very highly of you."

"Yes, fine. I know that," he said, giving up.

"And you thought highly of *him,*" she said, and she took hold of his hand and drew closer to him. "You were a good son to him."

"If you say so."

"Of course I say so! It was nice of you, for example, never to show that you knew your mother lived separately from him."

"Well, naturally. He would have felt humiliated," David said. (He didn't remind her that he *hadn't* known, in fact, until she herself pointed it out.)

"So, this is how it works," she said. "This is what families do for each other—hide a few uncomfortable truths, allow a few self-deceptions. Little kindnesses."

"And little cruelties," he said.

"And little cruelties," she agreed, and she swung his hand between them.

He was relieved that she seemed so unimpressed by what he'd told her. Suppose she had looked at him differently, all at once! Suppose she'd said, "Oh, yes, now that you mention it I see that you *are* unlikable."

But he should have trusted that she wouldn't. Not his Greta.

Nicholas waited till mid-morning before they set off, because he wanted to avoid the rush-hour traffic. As always in these situations, David teetered between dreading their leave-taking and wishing they'd just get it over with. ("I'd rather sit around the airport than sit around the living room," he used to tell Greta at the end of their visits to Emily.) So when Nicholas finally stood up and said, "*Well . . .*" David was almost glad. They all walked out front, the dog on his leash in case he balked at getting into the car, and David and Greta gave Benny a goodbye hug before Nicholas fastened him into his booster seat. John settled beside him, groaning to himself, and Nicholas shut the rear door and turned to his parents. "Thanks, you guys," he said. "I guess you'll be happy to have a little peace and quiet again."

"Oh, *right*," David said, and then they both hugged him and stepped back and watched until he had driven away.

"So," David said finally. "Here we are again, Mrs. G. Aging in place the same as always." And Greta linked her arm through his and they went back into the house.

They spent the rest of the day restoring some order, straightening the two guest rooms and moving David's things back into his study. At one point, while he was hooking up his computer, Greta turned from the bookcase and asked, "Have you seen this?" She was holding one of the family albums, the one that Nicholas had leafed through earlier. It lay open to a sheet of typing paper that had been slipped between two pages: a printed-out photo of David and Benny together in the garden. David was stooping a bit to examine the double handful of cherry tomatoes that Benny was holding up to him. "Benny with his beloved Grappa" was the caption, in Nicholas's blue-ink cursive.

"Aw," David said, because the sight of Benny's slightly grimy little fingers gave him a pang that was almost physical.

"I'm going to ask Nicholas to email me this so I can order a print," Greta told him. "It's my new favorite picture of you."

"Shoot: old guy with a scrawny neck," David said. But he was pleased.

For several days, they kept finding stray belongings here and there. A small sock left in the dryer, a rubber chew toy on the patio . . . Once David came upon Greta standing motionless in the kitchen, pressing her nose to a scrunch of fabric. She lowered it and looked up at him, her eyes suspiciously shiny. It was a child-size mask, he saw, with a crooked hem and a snarled trail of threads. He said, "Now, now, none of that," momentarily assuming the role of the sensible one in the marriage, and she gave an embarrassed laugh and handed it over. But as soon as he'd reached the study, where they were compiling a box of left-behind items to mail to New York, he pressed the mask to his own face and drew in a deep breath. He could still catch a trace of Benny's little-boy scent, salty but sweet, like clean sweat. He could still see Benny's seashell ears; he could hear his froggy voice:

Some people started singing it not knowing what it was,
And they'll continue singing it forever just because . . .

He shook his head and smiled, and he put the mask in the box and went back to Greta.

End

A NOTE ABOUT THE AUTHOR

Anne Tyler was born in Minneapolis, Minnesota, in 1941 and grew up in Raleigh, North Carolina. She graduated at nineteen from Duke University and went on to do graduate work in Russian studies at Columbia University. She is the author of more than twenty novels. Her twentieth novel, *A Spool of Blue Thread,* was short-listed for the Man Booker Prize in 2015. Her eleventh novel, *Breathing Lessons,* was awarded the Pulitzer Prize in 1988. She is a member of the American Academy of Arts and Letters. She lives in Baltimore, Maryland.

A NOTE ON THE TYPE

This book was set in Celeste, a typeface created in 1994 by the designer Chris Burke (b. 1967). He describes it as a modern, humanistic face having less contrast between thick and thin strokes than other modern types such as Bodoni, Didot, and Walbaum. Tempered by some old-style traits and with a contemporary, slightly modular letterspacing, Celeste is highly readable and especially adapted for current digital printing processes which render an increasingly exacting letterform.

Composed by North Market Street Graphics, Lancaster, Pennsylvania

Printed and bound by Berryville Graphics, Berryville, Virginia

Design by Maggie Hinders